BLOOD ON THE MOOR is both a moving love story and a vivid evocation of a turbulent past, poignantly written and lovingly created. When in the wake of the Battle of Culloden, defeated rebel Highlander Ross MacLean turns up nearly dead of his wounds on the doorstep of Arrandale House, gentleman lawyer Charles Lamont has no choice but to offer him refuge. But the dangers of harbouring a fugitive from Hanoverian vengeance soon become all too real for the compassionate solicitor and his household – most of all for Alice, the beautiful daughter of Lamont, who finds the fabric of her safe and predictable world torn asunder by the sudden arrival of the handsome Highlander so close to death . . .

ERIC MacSWEEN was born in Inverness in 1949. Educated at Inverness High School and at Napier College in Edinburgh, he is now the proprietor of a local business in the Highland capital. Though he has travelled extensively in Europe and in North America, his love for his native Highlands provided the inspiration for this first novel.

The author wishes to thank the following people for their assistance in the preparation of this book: Elizabeth Sherry, Dorothy Blake, Selma Cruickshank, Katharine Stewart, Tony Pledger and William Campbell.

A particular debt of gratitude to John Prebble, whose superb book *Culloden* provided much of the background information and military detail for the story.

Special thanks to Hunter Steele of Black Ace Editorial. Without his professionalism, you would not now be able to read the following pages in their present form.

Blood on the Moor

A Story of Love, Courage and Survival

Following the Tragedy of Culloden

Eric MacSween

GLEN BOOKS

First published in 1996 by Glen Books
47 Hilton Avenue, Inverness, IV2 4TJ, Scotland

© Eric MacSween 1996

Typeset by Black Ace Editorial
Ellemford, Duns, TD11 3SG, Scotland

Printed in England by Redwood Books
Kennet House, Kennet Way, Trowbridge, BA14 8RN

A CIP catalogue record for this book
is available from the British Library

ISBN   0–9528926–0–X

To my wife and son

1

The clatter of heavy hooves outside the window stopped abruptly.

And as the weathered oak door swung open, the flash of light from the four-stick candelabrum fell bright upon the bloodied figure of a rebel Highlander sprawled across the gravel drive. Drenched by the teeming rain, he looked up through haunted eyes at the bright, anxious faces hanging in the darkness above him. And in that instant before the black veil of oblivion cloaked his last conscious thoughts completely, somewhere in the distant back of his mind the skirl of bagpipes and the gruff voice of his sergeant pulled him back to that early April morning on the moor . . .

'Rise and shine, Captain — today, sur, if ye please!'

'Waken up, Hamish, or I'll put ye tae sleep fur good!'

'Angus! — there's a lassie oot here wi' a swollen belly an' her faither would like a word! — Come on, ye lazy wee tyke. Move yersel'!'

It was dawn reveille, and down by the banks of the Nairn River men of a Highland cavalry unit were stirring beneath their makeshift bivouac of horse-blanket and plaid as the music of the glens and the dulcet tones of Big Duncan MacLean intruded upon their dreams of gentler times and places.

Captain Ross MacLean stepped out into the rain and stretched his arms aloft to greet the new day.

'It's a snell wind, Duncan — it'll bring snow before the day's out, I'll wager,' he observed with some certainty.

Duncan rubbed his great red bush of a beard. 'Aye, sur, and what else will it bring, I wonder?' he returned coldly.

His young officer's worried eyes looked eastward, where already the sticks of Cumberland's drummers were beating the long roll of the General Call to Arms.

Meanwhile Duncan MacLean was casting a rueful eye over

his bedraggled men. They were a sad-looking lot; tired, hungry, and dispirited.

Their shabby clothes gave them a wildness of appearance that defied adequate description.

'Will ye look at them, sur! This lot would nae pass muster at a beggars' convention!'

But Ross MacLean was too busy running a critical eye over his own sorry state of dress; brown riding boots scuffed and wrinkled by sharp rocks and constant immersion in soggy earth. His faded trews were threadbare in places and the fabric of his tartan coat had long since lost its fashionable flair. The young Highlander looked up rather sheepishly at the older man.

'Now, I wisnae referring tae you, sur,' said Duncan holding up his hands apologetically. 'Impeccable as always. Though . . . maybe a wee shave would nae go wrong?'

Ross looked at the great bush of red hair which almost obscured his accuser's face and gave the older man an ironic stare.

'I wiz only being mindful o' the exalted company you've been keepin' lately in the mornin's,' Duncan reminded him. 'And ye ken fine that his Royal Highness prefers his pretty young officers . . . clean-shaven!'

'Now, now, Duncan,' warned the young man with a scolding finger. 'That kind of talk could get your neck stretched!'

'Aweel, I'm only voicing what others are thinkin'!'

Ross caught his friend by the arm and steered him out of earshot of the men. 'How are the food rations?' he enquired, adopting a more immediate tone of voice.

'Why, there's none left, sur! We ate the last biscuit during the night afore we turned in.'

'Do the men know?'

'Well, they must do, sur, for *they* told *me* – and in no uncertain terms, I can tell ye!'

The young man looked suddenly relieved, 'Ah well, so we don't need to hide the truth from them.'

Duncan scratched his beard in bewilderment; conversations

with his Captain often took a twisted path through the realms of logic.

The Prince's messenger careered into view and descended the steep hill at a gallop, stopping inches from the water's edge. Touching his blue bonnet, he addressed the young cavalry officer from the saddle:

'Begging your pardon, sir, but his Royal Highness requests your indulgence at the morning council, and begs your attendance at once. Sir!'

His message delivered, the boy rider turned his horse around and sped off up the hill.

Duncan rubbed his red beard once more. 'What's up wi' young Lachlan this mornin'? Ye would think someone had mentioned the word "food", the way he came doon yon hill!'

Climbing into the saddle, Ross fastened what was left of the buttons on his faded tartan coat.

'Well, how do I look?' he enquired of the men now gathering around him.

Captain Ross MacLean was a tall twenty-three-year-old with dashing good looks, whose sparkling blue eyes mirrored perfectly the good-natured humour that burned within. His dark shoulder-length hair billowed around his neck in the stiffening wind.

'Yer bunnet, sur!' shouted Hamish from under the tented horse-blanket. 'Dinna forget yer bunnet!'

The blue bonnet, adorned with eagle feathers, a sprig of crowberry, and the white cockade of silk, was ceremoniously handed up, and, after several adjustments to the angle of the tilt, the young cavalry officer enquired once more of his men:

'Well – now how do I look?'

'Bloody awful!' Big Duncan boomed from the background. 'But ye'll do!'

Turning his attention to Forbes, the oldest member of the assembled group, the mounted officer pointed to the river:

'Why not show the men that guddling technique of yours,

and see if you can't catch a big trout or two for our breakfast!' he suggested hopefully.

'Oh yes, and what would Sir like to go with his fish – a bottle of French or Italian perhaps?' replied old Forbes in his very best English.

Big Duncan pushed forward. 'Och, be off wi' ye noo and dinna keep the poor man waitin'!' he thundered as he slapped the powerful black charger on the rump, sending his young Captain off up the hill at full tilt.

Prince Charles Edward Stuart stood addressing an assembly of clan chieftains and military advisers from the eminence of a huge moss-covered boulder. He looked every inch the Prince: in tartan coat, cockaded bonnet, white breeches, and knee-length riding boots. A light broadsword hung in its scabbard from a wide leather belt. Though a young man of boyish face, he wore the mantle of authority with a confidence that belied his tender years.

He turned as Ross MacLean cantered towards him. 'Ah, good morning Captain! I am so pleased you could join us,' he said smiling. 'And how are my brave cavalry boys this morning? – out searching for horses to ride, I'll be bound!' jibed the Prince to a ripple of laughter.

The young cavalryman dismounted, removed his bonnet, and gave a polite bow in the Royal presence. He was not in the least offended by the remark, for it was well intended and uttered more in sympathy than in jest.

It was common knowledge among the men that Ross and his little band of mounted volunteers had lost the main body of their horses during a valiant rearguard action at Clifton on the long and bitter retreat from Derby. At Gladsmuir and Falkirk, the young cavalry officer had acquitted himself well in battle – so much so in fact, that many of the Highlanders in the rebel ranks, who had an inherent aversion to cavalry of any persuasion, were now looking through envious eyes at the unassuming young man. His dark beauty of a stallion whinnied in concert with the laughing men.

'I think you have your answer, your Highness – straight from the horse's mouth!' replied Ross to further howls of laughter.

'If we had a hundred like him,' said the Prince in admiration, 'I would feel more certain of the day's outcome, Captain.'

Ross bowed politely at the suggestion.

When the laughter had subsided, the Royal countenance took on a more serious expression:

'Now, gentlemen. You were gathered here yesterday expecting an attack from Cumberland which, we now know, did not materialise. Today, I have news that his army has been sighted in the fields above Nairn making ready to advance. I think we can safely conclude that he intends to meet with us and give battle. I must inform you now that I stand by my orders of the fourteenth . . . '

This intimation was greeted with much murmuring of discontent from the clan chiefs.

'Yes, I understand your concern, gentlemen. But please bear with me a moment. We have but three options available to us. The first is that we retire westward into the glens, where, it has been suggested, we fight a campaign of protracted warfare.' The Prince shook his head. 'The idea is absurd! We have already lost large numbers of men to desertion. A march westward would only serve to precipitate that process further until I would have no army, worthy of the name, left to lead!'

More discordant mutterings from the clansmen, at this slight to their honour.

'The second option suggests that we deploy our army south of the Nairn water, where the ground is more suitable for a Highland charge with broadsword and dirk.' Cheers of approval from the clansmen at this. 'But, gentlemen, if we avail ourselves of that possibility then we do so at the risk of Cumberland marching straight past us to seize the town of Inverness unopposed . . . '

More murmurings of disapproval.

'His army would be readily supplied and reinforced by ships in the Firth and we would be left out in the cold, starved of provisions and shelter . . . such a prospect is too painful to con-template.' Then the Royal countenance brightened noticeably:

'Our third and final option, and the one I favour above all, is for us to stand our ground here on the moor and face the onslaught head on. We have it in our power to deliver my cousin a birthday present he will not soon forget!' The Prince now removed his sword from its scabbard and pointed it skyward:

'Bannockburn! Go on, my lads!' he cried out in his lisping Italian voice. 'The day will be ours!'

And so the chant went up:

'Bannockburn! *Bannockburn!* BANNOCKBURN!'

Between the rousing cheers and huzzahs that followed, many of the clansmen drifted away amid mutterings of discontent. Cold reason had given way to hotheaded exuberance, and the clan chieftains were to find the wisdom of their long-held principles sadly vindicated before the day was out, and in the most bloody way imaginable!

Leading his horse from the scene, Ross MacLean, too weak from want of food and sleep to climb back into the saddle, was now feeling just as dispirited as the others by what he had heard from the Royal lips. Walking the sunken road back to the river, a familiar voice broke in on his thoughts:

'Ross! Ross! Over here, over here!'

The young man looked up to see the friendly face of his namesake Calum, grinning through an open window of a deserted outbuilding on the Culwhiniac enclosures.

'You'd petter pe careful you don't trip over that face – hass somebody died?'

'That almost isn't amusing, Calum,' replied his friend disconsolately and, coming over to the window, he leaned his elbow rather forlornly on the stone lintel.

'Himself hass decided then?' guessed Calum intuitively. 'The last throw of the dice here on the moor?'

Ross smiled back glumly. 'He is determined to have his way . . . I think they call it destiny.'

Calum gave a mocking laugh 'Destiny!' he repeated, shaking his head. 'Stupidity would pe the petter word for it!' And, breathing a deep sigh of resignation, he pulled out an envelope from his coat pocket and offered it through the opening in the wall. 'Then I had petter give you thiss,' he said solemnly.

'What is it?' asked his friend, looking suddenly perplexed.

'It's a letter for Mhairi, and I would like for you to deliver it . . . if it should prove necessary.'

Ross stared blankly at the envelope. 'Are you sure that I am the right man to carry this?' he said, taking possession of the letter.

'Och man, man, you surely don't pelieve the weird rantings of old Tonald John MacLean – the man's a doom merchant!'

But his young friend returned a haunted look. 'Nevertheless, he has the sight and I have never known him to be wrong . . . '

'Och, will you listen to the man!' growled Calum despairingly, 'Now look. I am asking you because I know the letter will pe safe in your hands. I hope, for both our sakes, that you nefer haf cause to deliver it, but I would pe failing in my duties ass a hussband if I did not ask the only man I can trust to convey my last thoughts to the woman I love . . . '

Calum looked searchingly at his friend.

'Now, will you take the damn thing or no?'

'Aye, Calum I will take it,' agreed Ross with a firm nod of the head. 'But I hope I never have reason to deliver it.'

His friend gave a sigh of relief. 'And what about you? Iss there . . . anyone?' he enquired, awkwardly.

Ross looked up with the shadow of a smile. 'Thank you, but no. There is no-one,' he answered.

With the dark business out of the way, Calum's face lit up like a summer's day. 'Would you pelieve, I almost forgot the reason I'm in here!' he exclaimed, beckoning his friend round to the doorway and ushering him into the dim interior of the thatched building. Pulling back a torn, tartan plaid to reveal a crate full of wine bottles, he proclaimed gleefully:

'French, Spanish, Italian, Portuguese – the finest vintage

from the pest cellar in the Highlands! You can take two, the rest are spoken for!'

Ross let out a long, low whistle of delight. 'Where in the world did you . . . ?'

But Calum's finger shot up against his lips, indicating silence and secrecy. 'Nefer ask your mother where you came from!' he reminded his friend.

During a reconnoitre in preparation of the Prince's visit, Ross remembered looking, with envious eyes, at the well stocked wine cellar of Culloden House some days earlier. He was quite sure that his friend's haul originated from the very cellar of the great house and he could only shake his head in admiration at the impressive booty on display.

'So which two do you want?' enquired the would-be wine merchant, holding aloft a bottle each of French and Italian.

'These two will do nicely!' grinned Ross, removing the precious bottles from his friend's grasp and secreting them hastily from sight in the deep pockets of his tartan coat.

Away from the sleety blast on the high plateau of the moor, the little band of horse soldiers were splashing knee-deep in the shallows of the Nairn River. Old Forbes had successfully tickled the bellies of six trout into submission as the others looked on, fascinated by the apparent witchcraft of the guddle.

When their Captain came over the rise, still half asleep, with his horse trailing by the reins some distance behind, Duncan went rushing to greet him.

'Ye'll never guess whit's cookin'?' he challenged with childish enthusiasm.

Ross dropped the reins and ran forward, slipping and sliding on the wet grass of the slope in his excitement. 'You're not going to tell me the old ferret has actually caught something?' he cried out as he skidded down the steep hill with his riderless horse following in his wake.

'Got it in one!' exploded the big man with an impromptu jig of joy.

The young man's face lit up with anticipation as the delicious aroma of grilled fish came to him from the happy group of men gathered by the river bank.

'What's going on in there?' Ross demanded with mock severity.

Forbes held aloft a speared fish on the point of his dirk. 'Welcome to the guddle huddle, Captain!' he announced to an explosion of laughter.

Angus came towards him, rubbing his hands with glee. 'The man's a magician, Captain! After he guddled the first two, the others just leapt out of the water and surrendered!'

Hamish pulled a worried face. 'Bloody uncanny, sur – the man should be burnt at the stake!'

Ross stepped into the huddle, breathed in a lungful of the mouth-watering aroma, and patted the chef warmly on the back. 'Forbes, you're a genius!' he proclaimed to cheers of approval.

'Och, but I've guddled bigger in a wee burn back home in the glen,' answered the reluctant hero dismissively. 'I don't know what all the fuss is about!'

Ross placed a grateful arm around his shoulder and beckoned the little group of men closer together.

'I'm fair taken by your fishing and culinary skills, Forbes. But unless I'm very much mistaken, I seem to recall you requesting my choice of wine to accompany the dish?' he reminded him with a mischievous wink to the others. 'And for the life of me, I can't see a bottle in sight!'

Forbes returned a bemused grin at this piece of farcical nonsense.

Their young Captain glanced at the wall of smiling faces for the moment of optimum impact, and in one swift movement, pulled the two bottles of wine from his coat pockets. '*Voila!*' he exclaimed in his very best French as the assembled eyes and mouths popped open in disbelief.

'Well, what'll it be gentlemen! French or Italian?'

Resting his head against the bright trunk of a silver birch, his blue bonnet scrugged low on his brows, Big Duncan MacLean gave vent to a long rumbling belch of contentment. Licking his fish breakfast leftovers from the hairs of his great red bush of a beard, he cocked an eye at his sleeping companions, who were now lying similarly reposed against trees of their own.

'I wonder whit the poor people are doin' this mornin'?' he enquired of anyone who might be listening.

'Sheesht!' someone demanded.

Young Angus sat bolt upright and cupped an ear to the wind. Iain and Hamish had heard it too. Even fisherman Forbes, whose hearing had long since lost its sharpness, had heard something.

Like a distant roll of thunder it came, vibrating on the air, down the valley of the Nairn the unmistakable anger of drums — and it was growing louder by the minute!

'Duncan! Grab your glass and come with me!'

The urgent command of his young Captain brought the older man abruptly to his feet. Fetching the small brass telescope from his saddle-bag, the big Highlander followed his officer along the river bank — with a fleetness of foot that would have seen him overtake a man half his age and size.

Keeping their heads down low and the high embankment to their left, the two men tracked the course of the river downstream toward the sound of the drums. Presently, after a mile or so of swift running, they came to a bend in the river where the steep bank curved gently upwards, offering a perfect vantage for observation. Crawling amongst the whins and junipers, they lay face down in the heather with the broad vista of rolling hills beneath them.

Duncan pulled his glass to the ready, but the sight which greeted the naked eye would have stopped the hearts of lesser men.

Cumberland's army, like a swarm of red ants crawling across the brown heather hills some miles off, marched westward. Soon it would swing south, seeking the high ground of the moor, and all the while, as it moved, the rolling thunder of the drums grew ever louder.

Other eyes too were watching the Army's advance that

morning. From the crows' nests of the Royal Navy's warships, lying at anchor in the Firth, sailors relayed news of the troops to shipmates on the decks below.

Duncan passed over the telescope and Ross peered through it in silent fascination. He would have wished for such an army. The third and final encounter between the Rebels and the Royals was imminent and, though he and his brothers-in-arms had claimed the first two victories, this one would be decisive.

The image Ross MacLean saw through the lens and through the sleet that fateful morning was as frightening as it was awe-inspiring. Three infantry columns of five battalions spread out beneath their flourishing standards, bending forward in the wind. To the right, regiments of St. Clair, Cholmondely, Howard, Fleming, and Pultney. In the centre, Price, Campbell, Bligh, Sempill, and Battereau. On the left, Munro, Barrel, Conway, Wolfe, and Blakeney. Marching in the ranks, men who had stood firm against the cannon fire at Fontenoy rubbed shoulders with others who had run like rabbits from the Rebels at Falkirk.

On the left of the infantry, a fourth column consisting of three cavalry regiments: Dragoons of Lord Mark Kerr and Cobham, and volunteers of Kingston's Horse – some three thousand in all, riding strutting black and bay horses, they advanced by squadrons, with the silk guidons of their regimental colours flapping above them.

Brevet-Colonel William Belford's artillery train made a fifth column on the right of the infantry. Gun carriages pulled by powerful draught-horses, gunnery teams of bombardiers, matrosses, and fireworkers. As the wheels squealed and the whips cracked and the drums beat, the young rebel watched as the artillerymen stumbled into a morass. Hub-deep in gurgling peat, the whole artillery column came to a rumbling halt.

Ross pulled the glass from his eye and gave a sideways glance at his bearded companion. 'It would seem that our spies were right after all, Duncan. Must be ten thousand of the lobsters at least!' he concluded assuredly. 'I fear our illustrious leader is about to fall rather spectacularly on his royal backside this day, my old friend.'

Duncan fingered his red bush pensively. 'Aye, Captain. But, I'm thinkin', no afore we fall very painfully on oors!'

The young Highlander pulled a worried face before raising the glass to his eye once more. Shire horses had been brought forward from the bat wagons at the rear of the columns to lend their considerable pull to the immobile cannon. Infantrymen from the right flank had been ordered to sling their muskets and put their shoulders to the wheel. After much heaving and cursing, the heavy guns were painstakingly extracted from the mire, much to the displeasure of the watching eye.

Though the main force was still some distance away, Campbell scouts and outriders of Kingston's Horse were reconnoitring the flanks. One of their number had strayed too far off line and forward.

Duncan touched his Captain's arm at the sound of approaching hooves. From their place of concealment, the two rebels watched as the scarlet frock-coat of a trooper, clearly visible through the overhanging branches, came splashing towards them on his dock-tailed mettlesome horse. The crown of his black tricorn beaver showed his head inclined downwards, his eyes apparently more on the river inhabitants than on the intended territory.

The big Highlander's fingers tightened around the hilt of his dirk as the horse drew near, the clatter of its hooves against the flat rocks of the river bed, muffled by the splish-splash of the crystal-clear water as it came on. He was so close now that the two rebels could almost reach down and touch the top of his head. As he passed directly beneath the hidden danger, Duncan was upon him in a flash. Exploding from the junipers, he sprang from the edge of the high embankment and caught the unsuspecting trooper in a ferocious bear-hug, tipping him from the saddle and over the animal's back to hit the water with a great splash.

His face lashed with spray, Ross, who had witnessed the ambush too late to prevent it, now burst from the concealment of the bushes as the long blade of the dirk flashed in the big man's hand.

'No, Duncan! No!' he commanded.

The tartan giant froze at the words and, with the hot blood of battle pumping through his veins, he dragged his semi-conscious victim by the broad leather shoulder-strap on to the wet grass by the river's edge.

Holding aloft a trembling hand of self-protection, the shocked trooper gazed up with abject terror into the wild bearded face of his attacker, the point of whose blade now hovered inches from his upturned jaw.

'It'll be wan less tae worry aboot Captain!' the big fellow growled angrily.

Leaping down from the bank to join them, the young Highlander knelt to examine the timorous white face of his enemy.

'Why, he's only a lad! Not much older than Angus!' he noted with obvious surprise.

'Aye, and just as deadly, nae doubt!' Duncan reminded his companion.

'What's your name, lad?' Ross enquired of the boyish-looking cavalryman.

'T-trooper G-George D-D-Duncan, sir!' came the terrified reply.

'Did you hear that, Duncan? The lad's only named after you!' exclaimed Ross, clearly amused. 'Now you wouldn't want to go stabbing at your namesake, would you? That would be a poor example of Highland hospitality!'

'Aweel, maybe no,' replied the other with some reluctance.

The younger of the two rebels turned his attention to the bay gelding, now standing in the river some distance downstream. Feeling slack reins, the horse had stretched his neck to chomp eagerly at the lush spring grass by the river's edge.

'What do you think, Duncan – could we make use of him?'

The older man looked rather disdainfully at the pretentious animal. 'I dinna hold wi' yon tail dockin' practice wan bit!' he complained, then, rubbing his chin, he reconsidered:

'It's a shameful sin on such a fine animal but, then again, beggars canna be choosers!' he convinced himself.

'P-please, d-don't take my h-horse!' came the pitiful cry from the prostrate trooper. 'They'll h-hang me f-for sure if I l-lose him!'

The two men exchanged bemused glances.

'Did ye hear that, Captain!?' thundered the older man at the very idea. 'Bloody savages!'

'Aye, and he may well be right, Duncan. I have heard talk of it. It would seem the King's officers are not the league of gentlemen they would have us believe.'

Fearful to look at the wild bearded one, the cowering boy trooper held the young rebel's rather sympathetic gaze, sensing that if his life was to be spared, then it would be due entirely to this intense young man with the piercing blue eyes.

Removing the trooper's carbine from its saddle sling and the dragoon pistol from the boy's broad leather belt, Ross hurled them into the river. He pulled the yard-long sabre from its scabbard and, swishing it against a tree, bent it upwards where it struck till it snapped off at the hilt. This, too, he threw in the river.

'Now then, Mr George Duncan!' said the young rebel in a concluding tone of voice. 'Perhaps one day, God willing, you will recall this little encounter for your grandchildren. Kindly point out to them, if they should be in any doubt, that you had the privilege to meet with two Highland gentlemen upon the moor this April morning, who had the good grace to leave you with your horse and your life!'

Signalling to his bearded comrade-in-arms, the young Captain indicated that it was time to leave. The big Highlander sheathed his dirk and, giving the boy redcoat a final hostile glare, he took off along the river bank in pursuit of his companion.

Still in shock, and with the rebel's parting words ringing in his ears, the boy soldier watched the retreating figures push their way through the tangle of overhanging branches until, at last, they were gone from sight.

* * *

Back on the broad plateau of the moor, the sound of Cumberland's advance was now in everyone's ears. The clan pipers, hearing the beating of approaching drums, inflated their bags, spread the drones and, fingering the chanter, sent up a rant of defiance; the strange squealing music sounding to English ears, hearing it for the first time, like some weird Highland beastie calling to them from the heather.

Immediately upon his return, Captain Ross MacLean called an impromptu council. And as they gathered around, the men could see by their young officer's demeanour that the subject on the agenda would contain little of the wry humour they had come to expect at such times.

'Now listen, lads!' he began in an earnest tone as they huddled in closer. 'Our friend Cumberland will be paying us a wee visit shortly,' he confirmed, nodding in the direction of the incessant din. 'Now this won't be another Gladsmuir or Falkirk. We'll be outnumbered two to one by my reckoning . . . ' Big Duncan nodded confirmation.

'Aweel!' said Hamish. 'Since any Highlander is worth two Sassenachs, it should be a fair fight!'

'Aye, I know Hamish,' agreed their Captain with a rather painful smile. 'But I am very much afraid that their guns and their horses, on this unfriendly moor, may prove too much even for us . . . '

There was such an outburst of dissenting voices at this suggestion that it caused big Duncan MacLean to erupt in fury:

'Shut yer bletherin' when your Captain is speakin' tae yiz!'

'Now look, what I'm trying to say to you lads is that you don't have to stay!' And turning to the big fellow, 'That goes for you too Duncan!' he said.

Blank faces and a shocked silence followed this thunderbolt.

'You swore allegiance to my father, not to me! It was he who begged your indulgence until the Prince took the throne. As it is clear such will never come to pass, your obligation to my father ended with his death at Falkirk. I know that you have stuck with me out of respect for him and for that I thank you most humbly.' He looked around at the wall of glum faces:

'You have no need to linger on my account. God knows you have had little change for your loyalty and courage these past months . . . ' And breathing a deep sigh of resignation, 'You are all free to go and with my blessing,' he concluded.

Dumbfounded by this unexpected turn of events, it was several moments before any of them could speak.

'And where does that leave you, Captain?' Dougal MacLean enquired, to shouts of accord from the others.

Ross glanced at the anxious faces. 'I will stay,' he answered softly. 'I promised my father.'

Big Duncan stepped forward. 'Why are ye doin' this, Ross lad?' he asked, with unaccustomed familiarity, 'I knew yer faither, better even than you! He widn'ae have wished for such a thing, and you mair than anyone have guid reason tae leave,' the older man pointed out with a knowing look.

'Aye, Captain!' cried the others.

Forbes, wearing a worried expression came forward to speak. 'You have not forgotten the words of the gifted one?' he challenged, with a sinister edge to his voice.

Hamish twisted the knife still deeper. 'The *saighdearan dearg* cannonball!' he reminded him in his Anglo-Gaelic way.

Ross straightened himself from the onslaught. If it was their intention to scare him into leaving, then they were doing a sterling job, but he would not wilt in the heat of the moment.

'If it must be, then it must be!' he told them bluntly. 'I cannot cheat the *taibhsear* so there would be no point in me leaving,' he declared to much-worried glances from the men.

'Then there iss no point in any of uss leaving,' Winky MacLean announced from the background. 'For we will not go without our leader!' he added, to howls of agreement.

Ross looked at the speaker, whose black eye-patch and long hair, tied back in a rough ponytail, made him look more a pirate than a cavalryman of the Highland army. He wondered why such a man, who had already suffered the loss of an eye in battle with the Royal troops, would wish to stay and risk his life, when he was free to return to the welcoming bosom of his family.

'But you have a wife, Winky, and obligations as a husband!' Ross reminded him.

The pirate emitted a sound like a suppressed laugh. 'Aye, it iss true what you say, Captain, but if you knew my wife ass I do, then you would know why I am more inclined to stay!' replied the errant husband, to guffaws of laughter.

'Weel! There ye have it, Captain!' said Duncan, putting a firm hand on the other's shoulder. 'Ye can like it or ye can lump it, but ye're stuck wi' us, and that's an end o' it!'

The men waited for some response but none came; only the bemused look on the young man's face gave any clue to his confusion. So the little group of men dispersed for their horses and, to the clatter of hooves, and the ringing of bridle chains, they started up the hill, leaving behind them the solitary figure of their young Captain, standing by the river's edge, brooding and perplexed.

For, at that moment, Ross was certain that he had failed them – why else would they refuse to leave?

But the men on the high slope could forgive him for not understanding; he was, after all, still very young and had much to learn of older values. Perhaps one day, God willing, he would come to know the reason why they chose to stay, for it was a simple truth and any of the men could have told him, if he had only thought to ask. The fondness they had felt for their chief, his father, they felt even more for his son . . .

That Ross could feel his father's presence was undeniable. He had felt the closeness for some days now, and there was comfort in the feeling. He would have wished for such a closeness in life, but sadly it had not been so . . .

With his eyes cast downwards in the water, and his hands resting on the basket-hilt of his hanging sword, he made a rather sad-looking picture as young Angus MacLean came towards him. The boy was concerned, more than anyone, for the future well-being of the Captain; his hero, his friend. And unburdened as he was by the complications of adulthood, he spoke directly to him:

'Captain, is it true you will die today?' he asked, with the blunt honesty of a child.

Ross felt the words as a sword through the heart. Turning, he gazed down at the worried face of his young inquisitor. 'You must not believe all that you hear Angus,' he answered.

'But the *taibhsear* has seen it. A redcoat cannonball. And the men say he is never wrong!' replied the boy in a rush.

Placing his hands on the young lad's shoulders, Ross smiled down reassuringly. 'It is just rumour and idle gossip – pay it no heed!' And with a swift change of direction:

'Where have you been?' he asked. 'I have been looking all over for you!'

'I was answering the call of nature downwind, as Big Duncan has ordered.'

The young man smiled at the answer. He was amused that Angus should think of such a consideration at such a time. Then, turning suddenly serious, he pulled a sealed envelope from his coat pocket and offered it to the bemused boy. As Angus reached out to take it, Ross tightened his grip, as though reluctant to release the envelope from his care.

'Now, you must listen to me Angus and listen good!' he said earnestly. 'I have here a letter for Cluny MacPherson. He is riding here from Speyside at the head of his clan. Seek the *bratach uaine* and deliver this to Cluny in person!'

Angus looked awe-struck at the envelope.

'It contains direct orders from the Prince, himself!'

'But . . . but, why me, sir?' asked the boy in amazement.

Ross cocked a dark eyebrow. 'Who else could he trust?'

Filled with the importance of the errand, Angus took possession of the letter, climbed on to the back of his little Galloway pony, then hesitated a moment as the realisation came to him:

'But, what about Cumberland? I should be with the men!' he reminded his Captain and himself.

Ross waved his hand dismissively:

'You will be back with Cluny in plenty of time.' And with urgency in his voice, 'Now go, Angus! His Highness is depending on you. We all are!'

Bursting with pride, Angus bade farewell to his young Captain, and started across the river. Ross watched him splash through the shallows to the opposite bank and ride some distance to the brow of a hill. There he hesitated, waving to the men on the far slope. The men, catching sight of him, waved back and for an instant he seemed rooted to the spot as though unwilling to leave. Then, all at once, he was over the top and gone from view.

Gathering the reins and clicking to his horse, the young cavalry Captain started up the slope in pursuit of his men. The gradient was steep lower down, where the land fell sharply to the valley floor and, still weary for the want of sleep, he felt double his twenty-three years as he climbed.

Duncan waited for his arrival. 'Have ye sent the wee lad back tae school?' he asked.

'If we can do it for one of theirs,' said the other, recalling the young trooper they had encountered downstream, 'then we can do it for one of ours!'

Duncan nodded approvingly.

'I only wish that I didn't have to lie to him. He deserves better!'

The big fellow rubbed his beard thoughtfully. 'Aye, ye did right, Captain! Tae tell the truth, I tried tae chase him yesterday but the thrawn wee tyke defied me tae ma face!' Duncan growled angrily and clenched his fist at the memory of it. But Ross could only smile at the older man's frustration, for he knew, better than anyone, the contentious nature of the boy.

Conscious that his time was growing short, the young man looked down, perhaps for the last time, at the green and fertile valley of the Nairn which had sustained his men and his horses while others above had starved. He glanced up at the heavy scudding clouds on Beinn Bhuidhe Mhor. Soon the sun would return from its long winter repose when the dead brown heather of today would know again the purple splendour of tomorrow.

He would remember it so, and turning, he put his shoulder to the wind and his eyes with the others to the moor.

At eleven o'clock the two armies came in sight of each other. Over the rising curve of the moor, Cumberland's vanguard moved forward in a feeling advance with fixed bayonets. They halted some five hundred yards from the Rebel front line, brought up their cannon from the rear and pulled them into line by pairs.

The forty-two-inch iron barrels were swabbed clean of mud and heather, the tompion removed from the gaping mouth, powder and ball rammed home, and a dribble of primer to the touch-hole. The bombardiers stood by their guns with their linstocks at the ready . . .

There was no movement from the clansmen who stood their ground, bashing the hilts of their broadswords against their bull-hide targets, yelling and taunting the enemy. Some of the Highlanders had hiked up their kilts and thrown off their plaids to free their sword arms in readiness. The Prince, riding a fine grey gelding, cut a dashing figure as he rode amongst the men encouraging them to be brave and do their duty for the King, his father.

And there they stood upon that windswept moor like two gladiators in the arena waiting for the signal. The Royals in the red and white livery of their King, and the Jacobites in the blue and tartan of theirs . . .

Then, suddenly, above the rant of the pipes and the tirade of the drums, a puff of white smoke belched from a Rebel gun; the muffled report blown back on the wind. The high, looping ball sailed over the Royal lines and came down in the ranks of the reserves, killing one soldier instantly.

A moment later, Brevet-Colonel William Belford's sword came down with the linstocks of his gunners and the battalion cannons roared into life in one devastating rolling discharge. The rapid fire sequence of the three-pounder guns sounded like ten claps of thunder in quick succession. The tremendous boom echoed off the hills and rolled out over the firth. The Royal horses reared with alarm as the guns bounced back on their wheels under the heavy recoil of the explosions. Gunsmoke swept across the moor on the wind, obscuring everything from sight. The acrid stench of burnt powder was everywhere.

Young Angus MacLean had barely reached the shores of Loch Moy when the distant thunder of the guns pulled him to a standstill. With his mind in turmoil, and all thoughts of his vital errand gone, the frantic boy turned his horse around and rode hell-for-leather back to the moor.

It took less than an hour for the little horse to retrace its own footprints. But in that short space of time the battle on the moor was already lost.

High on a hill, overlooking that sad stretch of ground, young Angus MacLean sank to his knees and stared down through disbelieving eyes at the scene of carnage below. The all-important orders for Cluny MacPherson, now a crumpled sheet of blank paper, blowing through the heather in the wind; his Captain's vital errand all too obvious now!

He watched and he suffered till he could watch no more. And with the sound of muffled gunfire and the distant screams of dying men ringing in his ears, the young Highlander slipped silently away . . .

2

The young man opened his eyes to a room filled with light and stared up at the ornate canopy of a king-size four-poster bed. A fire sparked in a hearth somewhere, and he could smell the familiar smoke of birch logs. Presently, into his line of vision came two large windows, where long velvet curtains of deep crimson hung tightly draped, allowing bright shafts of sunlight to intrude. The sound of a wood pigeon cooing its heart out and the alarm call of a distant blackbird came to him through the half-open window.

His head was throbbing, he could barely raise his right arm, and his left leg was numb below the knee. Any attempt at movement was accompanied by the most excruciating pain.

In an armchair by the bed a girl sat sleeping, her interlaced fingers resting prayer-like on the pages of an open book. Heavy lids betrayed big eyes, and the firm line of the jaw bespoke a determined spirit. The rich mane of honey-coloured hair, tumbling in golden disarray across her shoulders, framed a face of haunting beauty. She was wearing a taffeta blue gown and a gold necklace rested on a pair of perfect breasts.

The girl was enchanting and her spellbound admirer estimated that she could not be more than eighteen or nineteen years old. For a moment, he wondered if he had died and gone to heaven, for no angel could look more breathtakingly beautiful. But, the unremitting pain, and the blacksmith hammering at the anvil in his head, told him otherwise. And though he had an overwhelming desire to dwell on the vision of loveliness beside him, his eyes would not obey. Merciful sleep tiptoed upon him once more and stole his senses away . . .

Below the half-open window, two sombre figures walked the garden grounds in deep conversation.

'I've given him some laudanum for the pain. It should help him sleep,' one of them remarked to a nod of appreciation from his walking companion.

'You do realise the dangers of keeping him here, Charles? It's been three days now and, even as we speak, the soldiers are turning every stone for rebels – it's only a question of time . . . '

The other nodded, resignedly, and pulled a worried face as they proceeded along the path towards the yellow blaze of nodding daffodils, flowering en masse in the deep leaf mould of the giant beech trees.

'I have burnt his clothes and cast his weapons into the garden pond,' Charles informed his friend. 'If the soldiers come I will inform them that he is a nephew recovering from a nasty riding accident.' He gave a little knowing smile. 'Being prudent with the truth, Ronald, comes naturally to the son of a politician.'

But this light-hearted suggestion brought a reproachful shake of the head from the other. 'Do not underestimate the powers of the military, Charles,' he warned. 'Loyalty to King and country will count for nothing if you are found giving succour to a rebel!'

Charles pondered his friend's words a moment. 'And if . . . I move him?'

'Then, he will most probably die!' replied the physician with clinical certainty.

Charles stopped his companion's progress along the path with a restraining hand. 'Even if I wanted to move him, Ronald, I could not! Alice has taken it upon herself to play the guardian angel. She has scarcely left his side since he came to us that night – she would never forgive me!'

The gentleman with the leather bag showed his friend a raised eyebrow. 'Ah, yes!' he agreed. 'It would seem that young Alice is growing up rather quickly and, unless I am very much mistaken, she may already be smitten with the handsome rogue?'

Charles wore the look of the protective father at this piece of very unprofessional observation. 'Oh, yes!' confirmed his friend. 'Women have a way of melting at the sight of a helpless man. It has something to do with the maternal instinct; a need to help the helpless. I have witnessed many examples of it in my time,' he recalled, looking pointedly at the other's doubtful expression. Climbing aboard his parked carriage, he chuckled wickedly. 'Aye, the poor lad doesn't realise the danger he's in.'

'You're a charlatan, MacTavish!' grinned Charles, ushering his friend into his seat in faint rebuke.

Doctor Ronald MacTavish consulted his pocket-watch and frowned like a man late for an urgent appointment.

'Isobel Anderson is in the last days of her confinement; she's due any moment now and if I know husband Roy, he'll be running round the place like a headless chicken!' He choked down a laugh then, slapping the reins and clicking to the horses:

'Men! Totally useless in a crisis!' he complained.

Charles stepped aside as the wheels of the black curricle rumbled into motion and the two-horse team clattered down the drive with their ears pricked and their tails flicking as they went.

High above the chimneys, the giant beech trees creaked eerily as a rising wind tore the last dead leaves of winter from their swaying boughs, scattering them across the rooftops. Recalling his friend's words of warning, Charles glanced up at the half-open window and wondered at the man asleep inside . . .

Later that morning the wounded rebel received his first 'conscious' visitor. Awakening, groggily, from a troubled sleep, his eyes focused on a rather portly-looking gentleman at the bedside.

'Good morning! I trust you are feeling a bit better?' enquired the amiable face peering down from above.

Several disorientated seconds passed before the patient had gathered his thoughts sufficiently to answer the friendly greeting. 'Wh . . . where am I?' he asked weakly.

The question brought a broad, candid smile to the face of the clearly delighted visitor, who, suddenly remembering his manners, drew himself up to his full height and, showing the crown of his powdered periwig with a polite bow of introduction, declared in a rich, resonant voice:

'My name is Charles Lamont, and this is my home: Arrandale House!'

Charles Lamont was a man in his sixth decade of life, by the Highlander's reckoning. Although not overly tall, his broad frame and upright bearing gave him a rather large perspective. The features of his heavily lined face, aquiline and noble, mirrored perfectly that inscrutable quality of stoic Scottishness that would greet all of life's triumphs and tragedies with equal dignity.

Sombrely dressed in a dark suit of clothes, his large square cuffs and pocket flaps proclaimed a professional working gentleman. A tell-tale sheen above the fob-pocket of his black waistcoat, betrayed a frequent tendency to consult his pocket-watch, whose gold-link chain dangled, dependably, from its buttonhole anchorage. Knee-length stockings of white silk and a bright linen shirt, goffered at the cuffs and collar in the fashion of the day, owed their immaculate appearance to the tender loving care of a woman's hand.

'Arran . . . dale House!?' echoed the Highlander through a haze of confusion. 'How did I—?'

Charles Lamont's silencing hand allowed no further questions. 'You must not concern yourself with such matters now,' he advised. 'All will be revealed in good time. It is important only that you recover your strength and get well again.'

But the Highlander's thoughts were already racing ahead of him:

'I . . . cannot stay here,' he argued. 'It would be . . . dangerous!'

The gentleman of the house picked up a chair and pulled it in closer. As he sat down at the bedside, his deep voice took on an altogether more serious tone. 'Now look, my boy,' he said bluntly. 'You are going nowhere! You were lucky the other night. My friend, Doctor MacTavish, was our dinner guest and it was his timely intervention that saved the day. You have wounds to your head and shoulder, your left leg may be broken, and you've lost a great deal of blood. Another hour out there on the moors and you would have been lost to this world for certain!'

The wounded rebel could see the truth of these words in the frown lines of his visitor's brow.

'My daughter, Alice, will be keeping an eagle eye on you, and Doctor MacTavish will drop by from time to time,' he said, rising to leave. 'Oh, and Molly, my housekeeper, will be along shortly with some breakfast,' he added, checking his watch for the time.

The Highlander's muddled brain was having some difficulty assimilating the information. The word 'Alice' had registered, but little else.

Hesitating in the doorway before leaving, the master of the house turned back to face his convalescent guest. 'I'm afraid that I have taken the liberty of destroying your clothes and disposing of your weapons,' he informed him apologetically. 'I will of course replace the clothes with others of a less conspicuous nature.' Then, with a reassuring smile, he went out, closing the door quietly behind him.

Drifting on the edge of sleep, the Highlander was brought abruptly to his senses by the intrusion of an elderly woman, showing him a silver tray and a broad, welcoming smile. 'Hello, dearie! – how are you this mornin'?' she breezed in a bright and chirpy voice. 'You poor thing. You must be starvin' hungry after your terrible ordeal. Now, I've brought you some breakfast and Mr Lamont says that I'm to make sure that you eat it all up!'

The patient, attempting to arrange himself in a more suitable position for the intake of food, collapsed back into the pillows, exhausted by the effort. His elderly visitor, witnessing the guest's dilemma, put down the tray and was at his bedside in a flash.

'Now, you just stay right where you are!' she ordered and, with a gentle lifting of his head and a few mother-hen prods at the pillow, soon had him sitting upright and comfortable.

'Thank you . . . Molly. It is . . . Molly, is it not?' he enquired weakly.

'Aye, sir. Molly it is, and I'm right pleased to make your acquaintance!' she answered with all her heart in the words. 'Oh, but you gave us an awful fright, you know, turning up like that: half dead and covered in blood!' said the old housekeeper, now sitting on the edge of the bed and arranging a napkin on his chest with meticulous care.

'We thought you were lost for sure when Doctor MacTavish couldn't find a pulse!' Molly looked aghast and her voice dropped to an eerie whisper as she recalled the horror of the moment. 'How on earth you ever managed to find your way in the dark, out here in the middle of nowhere, is beyond me!'

He attempted to question her about that particular mystery, but to no avail, for the memory of his arrival that terrible night had the old housekeeper in a flood of excitement.

'The rain was pouring down cats and dogs! And you, sir, were drenched right through to the bone! We all helped to carry you upstairs: Mr Lamont and the good doctor at one end, and myself and Miss Alice at the other! My husband, Alex, put your horse in the stable and tended his wounds . . . '

The Highlander opened his mouth to speak, but Molly was in full spate. 'Oh, he'll be fine, sir. Don't you worry; just a few cuts and bruises – better than his owner anyway – and that's for sure!' she added, smiling hearteningly.

In common with most of the women he had encountered, during his short life, Molly the housekeeper had the uncanny knack of talking without drawing breath – a technique no man, to his knowledge, had ever been able to master.

She was now demonstrating her mother-hen qualities again with a spoonful of hot soup hovering expectantly under his nose:

'Now, open wide!'

Between grateful sips, he seized the opportunity to speak:

'Tell me . . . about Alice?' he ventured as the old woman's ear came within whispering range.

'Alice!' she exclaimed, surprised. 'Why, the poor lass is

sleeping like a log. Absolutely exhausted! She spent the last three nights mopping your fevered brow!' she informed him, waving the soup spoon around like an orchestral conductor. 'Aye, and pinning you to that bed, too, or else you'd have been on the floor – and, heaven knows, out yon window maybe!' she told him, pointing now with the busy spoon at the large bay window.

But the Highlander's eyes had already closed to savour the vision of lovely Alice mopping his fevered brow. Then he re-opened them, cursing himself for having no memory of it!

'She is . . . a bonnie lass!' he remarked, then noted a distinct change of expression on the old housekeeper's face as he said it.

'Aye – she is that!' she agreed under a raised eyebrow. 'But don't you go getting any ideas in that direction!' she warned, now thrusting the metal utensil, swordlike, towards him. 'You're in no fit state for those kind of thoughts!' she reminded him threateningly.

Her defenceless victim smiled rather disarmingly, then pulled a worried face, for in truth he had been aware for some time now that all sensations in the 'those kind of thoughts' region of his anatomy were alarmingly absent! Perhaps his injuries were worse even than Charles Lamont had described? He must question Doctor MacTavish at the earliest opportunity!

Molly, seeing that her charge had grown suddenly distressed, lifted her tray and crossed the room to leave. Pausing at the door, she glanced back at the worried face in the pillows and whispered to herself:

'Men! All the same! Every last one of them!'

In the late afternoon, while the wounded rebel slept soundly in his bed, the young lady of Arrandale House paid her first sneak visit to the four-legged invalid. Hesitating outside the stable doors, Alice screwed up her courage and slipped nervously into the dim interior. A splinter of sunlight, shining through the skylight window, fell bright upon the black brooding monster in the corner.

'Sixteen hands of pure equine strength!' Alex had enthused and Alice, seeing the stallion for the first time, gave a deep sigh of admiration, for she had never in her life seen such a magnificent-looking animal! Almost completely black in colour, save for the long white blaze, stretching from the base of his ears to just above the level of his nose, he stood dark and forbidding.

Though she had an irresistible urge to touch him, Alex had warned her not to take liberties in his presence, for the pain from his wounds had made him nervous around people, and a horse possessed of such power could be a dangerous proposition! Observing from a safe distance the deep cuts on his chest and flanks, she wondered with pity what horrific experiences the poor beast had suffered; instinctively, her heart went out to the big fellow.

Heart in mouth, and keeping well clear of his unpredictable hindquarters, Alice edged slowly towards the powerful beast, now pawing at the stable floor and snorting defiantly at her nervous approach. Then, with a tentative outstretched hand, she found to her surprise that she could clap his nodding head and stroke his mane of ebony hair with no sign of erupting violence. Pulling a handful of broken biscuits from her coat pocket, she offered up the tasty crumbs, only to find him munching happily from her open hand and then nuzzling her pocket for more of the same.

Alice chuckled with delight to discover that the black stallion, like most of nature's giants, who know the confidence of their own power, could be as gentle as a kitten in quieter moments. And he was enjoying one of them now as this sweet-smelling creature, with the soothing voice and the gentle touch, lavished upon him this very pleasant attention.

Teasing the horse's tousled hair between her fingers and whispering softly in his twitching ear, Alice glanced up to the distant window of the house where the wounded stranger lay, and puzzled at the man asleep inside. Though she now lived in the very heart of the Highlands, her knowledge of its people and of Bonnie Prince Charlie's followers was limited in the extreme. What she had read about them and heard from the lips of others painted a grim picture of an ignorant tribal people who dressed in strange patterned clothes and spoke in a totally incomprehensible tongue. Living in homes of sod, heather and stone, they scratched out a meagre existence from the hard land under an unforgiving sky.

But this handsome Adonis under her father's roof was an odd inconsistency and not at all the wild barbarian she might have expected. His clothes were indeed strange, but not without a certain charm and flair. His voice, though he had spoken only in troubled sleep, was soft and his words undeniably English.

Only the lethal-looking sword, broken inches from the hilt, which she had seen her father cast into the garden pond along with the weird-shaped pistols and dagger, tied him to the tribal image. But why on earth such a beautiful fellow would carry such things, she could not imagine.

Even as she watched, and stroked, and wondered, she could feel again that little stab of excitement that brought goose bumps to her skin. And it was a feeling like no other she had ever known . . .

The hours crawled by.

Afternoon came and went, and the April showers which had filled the dips and hollows in the gravel drive with many miniature lochs and streams, finally gave way to a warm blink of spring sunshine.

Awakening from the fragmented dreams of sleep, the wounded rebel opened his eyes to a dream of a different kind.

'Good evening, Captain! I trust you slept well?' beamed the young lady of the house at her still groggy patient.

'Why . . . Miss Lamont! Forgive me . . . I am a poor guest indeed . . . to sleep in such . . . charming company.'

'Oh, I think I could be persuaded to forgive you on this occasion, Captain, providing that you call me Alice. Miss Lamont is much too formal!' she insisted with a look of mild amusement.

'Then you must . . . call me Ross,' he answered. 'Captain is of no consequence now . . . ' Then, looking suddenly perplexed. 'But how did . . . you know to . . . call me so?' he asked.

'I'm afraid that you talk in your sleep!' she informed him with a knowing smile. 'You would be surprised how much I know about you already!'

Setting aside the book she had been reading, Alice rose from the armchair to collect a porcelain ewer from the dresser nearby and returned to sit on the edge of the bed. The effect of the cold refreshing water dabbed on his clammy face and forehead was immediate and he could soon feel his senses reviving. He smiled appreciatively.

'I know you must be very uncomfortable,' she said apologetically. 'But there is nothing more I can do until Doctor MacTavish examines your wounds,' she added and, taking his hand between her own, squeezed it gently with reassurance.

'You have done . . . a great deal for me already. Your father and Molly have told me . . . and I thank you . . . most sincerely for it.'

Alice returned a rather embarrassed smile and when their eyes met briefly she looked away with a faint blush, as though fearful that holding his gaze might betray some dark secret she was not yet ready to reveal.

There was something so natural in the way she had taken possession of his hand that it brought a smile of surprise to his lips. If only she knew what tingling sensations that simple act had triggered within him, she might snatch her hands away at any moment. But thankfully she did not. Perhaps, he thought, if she knew how many Royal soldiers the hand she was now holding had cut to pieces in recent months, she would very likely snatch them away – forever!

'What are you thinking?' she asked suddenly, her brown eyes alight with curiosity.

For a dreadful moment he felt sure that she had seen the image of his innermost thoughts reflected in the blue of his eyes and so instinctively he narrowed them.

'What are you thinking?' she insisted.

'I was just . . . wondering,' he answered.

'What exactly?'

'Why I should . . . fall off the edge of the world. Only to land in . . . in the sweetest safety net,' he admitted with a quick smile.

The girl's face coloured slightly but she did not answer, only a gentle squeeze on his hand gave any clue to her thoughts.

The Highlander was utterly entranced by her. Like the hapless moth drawn inexorably to the proverbial candle flame. With all his heart he wished he could be in this room alone with her under different circumstances. But, he wondered with growing anguish, would he ever recover sufficiently to realise such wishes again?

There came a soft, double knock on the door and Molly peeked in.

'It's Doctor MacTavish to see you, dearie!' she gushed.

Alice relinquished his hand and stood up abruptly as the doctor entered.

The Highlander shrank into the pillows at the sight of the newcomer; he didn't like doctors. They were painful, prodding creatures who treated people like the interesting exhibits they had once encountered at their medical university in Edinburgh. And this particular one looked capable of causing more than the usual amount of pain and suffering!

Doctor Ronald MacTavish was a large heavily-built man in the later years of his life, with a round face and ruddy complexion. A pair of half-moon pince-nez spectacles perched rather precariously on the point of his nose, giving him a decidedly owlish appearance. Placing a distressed leather bag on the bed, he sat down on the edge and peered over the lenses at his patient.

The Highlander glanced up at Alice for reassurance and braced himself for the onslaught.

The physician, following his patient's apprehensive gaze, caught Alice by the hand. 'If it wasn't for this angel of mercy, I wouldn't have wagered much on your chances!' he observed grimly.

'Do you wish me to stay, Doctor?' she asked politely.

'Yes, yes of course my dear! There is no need for you to leave. You've already seen everything that this young man has to offer!' he replied matter-of-factly.

Alice's instantly burning cheeks reflected the Highlander's acute embarrassment perfectly. But MacTavish, oblivious to the devastating effect of his remark, proceeded, unhindered, to examine his patient's head wound by first removing the dressing and handing it to his scarlet-faced assistant.

'You have rather a nasty gash on your head, my boy!' he assured him confidently. 'It will, no doubt, be painful for a while, but I'm fairly certain that it will leave no lasting damage.'

But the patient was much more concerned with the 'down below' region of his anatomy and wanted Alice away so that he might question the doctor in confidence.

'Alice, dear, would you like to do the honours?' MacTavish requested, handing the attentive girl a fresh linen dressing from the apparently bottomless bag.

Alice, reaching across to apply the dressing to his head wound, pressed her breasts innocently against his cheek; the sensation of which, accompanied by her heady perfume, caused his head to swim so wildly that he was obliged to close his eyes in order to regain equilibrium.

'Oh, forgive me!' she said, hesitating. 'Am I hurting you?'

'No, I'm fine . . . really!' he assured her, then smiled wickedly to himself, for he was suddenly aware of certain 'down-below' feelings returning.

When his arm and leg wounds had been painfully examined and their dressings duly changed, the patient was finally released from the physician's torturous probings.

Pulling a phial of laudanum from his cavernous bag, Doctor MacTavish handed it to Alice with precise instructions for its use, but was amused to find his patient in little need of the opium drug, for he was already sleeping soundly.

Snapping shut the catches of his worn leather bag, the doctor gave the young lady of the house a leaving smile and, with the promise to return the following afternoon, bid her good-day.

Hearing the front door close and the tramp of heavy feet on the gravel path below, Alice stood at the bay window and watched the visitor's black curricle rumble down the drive. Off to torture some other poor unfortunate soul, no doubt! She smiled at the thought. But little did she know, for her father had been careful to keep from her, the dangers that Doctor MacTavish and others of his ilk were risking in their 'treasonable' care of wounded rebels. The fetid gaols of the Highland capital now held some notable local physicians in irons for merely having the temerity to express their professional concern at the ill-treatment of rebel prisoners.

Sitting again in the armchair and taking up her book once more to read, Alice gazed at the mysterious young man in the bed a long while. She knew so little about him, and yet she had felt so comfortable in his presence. Indeed, for he had not been aware of it at the time, she had actually taken the liberty of catching hold of his hand unthinking! The realisation appalled her almost as much as the excitement of that touch itself! The intensity of his blue eyes, shining through the pain, had all but taken her breath away. Nobody had ever made her feel so alive, so vital before!

She wondered what strange magic was at work around her, for if she had conjured him from dreams, she could not have wished for a more perfect embodiment. He was everything and more, this handsome wounded rebel with the hint of danger; an all-too-heady potion for any fluttering female heart!

If only she could hold him in this room as he was now, helpless and vulnerable, her own personal prisoner. She could almost wish it. But — like the injured bird, caged with its broken wing — he too, she knew, would some day soon recover from his wounds, mount his magnificent black stallion, and ride off and out of her life forever.

But until then she would dream . . .

In the days and nights that followed, Alice would come to learn much about her mysterious Highlander and he in turn would come to learn much about her.

'Tell me about yourself?' he had enquired during one of her

frequent visits to his bedside. 'Have you always lived in this house?' he wanted to know, and she had sat down on the edge of the bed, starry-eyed and thrilled that he should be interested enough to ask.

'No, Not long, really,' she answered with a shake of her honey-golden hair. 'I was born on the island of Arran, hence the name of the house, Arrandale!' she told him. 'I lived there till I was two, then we moved to Edinburgh, where Father was a partner in a law firm. He travelled often to Inverness on business and fell in love with the beauty and remoteness of the Highlands. So much so, in fact, that he decided to move up here to live.' She broke off suddenly, trying to remember. 'That would be . . . almost five years ago!' she informed him, smiling sweetly.

Ross returned that smile, encouraging her for more.

'I fell in love with the house the first moment I saw it! It is very old, you know – over two hundred years!' she enthused. 'And would you believe', she added, introducing a distinct tone of mystery, 'that it comes with its own resident ghost?'

The Highlander's expression, which up till now could only be described as pleasantly attentive, looked suddenly shocked. Alice was delighted that she had, at last, stirred his curiosity.

'I have never actually seen it, but I have heard it!' she said, dropping her voice to an eerie whisper, her eyes alight with the memory. 'Not long after we moved in, I heard weird wailing sounds one night. It was awful! Like someone in terrible pain, crying out in agony! Molly swears she saw the large figure of a man climbing the staircase and . . . walking through the wall in the east wing of the house on the very same night!'

'MacTavish examining one of his patients!' said the High-lander interrupting.

'Oh, be serious for once!' she scolded. 'There's a room in the house,' she continued, 'which is kept forever locked! Only father has the key and even he won't go in there! I wouldn't feel safe in the house alone at night!' she concluded, rubbing her upper arms in dread at the very idea.

Though Ross had listened intently to her every word, she could not help but notice a strange faraway look in his eyes as she spoke.

'Do you believe in the supernatural? Ghosts, premonitions and the unexplained?' It was an innocent enough question but it had an odd effect on her listener. He flinched visibly as though something had struck a raw nerve.

'Ross, what is it?' Have I said something wrong?' she enquired with growing concern, but still he did not answer.

'Ross, please. You are frightening me!'

Certain he must be suffering some seizure, she moved to ring for Molly to fetch Doctor MacTavish at once, but before she could act upon her impulse, his hand caught her wrist and, turning back to face him, she could see that the faraway look had gone from his eyes.

'Forgive me . . . I did not mean to alarm you,' he said in a thread of a voice.

'Has it something to do with *taibhsear*?' she ventured hesitantly and saw his eyes flicker at the word, knowing instinctively, now, that she had found the core of his dread.

'What is the *taibhsear*?' she asked, stepping carefully toward the truth. 'You spoke of it in your sleep. Is it something to be feared?' she urged, taking hold of his hand in that way of hers.

The Highlander looked up at the frown lines on the usually smiling face and touched them gently with the fingertips of his free hand.

'You'll grow old before your time,' he warned, smiling evasively.

But she would have none of it:

'You must tell me what this *taibhsear* thing is!' she demanded. 'I need to know!' And the firm grip of her hand on his confirmed that she meant business.

'Donuil Ardgour is the *taibhsear*!' he told her, finally submitting to her insistent glare.

But her frown lines deepened. 'You mean that this *taibhsear* is a man?' she asked, her expression softening as the veil of mystery lifted. 'Why then is he to be feared?' she continued to probe.

The Highlander glanced down from her gaze. 'He is not the one to be feared . . . only what he sees.'

The girl's face was a picture of unfulfilled curiosity and Ross knew that he would need to explain further or be forever tormented.

'The man has the sight as his father had before him. He has foreseen many things which have come to pass. And he has never been wrong.'

'Has this Donuil Ardgour seen something for you?' she was anxious to know and watched closely for his reaction.

'Perhaps he thought so . . . but he was wrong,' answered the Highlander softly, then, seeing that she was studying him so assiduously lest he should keep anything of the truth back from her, broke into one of his evasive smiles again.

Alice remained unmoved. 'But you said he has never been wrong, so what was it that he saw for you?'

Ross could see that she was worse even than a West Highland terrier with a favourite bone, and cursed himself for ever having mentioned the word, even in delirium.

Sighing deeply, he glanced up with a look of complete sincerity:

'He told me that one day I would meet with a beautiful young angel with long golden hair and the biggest nut-brown eyes . . . ' he paused, smiling evasively. 'And that we would live happily ever after!'

Alice held her frown for a long and puzzled moment then broke into a beaming smile when the penny finally dropped. 'You lying toad! He told you no such thing!' And together they burst into uproarious laughter until he was forced to stop, abruptly, when the movement caused his shoulder wound to complain bitterly!

'That's what you get for telling such outrageous lies, Ross MacLean!' she giggled in that endearing girlish way of hers.

During those long uncertain days of convalescence Ross had time to dwell on deeper feelings and the creeping realisation of how much they had grown for Alice. Everything about her. The brightness of her eyes; childlike in their open, candid gaze, so easily surprised, and always sparkling with curiosity about him and his mysterious world. The radiance of her smile; captivating, enchanting, disarming and oh, how often had he been the victim of all three!

The rustle of her gown as she moved about the room.

The fragrance of her perfume that lingered on the air long after she had gone.

How his heart would lift at the sound of her approaching footsteps in the hall. The sinking disappointment of her leaving. And in the long, lonely absence, how his eyes would wander to the fireplace wall, where the heavy mantel clock sat ticking down the hours till she returned. Every waking moment, and in dreams, his heart was filled with Alice.

But behind the pain and the uncertainty there was dread; a terrifying dread that one day soon the soldiers would come. Then, early one morning, it happened . . .

At dawn on the twelfth day the Highlander was suddenly and rudely awakened by a near hysterical Alice and an equally panic-stricken Molly pulling back the bedclothes and dragging him unceremoniously to his feet.

'What! What's happening?' he stammered, still groggy from sleep.

'Quickly! Soldiers are coming. We must hide you somewhere!' shrieked Alice.

'The curtain!' gasped Molly. 'It's the only place – we haven't the time!'

There came a loud banging on the front door, a dog furiously barking, and a commotion of gruff voices in the downstairs hall.

The two women half carried the still helpless patient to the window on the far wall, remote from view of the soldiers below. Charles Lamont rushed into the room, his blood freezing in his veins as he stared in stark horror at the bloodstained sheets on the bed. Alice followed his gaze. As Molly concealed the Highlander behind the curtain, Alice leapt into the bed and pulled the sheets all the way up to her neck so that only her head was visible above the bedclothes.

An instant later a young fresh-faced soldier pushed past Charles in the doorway and stared suspiciously round the faces in the room, his eyes resting momentarily on Alice. A glint of early morning sunlight flashed off the polished brass buttons on his scarlet tunic as he moved towards the centre of the room. A dragoon pistol filled his right hand and Charles could see that the hammer of the flintlock was cocked in the firing position.

The intruder's gaze swept from the stupefied faces to a point on the floor directly ahead of him, where a bright dribble of fresh blood led a telltale path to the exact spot where Molly was standing. Slowly, relentlessly, the young soldier walked toward the window and, with one swift movement of his free hand, pulled back the curtain!

The Highlander closed his eyes as the cold muzzle of the gun pressed against his cheekbone. Beads of cold sweat issued from every pore as an agonising moment of pain and terror swept through the very fibre of his being. After an eternity of hopeless suspense, Ross opened his eyes to the inevitable – and the boyish face of trooper George Duncan, from the Nairn River encounter, now staring at him in a shock of momentary disbelief.

Then, without a single word passing between them, the startled trooper stepped backwards into the centre of the room and Charles Lamont watched in silent fascination as the pistol was safely uncocked.

With one last sweeping glance at the assembled faces, the young soldier slowly and carefully backed out through the open door.

'All clear in here Lieutenant!' they heard him say.

After several heart-stopping minutes, the front door slammed shut and, on the gravel drive below, the frantic clatter of heavy hooves, like thunder to their ears, gradually and mercifully died away in the distance.

In the stunned silence that followed, Alice, Molly, and Charles stared at the Highlander in a shared look of total astonishment. But Ross, who was now standing unsteadily against the window recess, merely glanced down at Alice in the bed and grinned rather painfully.

'May I come back . . . to bed now?' he pleaded in a breathless voice, then slid to the floor in a faint of exhaustion.

3

'*Vite! Vite!*' The French sea captain's urgent command cracked out in the night. Leaning on the gunwales of the heaving ship, he could see only the dimly moving shapes of his crewmen as they manhandled the heavy wooden crates from the creaking cargo hold into the flotilla of rowing boats, bobbing in the water alongside.

It was the last night of April when, under cover of darkness, the French frigate 'Bellona' and her sister ship the 'Mars' sailed into Loch Nan Uamh on the west coast of Scotland. Their mission, to effect a landing of stores for the rebellion – food provisions, 240 casks of brandy, arms, ammunition and money (35,000 louis d'or) – was a polite gesture from a friendly government. But, alas, it had come too little too late.

Neil Cameron leapt from the landing skiff and alighted unsteadily on the shingle beach. He was not much the sailor and was more than a little relieved to be setting foot on terra firma once again (albeit very dangerous ground). He puzzled at the absence of the Royal fugitive and worried the more for his safety. Time was of the essence, for British warships were guarding the western approaches and the young voyager was certain his two ships had been sighted off the coast.

He had advanced some way up the beach when he stopped abruptly. Faint on the wind he was sure he had heard voices – hushed voices and at no great distance. A redcoat patrol, was it? He touched his sword and cursed his damnable luck.

Back on deck, the captain stretched a worried face. The wind was rising, the ship was dragging anchor, and to top it all, the white sails of British warships were looming on the horizon.

'Neil! Neil! – we must return to the ship at once,' demanded the oarsman.

'See! – British ships are coming!'

Shadowy figures on the beach too were coming into view

now and ever closer by the second. Neil Cameron drew his sword and waited for the welcoming party.

'*Mo Dhia!*' one of the oncomers cried and Neil knew immediately that the strangers too, had seen the British sails, but more: he knew them to be Gaelic-speaking Highlanders. He lowered his sword as the strangers gathered around him.

'Do you speak English?' he enquired, his voice sounding remote in the darkness. There fell a long silence, filled by the distant voices of the ships' crew making ready to sail.

'Aye, we haf the English,' came the grudging reply and the young man breathed a deep sigh of relief.

'My name is Neil Cameron! I am a friend of the Prince and I am to meet him here!' he informed them in a rush. But this burst of excitement was greeted by yet another long silence; long enough for the speaker to wonder if his words had been understood. Then the spokesman – a tall, heavily-built fellow – pushed his face forward and Neil could see his bearded mouth go down in a mocking laugh.

'If I'd a guinea piece for efery time I've heard those words,' said the stranger in a voice that roared like the sea, 'I'd pe a prince masel!'

Behind them in the deep waters of the loch, the 'Bellona' was moving.

'Neil, Neil – *Mon Dieu!*' The oarsman in the little boat was frantic.

'Go back to your ship Meester Cameron!' the Highlander advised. 'The one you seek iss not here!'

But Neil, by way of reply, ran to the water's edge and pushed the boat clear of the shore. 'Go!' he commanded. 'Tell the captain I will return with the Prince at the next landing!'

The skiff had barely reached midway between the shore and the leaving ship when gun flashes illuminated the darkness as the British men-of-war fired warning shots across the Frenchman's bows. The 'Bellona' was lying luff to the wind with the 'Mars' covering her escape, returning fire on the rapidly engaging warships.

There came a blinding flash and wrecking of timber as the

horrified onlookers saw the little boat, which had taken Neil Cameron safely ashore, blown out of the water by a direct hit; the salt spray from the impact of the round-shot lashed the watching faces on the beach.

Numbed by the sight of it, the young man on the shore looked on helpless as the little craft and its oarsman slipped beneath the waves. Covering his eyes at the loss of his ship-mate, Neil crossed himself in the Catholic way as the big Highlander came to his side, the gruff voice rasping in his ear:

'Friend of the Prince, you say? A friend of the Almighty would pe nearer the truth, Meester Cameron.'

All along the shore other boats were leaving with shadowy figures aboard. There was some consolation in the young man's misfortunes, for not only had the cargo in his trust landed safely, but some gentlemen of the rebellion had, it seemed, seized their chance to escape.

'Come with uss!' the big Highlander suggested, the voice softer now, a note resembling sympathy in his words. Startled out of his preoccupation, Neil looked up into the deep-set eyes of the bearded one with the dawning realisation of a mission still incomplete.

'The Prince? – I must find him . . . ' he pleaded.

'Please, Meester Cameron – pefore the red soldiers come looking,' urged the others.

Wrenching himself from the scene, the young adventurer followed the strangers, single file along the sand, glancing all the while over his shoulder to the naval engagement in the deep waters of the loch. The two Frenchmen had turned now with the wind full in their sails and slipped past the heavier battleships – HMS 'Greyhound' and 'Terror' – all four heading out to sea.

When the guns fell silent and the loch was clear of sails, only the sad wreckage of the little boat remained to mark the landing . . .

Early next morning Neil Cameron awoke from a fitful sleep. He was wrapped in a warm, tartan plaid of a sett that was not his

49

own and the noise of his breathing came loud to his ears. The bed of sod and heather beneath him was as soft a mattress as he could wish for and the walls of a cave enclosed him. Water trickled down veins of purple and silver in the rock face and silicates of mica twinkled with the sun's rays where it filtered through a leafy opening.

His mind still swimming with the night's events, the young adventurer leapt to this feet and looked around his rocky bedchamber. Why, it wasn't a cave, he thought, but more of a cathedral in scale and grandeur; a great opening in the granite where some massive boulder had once stood! He remembered following the strangers from the beach up and up, climbing ever higher through the darkness. Once he had thought to slip and fall, only to be caught by a rough hand and pulled to safety – Yes, he remembered it now – all was coming back!

Running to the opening, he looked out upon the new day and drew back gasping at the sight which he beheld, for he must be hundreds of feet up a hillside! Below, as far as the eye could see, rocks and heather – miles of it – and beyond: the beach and the sea. His eyes held a wondrous look, like a child seeing snow for the first time.

The wildness of the scenery took his breath completely. 'Scotland!' he whispered to himself, then danced a spontaneous jig on the spot for the sheer joy of it. 'I have come home!' he shouted at the top of his lungs and heard his words repeating on the rocks in a long, dying echo.

'So, you haf come home, haf you now?' came the gruff voice from the Highlander of the previous night.

Looking up, Neil could see the great bushy face glaring down through a cleft in the roof of the cave.

'Then I bid you welcome, Meester Cameron,' he said with a look between a smile and a frown, 'but would ask that you please keep your voice at a peep pefore the whole of Scotland hears of your good fortune!'

For an instant, the face at the opening vanished from sight only to be replaced by a pair of the biggest buckled brogues Neil had ever seen. The legs and body quickly followed and, in a great blossoming swirl of tartan plaid, the big Highlander dropped to the stone floor with a grin on his face as broad as the ocean.

Of giants, Neil Cameron had read much in his childhood but in all his life he had never seen one loom so large as the man who stood before him now.

He must be all of seven feet tall if he was an inch and the broad shoulders went out almost as much again!

With his thick mane of tousled black hair and beard, and wrapped as he was in his clan tartan plaid, a brace of claw-handled pistols thrust into a broad leather belt, the giant Highlander was a magnificent anachronism – like some medieval warrior lost in time.

'So, you haf come home, haf you now?' he repeated, beaming through that ferocious ebony beard. 'Then it iss a fortuitous mingle of good blood that brings a Cameron to a MacDonald!' he bellowed.

'Coll MacDonald of Barrisdale at your service!' he proclaimed with a curt bow of the head and a hand that shot out as big as a fish-plate; the grip of which popped Neil's eyeballs from their sockets.

'So, it's Neil Cameron, iss it?' grinned the Highlander, his eyes sweeping the newcomer from head to toe with undisguised amusement.

'I can see from the cut of your cloth that you would pe a young gentleman of sorts,' remarked the giant with a twinkle in his eye. 'And all the way from France, no less!' The big fellow couldn't keep the smile from his face and Neil very soon realised that he must, indeed, look rather odd to the big Highlander, dressed as he was in such silk finery as would befit a King's banquet – and out here in this heather wilderness of all places!

But the genial giant's face suddenly darkened. 'My men recovered the body of your oarsman from the loch early thiss morning and gave him what Christian burial we could pefore the *saighdearan dearg* come looking.'

Neil smiled back appreciatively. It was a kindness he would

not have expected from such heathens as he took these fellows to be. Clearly, he had much to learn about his new friends.

'And you are a friend of Thearlaich, are you now?' enquired Coll doubtfully. 'Aweel, maybe you are. And then again, maybe you're no. But any man who sails yon dangerous waters to bring such bounty to these shores iss a friend of Coll MacDonald. And right now, Meester Cameron, that counts for a damn sight more!'

Neil was more than a little relieved to hear himself called 'friend' but pulled a long face nonetheless, for he was ever-mindful of his true reason for being here at all. And, even as he formed the question in his head, he found to his surprise that the big man had read his thoughts.

'He of the whispered name iss not here!' Coll told him bluntly and, pointing beyond the cave entrance:

'Out there iss where you'll find your Prince, Meester Cameron, where the Atlantic waves break on the outer buckler of the Hebrides. North Uist!'

The news hit Neil Cameron like a thunderbolt. 'North Uist?' was all he could think to say, and with such a look of perplexity that it set the other smiling again.

'Aye, and a right windswept devil of a place it iss to be afoot, and that's a fact!' said the Highlander contemptuously. 'Och, but neffer you heed,' he added cheerfully. 'I haf friends and a boat that will take you there if you haf a mind.' And with a dismissive wave of his rough hand:

'But more of that later!' he bellowed, walking now to the gloomy interior of the cave. There the big man pulled back a lattice of twigs and heather to reveal an inner chamber, stacked to the roof with crates and creels and barrels of all shapes and sizes.

Neil Cameron gave vent to a long, low whistle of amazement for if he had harboured any doubts about Coll MacDonald's true profession, then they instantly vanished at the sight of the booty on display. Coll and his men were smugglers for sure – and obviously very successful ones at that!

'A man who hass come home iss deserfing of a proper

welcome!' declared the smuggler. 'And if I had a MacCrimmon piper, I'd give you a tune that would swell your heart and bring a tear to your eye all at the same time,' he said apologetically. 'But, then again under the circumstances!' he added, indicating with a firm finger against his lips the need for silence.

'Aye, but wait you!' he reminded himself. 'We can supply the other half of the welcome or my name's no Bienn Coll MacDonald!' And, pulling a bottle from his store:

'A *stoig-chrich* from the *spreidh*!' he proclaimed rapturously, and peered at the label, for all the world like a canny wine merchant selecting a bottle of the finest for his best customer.

'Now then!' he said, returning with a bottle of his choice and handing his bemused guest as fine a crystal glass as would brighten any table in the Kingdom.

'You'll pe haffing a wee dram of the *uisge-beatha* to celebrate your homecoming!' announced Coll with a roguish grin.

At the pop of the cork, the big man's face lit up like a summer's day, for behind every nook and cranny of the cave entrance the eager faces of his men appeared as if by magic.

'Will you look at that now!' grinned the delighted giant with a broad sweep of his huge hand. 'The lads can hear the pop of a cork at a thousand paces and pe back on the spot pefore the first dram iss poured!' he gave a thunderous belly laugh. 'Och, man, man, iss it any wonder they call it the water of life!'

Neil, who had been struggling for some time to keep the smile from his face, could resist the temptation no more and finally erupted in laughter at the sight of the big man's shameless pleasure.

Seeing their leader in fine fettle, and more especially the large bottle of *uisge-beatha* on display, it wasn't long before all the smugglers had come in to join the *ceilidh*.

'Weel, bonnie lad,' sighed Coll raising his glass. 'You haf not a smeek of the *Gaelic*, nor a stitch of the *breacan* to your name, but I bid you welcome – *Ceud mìle fàilte agus slàinte mhór!*'

Through the cave opening and away out to sea, blue sky was showing through the clouds, the sun was out, and the rugged islands of Eigg, Muck, and Rhum were stirring under the dawn mist. But something else too was stirring; deep in the breast of the young Cameron, the sheer wild beauty of this West Highland place had put a swell of pride in his beating heart, as only a man who has come home could ever really know. Looking once more at the expectant faces gathered around him, Neil raised his glass to salute his new-found friends:

'Aye,' he said, and, with all his heart in the words, 'I have come home . . . '

4

Brooding under a dense blanket of cloud, Ben Nevis stood stark and silent. Still snow-capped from the harsh winter, this massive shoulder of rock dominated the skyline at the western tip of the Great Glen, where it cast an omnipresent shadow over the sleeping garrison at Fort William below.

Captain Caroline Frederick Scott wiped the condensation from his office window and observed, with more than a passing interest, the arrival of Lieutenant Bush and his night patrol. The detachment of weary troopers had ridden long and hard through the rain-soaked air on their steaming horses to arrive saddle-sore and bedraggled at the welcoming gates of their fortress headquarters.

Placing his writing quill in the inkstand, Captain Scott set aside the field report he had been so diligently composing, leaned back in his chair and, resting his interlocked fingers upon the leather-top pedestal desk, closed his eyes in thoughtful meditation. His mind drifted back, back to that day in March when he first set foot in this God-forsaken mountain wilderness . . .

The fall of Fort Augustus on 5th March 1746 had sent the rebels, flushed with success, up the glen to seize the greater prize – Fort William! Like a stranded leviathan on the shores of Loch Linnhe this odious symbol of English power had stood defiant throughout the rebellion and, oh, how ardently the Highlanders had coveted its capture!

However, the sitting tenants, Major General Campbell of Mamore and his five-hundred-strong garrison, were none too keen on being evicted by a horde of tribal savages!

During those early days of siege, the fort's defences slowly wilted under the relentless battering by round-shot and mortar fire. Morale hit rock-bottom and desertions to the rebel cause threatened the very life-blood of the garrison itself.

Against a background of mounting anxiety, the military hierarchy in London ordered the immediate despatch of warships to revictual the fort, and a certain Captain Caroline Frederick Scott with orders to hold Fort William at all costs. It was a do-or-die mission demanding every ounce of determination this zealous officer could muster. To galvanise the fort's defences, stand firm against the bombardment, and repulse every rebel attack until relieved.

These orders he carried out to the letter until, finally, on the night of 3 April, their resolve broken, the rebels spiked their cannon and, under cloud of darkness, withdrew. The month-long siege was over . . .

He could smile triumphantly at those memories now. How sweet the taste of victory had been. There was talk of a personal visit by the Duke of Cumberland himself, to bestow the King's blessings upon him. Only the capture of the elusive Royal outlaw would bring a greater glory!

The loud knock on the captain's door broke the spell.

'Come!' thundered Scott in his deep, gravel voice and the door swung open to admit a mud-spattered young Lieutenant with a smart salute.

'Good morning, Captain!' said the officer, pulling himself to attention. The man behind the desk glanced away through the window, watching the dispersing patrol lead their spent horses to the livery stable then, with a slow sweep of the head, he fastened his steely gaze upon the young man standing bolt upright in front of his desk.

'No prisoners today, Lieutenant?' he enquired through a perverse smile.

'No, sir,' replied the nice young officer politely.

Scott studied the fresh face across the desk a long moment in silence. The young lieutenant was popular with the men, fair-minded, and always irritatingly polite. But above all it was his naive military correctness that irked Scott the most.

'You don't like it here, do you, Mr Bush?' the boorish Commander reminded his subordinate. 'And I suspect that you don't much like what we do here?'

The young Lieutenant shifted uneasily.

'Well — laddie?' barked Scott impatiently.

'I do my duty, sir — I obey orders.'

Captain Scott pushed back the chair and, rising to his feet, proceeded to pace the floor with his hands clasped firmly behind his back.

'Aye,' he replied churlishly. 'You obey orders.'

Pausing at a wall chart of the western Highlands, he peered closely at the fine detail, studying every inch of coastline with a show of intense interest.

'This is the devil's own country, Mr Bush — and no place for Christians!' He spun round on his boot-heel, his dark eyes staring owlishly. 'Do we understand each other — laddie?'

The fair-haired Lieutenant drew himself up, deciding it better not to answer.

'If I get wind that your heart is anywhere other than your work,' Scott threatened, 'then, so help me boy, I'll have you scraping Flanders mud off your boots before you can say hallelujah! — Do I make myself clear?'

'Yes, Captain — perfectly clear,' replied the nice young officer politely.

The hard-bitten fort commander turned away in disgust, studying the wall chart again with that same intensity of interest.

'Well, Lieutenant,' he added dismissively, 'unless you have anything further to report?'

Lieutenant Bush summoned up his courage:

'Two French frigates landed a party of men and supplies on the night of the thirtieth, sir!' he informed the other in a rush.

The man studying the wall chart spun round on his heel; the look on his face was positively apoplectic!

'What? Where, damn it?' he thundered. 'Come, come, man! Show me, here on the map!'

Rushing forward at the double, Lieutenant Bush indicated, with a gloved forefinger, the exact spot on the map where the two ships were sighted. 'Right about here, sir — Loch Nan

Uamh!'

Captain Scott stood back from the chart with military straightness, his left eyelid fluttered intermittently and in his eyes there came a distant haunted look, as though the bogey man from his childhood had come back to confront him.

'Loch Nan Uamh . . . ' he whispered, nodding his head with a dawning understanding. 'The Young Pretender's original landing place!'

Scott's face, which was glowing redder than his scarlet uniform, suddenly darkened. 'Did either of these two ships leave with anyone of consequence, Lieutenant?' he enquired in an oddly detached, malevolent voice.

'Our intelligence is patchy, sir,' Lieutenant Bush reminded him. 'But it would seem unlikely.'

The grim-faced Captain relapsed into silence, his eyes once more glued to the map. Only the rapidly beating eyelid betrayed some deep, inner conflict.

'There was just one other piece of information, sir . . . ' the young officer ventured bravely.

'Mmh — what is that you say, Lieutenant?'

'It would appear that a young gentleman came ashore on the ship's open launch, sir. And, according to our reports, he alone remained behind after the ships departed.'

Scott's eyebrows went up. 'A young gentleman, you say?'

'Aye, sir. A young gentleman proclaiming himself a friend of the Royal fugitive,' Lieutenant Bush informed him further.

'Well, well, well — now there's a thing,' remarked the captain, who, having pulled himself upright, was now drumming the fingertips of his cupped hands in front of his lips in stunned fascination.

'And what do we know of this mysterious young gentleman, Mr Bush?'

The lieutenant's eager face pushed forward:

'Only that he has fallen in with a gang of smugglers led by a certain Coll MacDonald of Barrisdale, Captain.'

At the mere mention of the name, the redcoat officer's eyes closed and a sadistic grin of pleasure played upon his thin lips.

'You know this Barrisdale MacDonald then, sir?' the junior officer enquired as his Captain's face showed him a picture of unfulfilled vengeance.

'Oh yes, Mr Bush – through hell and burnt powder I know him – and by God, so help me, I mean to know him again!'

Captain Scott drew himself up and straightened his uniform – a sign his junior officer knew as the prelude to some pending action.

'Rouse the bugler, Lieutenant!' he thundered. 'Boots and saddles at the double! I want our best men and our swiftest horses fed, saddled, and ready to go within the hour!'

'Go? But where, sir?' the totally perplexed lieutenant wanted to know.

'Why, Loch Nan Uamh of course!!' Scott grinned. 'Time is of the essence!' Pulling his tricorn beaver from the hat stand and jamming it on his head at a rakish slant, Captain Scott followed his bemused junior officer through the open door, down the wooden walkway, and out on to the broad quadrangle. Like a stag at the rut, he stood with his head raised upwards, scenting the fresh mountain air.

High on the white painted flagpole, the union colours quarrelled with the wind, and beyond: dark clouds were gathering, the weather was closing in, and yet another rainstorm looked likely. He cursed under his breath the inevitable climate:

'Wind and rain, wind and rain . . . '

Meanwhile, at the opposite end of the Great Glen, some fifty miles northeast of Captain Scott's Fort William location, Captain Ross MacLean was looking up at a very different sky. The early morning sunshine in the hills above the village of Dores held the promise of a glorious day, for such was the habit of the Highland climate, to frustrate and deceive.

But even the welcoming warmth of a spring morning could do little to brighten the sombre mood of the rebel fugitive. The sudden appearance of the soldiers at Arrandale House had convinced him to leave immediately for fear of placing the Lamonts' lives in danger. And though he was far from well, no amount of persuasion by Charles or Alice would make him change his mind.

Fate had indeed been kind to him since that tragic day on the moor. His timely arrival at the big house had surely saved his life and, thanks to the skill of Doctor MacTavish, his wounds were slowly but surely on the mend. Charles Lamont had proved a rock, and a truer friend would be difficult to find in these troubled times.

And, of course, there was Alice.

Such was her impact upon him, that he could scarcely believe that he had ever truly been alive before she came into his life. But with the overwhelming joy she brought him, there came a tinge of sadness, too. For just as surely as a rose has its thorns, the young man knew that he could bring her only danger and heartbreak. And yet, through all the pain and dark moods which had dogged him since Culloden, being apart from her now was the deepest wound of all.

Old friend and comrade Ewen Grant, who had abandoned his hill croft to follow Prince Charlie during those heady days of the '45, had promised Ross a welcome door. That the old man was still absent, and the place devoid of life, bore testament to his fate on that infamous day. And so it was, here in the wooded heights above Loch Ness, that the rebel fugitive had found his refuge.

He would lie low until his wounds healed, safe in the knowledge that the redcoats would take their search westward into the glens. And although Inverness, the Highland capital, lay a mere seven miles or so due east, and was still heavily occupied by enemy soldiers, Ross reasoned that it would be a very foolish quarry, indeed, that would dwell so close to the hunter's gun. His instincts had taught him always to do the unpredictable and now, more than ever, he needed those instincts to come good.

The young man took stock of his situation: there were adequate food supplies; potatoes stored from last year's crop, trout from a nearby stream, and rabbits in the meat larder. Charles Lamont had presented him with a bottle or two of his best vintage. Molly had baked fresh bread and scones which he had greedily consumed the first day of his arrival. And Alice, with tears in her eyes had presented him with a small sack of oatmeal and a comprehensive recipe book – but what on earth he was expected to do with that, he could not imagine!

The croft was dry and comfortable and proved an ideal place of concealment. Secluded in pine trees and accessible from only one direction across the open moor, it afforded him time and opportunity to escape should the need arise.

On a slight rise of ground behind the outbuildings, a colony of raucous crows had taken up residence in a nearby copse and, though they tolerated the human presence with a grudging acceptance, the approach of intruders was accompanied by the most unrelenting alarm call imaginable.

And, so it was, upon this fine May morning, that the black-winged neighbours became unusually restless – hopping fretfully between branches until, all at once, with a single mind they burst from the tree-tops and filled the air with the cries of a thousand banshees!

Ross MacLean strained his eyes over the moor for the cause of the commotion overhead. Presently, the distant image of a horse and rider appeared on the horizon, heading towards him. Limping to the woodshed, he grabbed the loaded flintlock pistol and rusty broadsword he had discovered hidden by their owner.

Pausing in the doorway, he stood transfixed by the sudden appearance of the stranger. Was it Charles Lamont come to visit? He thought it unlikely for it was not the appointed day. And yet, even as he looked, something familiar in the rider's posture in the saddle struck him. The stride pattern of the little horse, too, was distinctive. Gradually, as the rider drew near, the realisation dawned, though he could not believe the evidence of his own eyes until the horse was almost upon him.

'Angus . . . Angus, is it you? – God in heaven!'

As the horse came to an abrupt halt, the rider leapt from the saddle amid a cloud of dust.

'Captain! So it's true — you're alive!'

Man and boy stood and stared at one another in a moment of shared disbelief; the look of incredulity on the one face matched only by the smile of recognition on the other. Then all at once they caught hold of each other in a vigorous bear-hug and danced an impromptu jig of joy in the heather until Ross was forced to stop for fear of hurting his injured leg.

Angus pulled a worried face. 'Has your leg not yet healed?' he gasped, still breathless from his journey.

'Och, it has a mind of its own, Angus, but it is slowly coming round to my way of thinking,' said Ross, laughing at the look of apprehension on his visitor's face. 'It is true that I am not the man I was, but I have it on good authority that I am fortunate to be alive at all.'

Angus smiled back encouragingly as his Captain put an arm around his shoulder and guided him towards the house.

Moments later, the two Jacobite rebels were settled at opposite sides of a broad oak table with full glasses of Charles Lamont's red wine filling their hands.

Angus could only shake his head at the wonder of it all. 'You and your wine, Captain! And this grand wee hideaway too. Who would think to look here, of all places?'

The young lad studied the glass of wine in his hand, ever-mindful of that day on the moor when the man opposite had produced two bottles of the finest, like a magician pulling rabbits from his coat pockets.

'Out here in the middle of nowhere,' sighed Angus in amazement. 'A bottle of the French claret!'

Ross raised his glass. 'This is the first time I've had reason to celebrate since I don't know when,' he smiled. 'To absent friends! And to you young Angus MacLean — come back like the prodigal son. *Slàinte!*' Ross put his empty glass on the table, leaned back in the chair, and looked rather quizzically at his smiling companion.

'How did you know about my leg?' he enquired after some deliberation. 'Outside, just now, you said, "Has your leg not yet healed." And how did you know to find me here? Only one man knows of my whereabouts.'

Angus shifted uneasily in his chair and, emptying his glass with a hurried gulp, looked back rather sheepishly at his host.

'I am very much afraid that I have disobeyed an order, Captain,' he replied. But Ross shrugged his shoulders in ignorance.

The visitor fidgeted with his empty glass and, with his eyes cast downward, began to explain:

'That day on the moor when you sent me away with the message for Cluny MacPherson, I did not deliver it.' Angus looked up into the intense blue eyes of the man opposite. 'When I heard the distant roar of the guns, I doubled back to the moor as fast as I could . . . ' he broke off, looking suddenly wretched. 'But it was too late . . . ' He glanced up, tears in his eyes. 'I should have been there and taken my chances with the men . . . '

Ross reached across the table, grasping the young lad's arm to console him:

'No, Angus. It was not meant to be. You would have perished with the others. There would have been no point to it. The cause was lost long before Culloden, believe me . . . I'm sorry that I lied to you, but there was no other way . . . ' Ross stood up from the table and paced the floor. 'But I still don't understand how you knew about my leg, and how you came by this place? Nobody is supposed to know that I am here.' Grasping the back of his chair with both hands, he gave his young companion a fixed stare which demanded of him an explanation.

'It's a long story, Captain,' replied Angus evasively.

'And I have all the time in the world to hear it,' returned the other unswervingly.

The young lad's head went down again for a moment before continuing:

'After the battle I went away but returned at dusk. I had to know if any of our men had survived. I searched along the river and as close to the field as I dared, for sentries had been posted to keep people away. I searched for over an hour and had all but given up hope of finding anyone alive,' he hesitated, looking suddenly incredulous. 'Then all at once there he was: large as life, grazing by the river's edge – your horse, Captain! And you slumped forward in the saddle!'

Ross, who had all this time been standing listening in silence, pulled back the chair and sat down in wonderment.

'Under cover of darkness I led the horse upstream and away from that terrible place as quickly as I could.'

Ross replenished the wine glasses as the boy's story unfolded:

'I was unsure what to do, knowing only that you were alive and in need of urgent attention. And then I remembered Doctor MacTavish. I had noticed the nameplate on his gate earlier that afternoon and so I decided to head there as fast as the horses would allow . . . ' he paused, shaking his head. 'But when I arrived at the doctor's house, pleading for help, I was told that he was dining that evening with the Lamonts and was not expected back until midnight.' He shook his head again at the dilemma. 'I knew that you would never last out till then so I set off across the moor, following the housekeeper's directions, until I arrived, mercifully, at the gates of Arrandale House.'

Ross MacLean's eyes widened at the words.

'I slapped your horse up the gravel drive and then hid myself in some laurel bushes near the door. Almost at once, two men and two women came out. I watched them carry you inside, then a third man appeared and led your horse off to the stables. I waited a while till the coast was clear; then I crept out from the bushes, remounted my horse and galloped like the wind for town!' His story complete, Angus looked across the table at his friend with uncertain feelings, for the other's impassive features were difficult to read. Perhaps the tale was too incredible for him to believe, though it had been, every word, the truth!

Ross sat back in his chair dumbfounded. Unbelievable though it was, the pieces of the picture fell so neatly into place that it could only be the truth; nothing else could explain his timely arrival at Arrandale House that night.

Rising to his feet in silence and making to leave, Ross paused for a moment in the open doorway then rounded unexpectedly on his visitor:

'Have you any idea what Cumberland's butchers would have done to you if you had been caught? Hung, drawn, and quartered, to be sold as rebel pie in the street markets of London! Good God Almighty, Angus! When will you ever learn to obey orders?' he bellowed angrily and stomped out.

Angus sprang up from the table, followed through the open door, and shouted after him.

'What would you have had me do? Leave you there — to die?'

The words stopped Ross in his tracks. Clutching his throbbing head where the red line of the wound was threatening to burst open with the rising pressure of blood, he stood for several moments. When the pain had subsided, he turned and walked back to the young lad, whose eyes were now cast dejectedly downwards to the earth.

'Forgive me if I have made you angry, Captain,' croaked Angus disconsolately. 'But I could do only what I thought was right.'

With one hand resting firmly on the boy's shoulder and the other to lift his face so that he might read it more clearly, Ross sighed deeply:

'But I am not angry with you Angus,' he explained gently. 'Only at a loss to understand why this worthless life of mine should be the cause of another risking his own — it is quite beyond me.' He shook his head, looking totally flummoxed.

Angus shrugged his shoulders by way of explanation. 'I have no family of my own,' he began. 'No brothers or sisters. My mother and father died of the fever when I was a bairn — I never really knew them . . . ' he said, fighting back the memory. 'It was my old granny that brought me up,' he added warmly. 'In spite of all that has happened, this past year — with you,

Duncan and the others – has been the happiest time of my life . . . just being a part of it all . . . ' he hesitated, looking suddenly embarrassed. 'And you, Captain, you were the big brother I never had.' His head dropped again. 'Is it so strange that I should try to save that which I hold most dear . . . ?'

Ross MacLean closed his eyes a long moment then squeezed the boy's shoulder reassuringly. 'Any man would be proud to have such a wee brother, Angus . . . ' he said quietly, it not being easy to talk with a lump in the throat that choked down the words.

'So it was Charles Lamont who told you where to find me?'

'Aye, Captain.' Angus nodded. 'I rode over to Arrandale House earlier this morning to ask after you and I told him the whole story.' He paused, looking disappointed. 'But he did not believe me at first – not until his daughter, who overheard the mention of your name, came to the study and convinced him that I was, indeed, the same Angus that you had told her about.'

'You saw Alice this morning?'

'Aye, Captain! She is worried about you and anxious to know of your whereabouts. Her father pretended not to know – until she was gone from the room. Only then did he tell me and bid me swear secrecy on it.'

Ross rubbed his chin, as was his way when deep in thought.

'How was she?' he asked.

Angus grinned, for he had not seen the other sparkle so in the eyes for many a long month.

'Like a Princess!' he whistled enthusiastically. 'But there was something she said that I could not understand.'

The young lad's eyebrows went up in curiosity.

'She said that if I was to find you, then I should remind you of the promise.'

Ross beamed back a smile of understanding. It was typical of Alice to hold him to a reckless pledge she knew that he could never fulfil. He shook his head at the memory of it. How on earth would he ever bake a traditional cake from the recipe book she gave him?

Throwing a playful arm around the boy's shoulder, Ross steered him back indoors. 'Now tell me about this old granny of yours, Angus. Can she bake oatcakes and scones?'

5

Pebble after pebble plopped into the deep pool of dark water, sending ripples outward from the centre in ever-increasing circles. There was something symbolic in the way of it all and Alice fancied, in her present mood of despair, that she was like the pool, and Ross was the pebble. And the ripples were the feelings his sudden appearance had set in motion. She wondered if fate had brought him to her door that night like some gift from the gods. But whether by chance or design, she knew now for certain that because of him her life would never be the same again.

'Penny for them!' smiled her father as he sat down beside her on the banks of the garden pond. Glancing up dreamily, she managed a little half smile as he placed a comforting arm around her shoulder. Snuggling in close against him, she breathed deep the wonderful aroma of pipe tobacco which lingered always on his clothes.

She was suddenly reminded of those childhood days when, as a little girl, she would climb on his knee for comfort. And there she would sit, watching intently as he pulled and puffed with the one hand on the long stem of his curved pipe, while the other dangled his gold pocket-watch from its chain close to her ear so that she could listen, with wide-eyed curiosity, to the magic ticking sound which emanated from the mysterious metal case. It was a sound and smell she would always link with her father and she would cherish the memory of those childhood moments for the rest of her life.

'It's Ross MacLean – he's the cause of this long face?' guessed her father intuitively, and squeezing her with reassurance as he said it.

'I do so worry about him, Papa. Doctor MacTavish said that he was foolish to leave when he was clearly far from well.'

Her father listened attentively, as he had always done when

she was upset, and patted her sympathetically in the same caring way.

'You would think that the ungrateful toad couldn't get away quickly enough!'

But her father shook his head at the suggestion:

'Now that's not true, and you know it! Ross left because he was afraid – afraid that his presence here would prove dangerous for us all. After that unfortunate visit from the soldiers, you could hardly blame him for thinking so.' Her father sighed rather thoughtfully. 'I worry about him too, you know,' he admitted, 'he reminds me of me when I was his age,' he said, squeezing her affectionately, 'and you are so like your mother.' He smiled reminiscently. 'There are certain parallels.' He pulled out his pocket-watch to check the time. 'Well, bless my soul!' he exclaimed, suddenly realising the lateness of the hour. 'Let's get back indoors before Molly sounds her infernal dinner gong.'

Late that same evening, as the scavenging crows winged their homeward way to roost, Charles Lamont arrived at the secluded hill croft. His visit had as much to do with the promise he had made to the new tenant as it was out of concern for his daughter's peace of mind.

Ross MacLean, who had studied his visitor's approach closely from his place of concealment, came out at last to greet him.

'Good evening to you, Charles! You must forgive my two companions,' he said, showing the older man the pistol and broadsword, he was holding, 'but I never quite know who to expect up here these days.'

Charles returned a knowing smile:

'I take it Angus found you then?'

'Aye,' grinned the Highlander, 'the wee tyke has a habit of turning up like a bad penny when you least expect it.'

'And lucky for you that he does! wouldn't you say?' his visitor reminded him; to which the Highlander could only nod his head, though a little reluctantly.

After a brief guided tour of the outbuildings, Ross invited his guest indoors, where he toasted his arrival with a large measure of his favourite malt tipple. 'Did you come across any hostiles?' he enquired of his guest as they sat at the broad oak table.

'Not a sight and, in any event, I have my story well rehearsed,' replied the solicitor, raising his glass in gratitude. 'I am a harmless old lawyer visiting a client in connection with a tenancy agreement.' He gave a sly grin. 'Scots Law is totally beyond them and I have prepared suitable documents in my saddle bags if proof should be required.'

Ross could only smile back in admiration at the cunning contrivance of this ostensibly law-abiding gentleman sitting, the picture of innocence, across the table.

'You are to be commended on your choice of living quarters,' said the visitor, looking around him with more than a little interest in his friend's new home. 'A very comfortable residence and, indeed, no easy place to find.'

'The former tenant was a fey old man who kept very much to himself,' Ross informed him, 'but the place does him credit for he was hard-working and tidy in his ways.' He broke off, looking suddenly pensive. 'I can only trust that he will forgive my intrusion.'

'A friend's gain is no loss,' Charles reminded him after a satisfying gulp of the golden liquid.

Removing a sheet of folded notepaper from his coat pocket, the lawyer placed his reading glasses on his nose and positioned himself in such a position as to allow the late evening sunlight, which peeked through the window, to fall obligingly on the writing.

'I paid a visit to General Hawley's headquarters at the Town House this morning,' Charles informed the Highlander. 'Just in time to witness the hapless Provost Hossack being escorted through the building by the scruff of the neck for daring to speak out against the army's harsh treatment of the townsfolk.' He hesitated, raising his eyebrows. '"Damn you, puppy. Do you pretend to dictate here?" was Hawley's snappy response.

Whereupon the poor fellow was manhandled to the top of the stairs and received such a kick that he never touched ground till his backside met the cobbles in Castle Wynd!'

The two men couldn't conceal their amusement at the misfortune of the town's principal dignitary. 'Apparently he has already been dubbed *The Kicked Provost!*' added Charles ruefully.

Ross was not the least surprised, for such was the custom of the Highland sense of humour, to link the victims by soubriquet to their own misfortunes.

That lighthearted moment over, Charles shook the notepaper he was holding and looked over his lenses at the young man opposite before proceeding:

'Ross, I have made many enquiries in recent weeks and have compiled a summary of my findings. I have to tell you now that much of what I have discovered does not make for pleasant reading,' he paused, looking intensely concerned. 'If you would prefer not to hear what I have written, then I will fold this sheet of paper and tuck it out of sight once and for always and we will say no more about it.' The older man stared across the table at the younger, whose face was distinctly uneasy.

'When I begged your indulgence, Charles, I held no illusions as to what you might uncover. The fate of my men, I knew already in my heart to be forlorn . . . ' he broke off. 'I sensed it with Angus, though he was careful not to make mention of it,' he looked up, a painful, haunted look. 'There are more secrets to be revealed in silence than ever in words. Pray, Charles, continue!'

The lawyer cleared his throat and took a deep draught of the golden liquid before commencing:

'According to the official lists two hundred and twenty-two French and three hundred and thirty-six Scots prisoners of various clans are presently under lock in the town's gaols.'

There fell an awkward pause.

'There does not appear to be any record of the wounded,' added the reader solemnly. On hearing only a profound silence,

Charles thought it better to press on regardless. 'The Prince is believed to be in hiding somewhere in the Western Isles and has so far evaded all attempts by the military to secure his capture. Not even the very considerable reward of thirty thousand pounds sterling, for information leading to his arrest, has tempted a single whisper of his whereabouts.' Charles glanced over his spectacles, but the face of the young man opposite was an unreadable book.

Replenishing his empty glass, the lawyer continued at pace:

'Lord George Murray, Lochiel, and a handful of other clan leaders were fortunate to escape with their lives. Murray retreated in good order with the remnants of the Highland army still intact and headed south to Ruthven in Badenoch, where they regrouped to await further orders from the Prince. But when the *sauve-qui-peut* message arrived the following day and it was clear that the Rebellion was over, the clans disbanded and went home to their glens . . . Murray himself is believed to have gone to ground somewhere in Glenartney . . . '

The reader looked up from the paper and over his lenses to the listener opposite, who was now sitting in a state of stunned silence. Though Charles could feel the anguish in the stillness of the room, he decided to press ahead with his report:

'Cameron of Lochiel was carried from the field with both ankles broken by grapeshot and somehow, incredible though it sounds, taken the fifty miles back to Loch Arkaig, where he is believed still to be. Ian Garbh Cameron bore the wounded Grant of Corriemony on his back all the way to Glenurquhart . . . ' Charles broke off, shaking his head in admiration.

But still there was no response from the Highlander opposite.

'Keppoch, badly wounded in the charge, was taken by his men to a bothy some distance from the battle. There he later died of his wounds. Gillies MacBean of Clan Chattan, badly wounded, with his back to a wall and broadsword in hand, is said to have accounted for thirteen of the enemy before the horses of the dragoons trampled him underfoot. Even then, he refused to die and crawled to a barn at Balvraid, where he lived until evening. Robert Mor MacGillivray, trapped and unarmed, seized the wooden shaft of a peat cart and despatched seven of his pursuers before he was finally overpowered . . . '

Glancing up from the paper to the young man opposite, Charles could see that his eyes were by now red and moist. Though there was more to tell – much more, in fact – it was clear to the older man that the listener had already heard enough. Folding the notepaper in his coat pocket along with his spectacles, Charles pulled out his pipe and tobacco pouch and made ready to smoke.

The Highlander rose from the table, walked over to the window, and gazed out across the moor. The room fell suddenly silent; one man unable to speak, and the other lost for appropriate words.

Eventually the younger man spoke first:

'I've done a lot of hard thinking since I came up here, Charles. Something in the tranquillity of the place has a way of reaching into a man's soul and unlocking all the hidden truths he would sooner choose to forget . . . And, believe me, I have tried to forget, but I cannot . . . If I had known then what I now know to be true, I would have broken my sword at Loch Shiel and turned my back on the whole sorry affair.' He paused, his voice filled with emotion. 'Oh, but it was a bonnie dream we were sold, Charles, and it burned so fiercely in the dreamer's heart that it caught fire in us all. And for a time, it seemed, the whole country was ablaze with it . . . even through that long and bitter winter, it warmed us still . . . until that day on the moor when the flame flickered and died and we saw the dream for the nightmare it had become . . . '

There fell a hush upon the little room, only the puffing of the visitor's pipe above the silence until the plaintive cry of a distant curlew broke the stillness of the moment.

'Angus has told me tales of homes in flames, of sheep and cattle driven from the glens, women and bairns wandering the hills. Whole families destroyed,' he half turned from the window, his eyes cast downward. 'It is a heavy burden I must

73

bear, Charles, and one I feel less and less able to justify with each passing day . . . '

Charles Lamont, who had all this time sat quietly in the dim interior of the little room, rose ponderously from the table and drank the last remaining drops of liquor from his glass. He moved to the fireplace where he tapped out his pipe on the stone hearth. Then, returning to the table, he picked up his hat and cane, walked over to the window where the Highlander was standing, and placed a comforting hand upon his shoulder.

'I think you are being a little too hard on yourself, my boy,' he said, 'Nothing cuts so deep as the self-inflicted wound. You have your whole life ahead of you. Don't waste it looking over your shoulder to the ghosts of the past.' Charles guided the sullen young man away from the window. 'Let's go outside and get some air. Walk with me to my horse,' he suggested with an encouraging smile.

Outside the smoke-filled room the evening shadows had lengthened considerably, and the sun, which had burned steadily through that long afternoon, had now all but slipped from view behind the hills to the west.

Charles Lamont conducted his walking companion down the short path to the gate where his docile old mare stood tethered and waiting.

'There is a little matter of a — shall we say? — *delicate* nature I would like to discuss with you,' said the lawyer after much deliberation and with his hand still on the other's shoulder. 'It will not have escaped your attention, Ross, that during your stay with us at Arrandale a certain young lady showed more than a passing interest in your well-being. I had rather foolishly believed that once you had left, things would have returned to normal,' he shook his head, looking perplexed. 'It appears, however, that I have been proved very much mistaken! Why, even an old fool like me would be hard pressed not to see the change which has come over the girl since your untimely departure.'

The Highlander opened his mouth to speak but found his words stifled on his lips.

'No. Please, Ross, let me finish! What I am trying to say, my boy, is that when it comes to affairs of the heart, things are always best brought out into the open. No good ever comes out of one party thinking one thing when the other is, well, thinking something — something altogether different.' He looked at the Highlander pleadingly:

'You do understand what I'm driving at, don't you, my boy?'

Ross opened his mouth to answer but again found himself speechless.

'There now, I've said it. And I'll say no more on the matter!' concluded the lawyer with a dismissive wave of the hand. Then, climbing laboriously into the saddle, the departing visitor collected his reins from the bemused Highlander.

Behind them, silhouetted against the fading light, the last straggler flew into the pines and settled his black wings in preparation for the approaching darkness.

Charles Lamont pulled his coat against the chill night air. 'It has been a grand old day, Ross,' he remarked, 'though somewhat cold behind the sun, as you Highlanders would say.' He gave his young friend a leaving smile and, clicking to his horse, turned her slow feet homeward.

After his visitor had gone, Ross took himself off across the moor to a place some distance from the house where he sat down under a tree overlooking the loch. There, pulling a blanket around his shoulders, he settled in for the night. But there would be no sleep for him tonight, as there had been none the night before. In truth he had not slept soundly since the morning of the battle, when overwhelming fatigue had overtaken him and his men upon their return from the abortive night attack on Cumberland's slumbering army.

Across the loch, on the verdant meadows of Fort Augustus some miles to the south west, the glow of Cumberland's camp fires shining through the darkness were a constant reminder of the new order. Three battalions of the King's Foot had marched there from Inverness on 16 May. Howard's Buffs, men of Cholmondeley and Price, and eight companies of Argyll

Militia: the advance party of Rebel hunters who would begin the pogrom. Or was it genocide of the clans? It was difficult for Ross to believe that anything else could be their intention.

Tonight in the woods the bark of a roe deer, and in the air above the shriek of a mousing owl on silent wings, would be his only companions. Tomorrow, Angus would return. Ross would never have believed how precious human company could be, for at that moment, as the darkness closed in and the long night beckoned, he had never felt so utterly lonely in his life . . .

Next morning, Angus glanced up at the vociferous crows circling overhead, pulled the small telescope from his coat pocket, and studied the rider heading towards them.

'How many of them?' enquired Ross, emerging from the woodshed with the familiar pistol and broadsword at the ready.

After some nervous moments, Angus closed the telescope and popped it casually into his coat pocket. 'Only one!' he replied. 'And you won't be needing these,' he added removing the sword and pistol from his friend's grasp. 'It's a lassie!'

Puzzled, Ross stood squinting against the sun as the rider drew near.

'Alice! What in the—?'

The high-stepping sorrel cantered to a halt and Alice, resplendent in a deep-crimson riding habit of velvet, trimmed with gold, beamed down at him from the saddle.

'Surprised to see me?' she asked, her eyes flashing defiance.

But Ross was too thunderstruck to answer.

'Well, are you going to do the gentlemanly thing and help me down?' she enquired with a provocative flick of her long golden hair.

Ross, still stupefied by her sudden appearance, reached up to help ease her down from the saddle, when his unreliable leg buckled beneath him, sending them both crashing headlong into the heather; he landing on his back with Alice on top. For an instant, they stared in mutual shock at each other, then exploded into laughter.

'I was about to ask if your leg had healed,' she gushed between giggles, 'but I think I have my answer!'

Attempting to get up, Ross found to his surprise that the lady was not for moving. And there was a strange sparkle in her eyes such as he had not seen there before. 'Why, Miss Lamont, I do believe that you are taking advantage of an invalid!' he observed with a cocked eyebrow.

'Why, Captain!' she replied with equal aplomb. 'Whatever gave you that idea?'

Angus appeared at the doorway shaking his head disapprovingly 'Where I come from, Captain, people generally shake hands when they haven't seen each other for a time.'

Ross got up quicker than he had gone down and pulled his red-faced visitor to her feet as the young lad came over to greet her.

'We meet again, Miss Lamont,' said the boy politely.

'Angus,' replied Alice sweetly and in an instant, he had seized the outstretched hand and placed a courteous kiss upon it, whilst affecting the most flamboyant bow.

Ross threw an upward glance at this display of ostentation while Alice positively beamed with delight.

'It is so refreshing to meet with such a gallant gentleman. Sadly, there are so few left nowadays,' she remarked, looking teasingly at Ross. 'Don't you agree, Captain MacLean?'

Ross retrieved his hat from the heather and dusted it down in silence. Angus decided to retreat graciously from the scene and, gathering the loose reins, walked away with the visitor's horse while whistling a popular love tune of the day.

Alice glanced knowingly at Ross then stepped forward and took possession of his hand in that way of hers. 'It's a beautiful day – let's go for a walk,' she said, gripping his entwined fingers more and more tightly as they went.

Down a narrow footpath through the pines, Alice stopped to gather discarded cones beneath the trees. She puzzled at their half-eaten appearance until Ross explained that they were the left-over dinner of the red squirrel, dropped from the branches above.

Pushing breast-high through the bracken, they came upon a stream threading its way lazily across the moor. Here, on the banks of a deep pool, Ross pointed to the myriad darting fish and flying insects, to the kingfisher as it flashed from a rock, and the zig-zagging sand martins on the far bank opposite. A roebuck came to drink, unaware of the human presence. Alice stood fascinated by the noiseless vision of this enchanting creature as it drew ever closer. Never had she seen the small fairy-like deer with its large and limpid eyes, its busy twitching ears, and nervous glances so close before. An all-too-fragile being, she thought, for this turbulent world.

It was a faultless day with not a cloud visible in the noon sky as they walked on in perfect silence, each rapt in the presence of the other, daring not to speak lest they should break the spell of magic between them. Then, all at once, over the brow of a hill, they came upon the loch. The moody magnificence of Loch Ness spreading out below them and off into the distance as far as the eye could see quite took the breath away.

Foreboding, melancholy, mysterious, it was many things, but on such a sun-drenched day as this, the vast expanse of crystal-clear water glistened like some gigantic jewel in the glen.

Alice sank down among the spring flowers, pulling Ross down beside her. Leaning back on her elbows, she shook free her golden hair as the warm scents of yellow gorse breathed over them.

'Oh, Ross, it's so peaceful up here,' she sighed admiringly.

But the Highlander, who was now lying propped up on an elbow was too busy studying another of nature's splendours to notice. She looked even more beautiful than he remembered. Like good wine, time had a way of sweetening the memory. If she only knew the effect she had upon him, he felt certain she would pick up her skirts and run home to safety!

Feeling his eyes upon her, she turned to face him but his gaze went down in fear that she might see his innermost desires. She saw only the long dark lashes which concealed the truth. Those eyelashes, she thought, most women would kill for. How positively unfair of nature to bestow such weapons of flirtation on a mere man!

Of all the things she had thought to say to him when next they met, for the life of her, she could not think of a single thing until she remembered the letter she was carrying. Now, she thought, would be the time to learn the truth – however painful it might prove.

Sitting upright, she removed the crumpled envelope from her riding jacket. 'I trust you will forgive me, Ross,' she began nervously, 'but before Father destroyed your clothes, the morning after you came to us, I took the liberty of searching through your pockets. I thought there might be something you would wish to keep,' she paused, handing the distressed envelope to him. 'I found this letter. I'm afraid it is rather the worse for wear, and has some of your blood on it,' she said apologetically.

Ross pulled himself upright, looking intensely curious. One of the ghosts of the past which her father had warned against had come back to haunt him.

'Mhairi? It is a woman's name?' Alice inquired, though he barely heard the words. 'Is she someone you know? Is she someone special?' Biting her lip as she said the words, Alice stole a sideways glance at Ross, who appeared to have recovered some of his composure.

He looked away momentarily, a painful memory etched on his face. 'Yes, she is someone special,' he replied softly.

'Oh, I see,' was all she could think to say.

'She is the wife of a very old friend,' he informed her and Alice could feel her heart sail once more.

After much deliberation and gathering of courage, she ventured to probe deeper. 'Then it was her husband who gave you this letter to give to his wife?'

Ross simply nodded.

'So that you might deliver it to her if anything was to happen to . . . ' her voice tailed off as she realised that she had answered her own question. Pulling her knees up close against her chest, she gazed off into the distance.

Ross, sensing her anguish, beamed her an encouraging smile. 'Thank you for rescuing it. With all that has happened these past weeks, the business of the letter had completely slipped my mind.'

She turned to him again, the flutter under her ribcage beating more rapidly now. 'And did your friend take possession of a letter for you?' she asked, hardly daring to hear the answer that might shatter her fragile illusions.

But Ross could only sigh deeply and, gazing into her brown pools of doubt:

'Alice, there was no letter, for there is no-one,' he assured her, and with a degree of conviction that even her disbelieving heart could not deny.

Taking possession of his hand, she held it as a drowning man might clutch at a straw. 'Ross, you must forgive me if at times I seem insensitive. I feel so happy when I am with you that in my eagerness for you to be happy too, I am inclined to forget what you and your friends have suffered. Sometimes I say things and then instantly wish that I could cut out my tongue for having said them!' She looked at him pleadingly. 'You do understand? Please say that you do!'

The Highlander smiled tenderly and squeezed her hand as he did so. 'You must not feel that you have to walk on egg-shells when you are with me. My heart is not made of glass. There is nothing that you cannot ask of me. There must be no secrets between us!' he declared, searching her eyes for some flicker of accord.

'No secrets – Yes, you are right. There must be no secrets between us!' she agreed wholeheartedly and, in doing so, had walked unsuspecting into the trap he had so cunningly set for her.

Ross gave the wicked grin of a poacher who has just stolen a pheasant from under the gamekeeper's nose.

'Then, if there are to be no secrets between us, you must tell me how you came to find me here? Angus has told me that your father kept the truth of my whereabouts from you.'

Alice looked up from the impasse in the way of a chess player who has just witnessed her King being checked and cornered by an opponent.

'You cheating toad!' she scolded.

But the Highlander's eyebrows went up in anticipation. 'Well?' he insisted.

'I followed my father up here last night, if you must know!' she admitted unashamedly.

Ross could scarcely conceal his disbelief and looked away gasping reproachfully. The girl was impossible; he had never known another like her!

She peeked round his shoulder, looking at the stern face through big, innocent eyes. 'Do you think me a recalcitrant female?' she enquired in the way of a child seeking forgiveness.

'I might!' retorted Ross furrowing his brows, 'if I knew what the hell it meant!'

For an instant she looked shocked then, all at once, triggered that uncontrollable giggle of hers; so infectious that it set Ross laughing too.

'Oh, Ross!' she scolded between breaths. 'You're totally incorrigible, you really are!'

There fell a hush after the laughter died away and Alice, her brain racing to form the words she had come up here so determined to convey, seized her moment in the silence.

'Father has gone to Edinburgh for a few days,' she announced matter-of-factly. 'I have given Molly and Alex leave to visit a sick relative in Nairn,' she paused, looking hopeful,' I was wondering if you would do me the courtesy of accepting my invitation to dinner this evening?' Her eyes were wide now with anticipation. 'Providing, of course, that you have no pre-arranged plans?'

Ross sat bolt-upright, looking intensely curious. 'You mean to tell me that you are all alone in that big house?'

'Molly and Alex will return tonight – sometime,' she retorted.

But the Highlander looked perplexed.

'Ross, I am not a child!' she reminded him sharply. 'In case you hadn't noticed!'

Ross glanced down from the defiant glare to the sensual swell of her breasts and could only raise his eyebrows in agreement.

'Well?' she insisted.

But the Highlander's reply died on his lips as the beating of distant drums came to them from the valley floor below. In an instant he was on his feet and off down the gentle slope of the hill, stopping at a flat rock where he lay face down, scanning the dirt road far below.

Alice came to join him.

'Soldiers – hundreds of them!' he informed her as Alice peered through the tree tops for a sight of them. Angus, who had also heard the din, appeared with his telescope and lay down beside them on the rock.

'Looks like they intend to bivouac at Dores!' he told them after some moments of study through the glass.

Ross MacLean rubbed his chin; more of Charles Lamont's ghosts of the past – eight battalions of them were marching down the glen in a great thunderstorm of drums with none other than the Duke of Cumberland himself, flanked by vedettes of Kingston's Horse, leading the way.

'Alice, it is not safe for you here!' declared Ross, turning suddenly urgent.

'You must return home at once. Angus will escort you!'

Tossing the telescope to his Captain, Angus jumped to his feet and hurried off to prepare the horses. But Alice would have none of it and argued against the decision as Ross pulled her to her feet.

'But you must come with us!' she pleaded. 'If it is unsafe for me then it is unsafe for you also.'

But the Highlander shook his head against the idea and, placing his hands upon her slender shoulders, he smiled down reassuringly. 'They have no business here,' he told her and, mindful of the incident with the young trooper he and Duncan had encountered on the Nairn River the day of the battle. 'I fear only that one of their absent-minded scouts might stumble upon this place accidentally. I have known it happen,' he explained.

But Alice remained unconvinced and pulled a worried face for his safety.

'I have my hiding places. They will not find me – I promise!' he assured her. 'In any event, it will pass the day for me,' he said showing her the telescope. 'I can watch them eat, and see if I can't learn some of their English table manners.'

But Alice stood yet immovable.

'So that I might know how to behave at dinner this evening!'

Her expression softened as she realised that he had, at last, accepted her invitation.

Angus reappeared and signalled that the horses were ready to depart.

'Go now!' urged Ross, and Alice picked up her skirts and raced off quickly – only to stop some yards away to turn and look back.

'Eight o'clock! Tonight! Be there!' she commanded.

Ross smiled back obediently and watched her run down the narrow path through the pines with Angus in the lead.

Satisfied that she was safely away, he turned a worried face once more and lay upon the rock to watch the enemy below.

The long red line had broken and now spilled out across the green meadows on the shores of Loch Ness in a great hubbub of noise and activity. And all the while, the unseen rebel on the hill studied every movement, meticulously, through the lens of his telescope.

If any of their scouts happened to come by, then the crows would tell him. But the colony remained quiet that afternoon, for the redcoats, so preoccupied in the business of their camp, had neither the time nor the inclination to wander any great distance from the security of the loch shore.

The grandeur of Loch Ness, as it lay dark and silent in its deep mountain trench, unsettled the soldiers. Many had never seen such wilderness before. The high mountain walls and sheer ravines of grey and red, looming above them, were alien features to lowland eyes. And though it was almost summer there was a chill in this Highland glen and a strange stillness in the air which served only to remind them of the hostile territory that lay a hard day's march ahead.

Throughout the long afternoon Ross watched silently, and in the evening, when the bivouac fires were lit and the outlying pickets posted, the lengthening shadows told him that it was time to go. After all, he had more important things than enemy soldiers on his doorstep to think about. A hot bath and a change of clothes for his dinner engagement with the most beautiful girl in the Highlands!

Angus arrived back as Ross was making preparation to leave.

'I had to be sure that you were still safe, Captain!' the young lad explained to his somewhat irritated companion.

'I'm beginning to wonder which of us is the wee brother in this relationship?' Ross mumbled, but it was water off a duck's back to Angus, who simply smiled back, imperviously, as he handed over a paper bag between horses.

'I brought you something!' he announced proudly.

Ross peeked inside. 'Scones!' he exclaimed triumphantly.

'Aye, and freshly baked too!' Angus informed him. 'And she had better like them for I took a skelp on the lug for the asking!' he added ruefully.

Ross chuckled at the idea of the aggressive granny. 'Och, but it was well worth the wallop!' he assured the boy.

'Aye, it's easy for you to say,' complained the boy, holding his tender ear, 'She said I had a damn cheek asking if she could bake scones when I'd only eaten them for the past fifteen years!'

Ross placed the priceless cakes carefully in his saddle bags as Angus looked on.

'Alice will never believe it!' he grinned as he gathered the reins to leave.

But Angus had pulled his worried face again. 'Captain, be careful down there!' he warned earnestly.

Ross stared at the boy in bewilderment then shook his head

in dismay. 'For pity's sake, Angus, she's only a woman — what harm can she do?' Not wishing to hear any more on the matter, he whirled his horse around, in a great flurry of dust, and galloped away.

Angus sat impassively in the saddle, watching the rapidly departing figure disappear over the hill. 'I was meaning the redcoats, Captain!' he murmured quietly to himself . . .

6

Arrandale House stood in a natural woodland of Scots pine and silver birch. The garden grounds, enclosed on all sides by a high perimeter wall, had two sculpted eagles perched high on lofty stone pillars overlooking the always-open wrought-iron gates. Here, an avenue of overhanging trees formed a perfect tunnel of foliage above the long driveway which swept gently to the front entrance.

The garden — with its manicured lawn and ubiquitous spring flowers — was ablaze with colour.

The house itself was a large rambling building of red sandstone with towering chimneys and a moss-covered slate roof. The centre structure was very old, possibly sixteenth-century, but the east and west wings showed evidence of a more recent design.

The place had a timeless quality which could not fail to impress even the most insensitive observer.

At eight o'clock precisely Ross MacLean stood on the deeply curved stone doorstep, gave a quick tug at the bell chain, and watched the weathered oak door swing open.

In the twilight of evening Alice looked stunning in a pink satin off-the-shoulder gown. Her hair was teased up in a fashion he had not seen on her before. Pearl-drop earrings and a fine, gold-link chain necklace glistened against the smooth texture of her skin. She looked beautiful. The very quintessence of perfect young womanhood.

He hadn't uttered a word, but his face must have betrayed him.

'Well?' enquired the lady. 'Are you going to stand there with your mouth hanging open all night, or is it your intention to come in?'

Snapping out of his trance, Ross stepped across the threshold and wiped his boots enthusiastically on the doormat.

'Good evening, Miss Lamont!' he announced with a courteous bow of the head and a flamboyant sweep of his three-cornered hat.

Alice returned a polite half-bob of her own.

'Why, Captain!' she said, admiring his fine suit of clothes and polished appearance. 'Forgive me if I stare – but you look so incredibly different!' She took his hat and cloak. 'And you won't be needing that!' she scowled, pointing an accusing finger at the light sword hanging from his belt.

He undid the buckle and surrendered the offending weapon. 'In case of eventualities!' he explained.

'Not in this house!' she told him.

As she hung up his travelling clothes, he gazed longingly at the back of her neck; the bare flesh looked so inviting. He had to stop himself from kissing it. What if she was offended? Him taking liberties like that! She might get mad and send him packing. He resisted the temptation.

She turned suddenly, showing him a worried face. 'Oh, Ross!' she gasped earnestly. 'All afternoon I've been on tenterhooks for your safety. I was so sure that the soldiers would find you. I should never have left you there . . . '

He silenced her protests with a finger on her lips and a glint of a smile in his eyes. He was pleased that she was worried for him; it signified deeper feelings.

'But I am here and I am safe!' he assured her. 'So there is no need to worry.'

But her doubtful look remained.

'Why do women always seem to worry over nothing?' he wanted to know, 'Is it some prerequisite of birth?'

She hit him playfully on the arm. 'Because we have to look after careless little boys like you!'

He looked searchingly around. 'I do believe I have a dinner engagement,' he reminded her. 'Do you think the young lady of the house is ready to receive me?'

Alice gave a silent reply, as women do when slighted by discourteous gentlemen. Bidding him follow, she led him down the hall to the drawing room. Smiling sweetly, she opened the door and ushered him in. 'And I'll have less of your cheek,

Captain MacLean. Unless you fancy being the main course this evening!' she warned.

He responded by swiftly pulling the bag of scones from his pocket and handing it to her. 'Truce!' he grinned as she peeked inside. 'As promised!' he reminded her proudly.

'But you didn't bake these?' she questioned. 'You couldn't have!'

'Don't pass judgement until you've tasted them!' he advised.

She looked distinctly suspicious but could read little in the inscrutable smile he beamed back. 'You haven't heard the last of this, Ross MacLean – I'll get to the truth of it – you see if I don't!'

'Oh ye of little faith!' he complained, looking suitably wounded.

Pouring a large measure of her father's malt whisky, Alice handed him the glass then crossed the room, opened the French windows on to a wide veranda, and stepped out leaving him watching. Leaning against the low stone wall she inhaled the sweet scents of evening then turned slowly back to face him.

'It's a wonderful evening!' she enthused. 'I love how the twilight lingers so long up here in the north. I think it is my favourite time of day and spring is my favourite season.' She closed her eyes, breathing deeply. 'You can almost hear nature stirring from the long sleep of winter . . .'

All this time, the Highlander had stood trancelike, hanging on her every word. Her movements seemed dreamlike in their slowness, as though time had stretched from seconds into minutes. The image of her beauty at that precise moment as she leaned serenely on that low-pillared wall – a silhouette against the last dim lambency of sunset would remain with him forever.

'Are you feeling unwell, Ross?' she stood up from the wall, looking suddenly concerned. 'You seem distant somehow. Perhaps you should sit for a moment.' She came over to him, took hold of his arm and led him gently to an armchair by the fire.

'You are not well!' she scolded. 'I knew that you should

never have left here so soon when it is quite clear to me that you are far from recovered!'

He raised a silencing hand as he sat back in the chair. 'You . . . you look beautiful!' he admitted, in spite of himself, and a trace of colour came to her face.

Then Alice looked suddenly embarrassed. 'I was beginning to think you hadn't noticed,' she murmured.

'Did you encounter any difficulties on your way over?' she asked, cleverly steering the conversation from further blushes.

He smiled at the evasive nature of the question. Perhaps if he told her that he had met with a redcoat behind every tree, she might show some surprise. But it was doubtful. He was more certain that she would smile back sweetly with an *Oh, how nice!* Such was the absence of her mind at that precise moment. Instead he said:

'I cut across the moor avoiding the road as much as possible, but there were no "difficulties", as you put it.'

Alice nodded dutifully, but without much perception, then gradually the light of understanding returned to her eyes. 'I am growing tired of the sight of them!' she groaned. 'When I accompany Father and Molly to town, their leering faces stare in that unspeakable way as though they considered every woman a part of the spoils of war.' She looked away, fleeing from the unpleasant memory. 'Some of the women chase after the soldiers with plaids and trinkets to sell. You would almost think that they enjoyed having them here!' she complained bitterly.

Ross nodded sympathetically:

'Yes, I believe some of the lassies are doing quite nicely out of it.' But his meaning was clearly lost on her innocent ears.

The delicious aroma of food came to them and Alice remembered the dinner.

'Back in a moment!' she told him, springing to her feet and rushing off.

When she had gone from the room Ross rose to his feet and took in the opulence about him. The room was a peculiar mixture of dates and places. The heavily oak-panelled walls belonged to a century or more earlier, adorned on all sides by gilt-framed oil paintings and a few contemporary water colours. Heavy velvet curtains draped the two large windows overlooking the front lawn, where a giant, spreading beech tree stood. The fine English furniture looked, as far as he could guess, to be of mainly Elizabethan period, though an elaborate escritoire of walnut, and a *bonheur-du-jour* in rosewood, had a distinct Frenchness.

On the wall, above the blazing log fire, hung an oil painting of an American Indian on a striking palomino stallion. Something of the subject struck a harmonious chord. Here was a tribal people persecuted by the very powers who now threatened the Highland way of life. The similarities were all too obvious and the Highlander could not resist the temptation to raise his glass and salute the unknown warrior.

The dinner gong sounded in the hall. 'Dinner is about to be served, Captain! Come this way, if you please.'

Alice had returned to the servant role once more, much to his amusement. He followed obediently. In the dining room he gave a gasp of approval at the sight of the luxurious table laid before him. The silver cutlery and crystal goblets she had placed strategically opposite each other, either side of the long mahogany table. Only the light from the heavily ornate four-piece candelabrum, positioned centre-table, to the left of the place settings, illuminated the room.

It was clear that she had gone to a great deal of trouble to make the evening special and he felt suitably honoured that it was for him.

'Please be seated!' It was the servant again, pulling out a chair from the table and inviting him to sit.

'You spoil me with all this attention. How will I ever repay you?'

'Now, Captain, we mustn't be flirtatious with the servants!' she answered teasingly.

The silver entrée dish arrived on the table with a proud clatter. 'Salmon *à la mont!*' she announced, lifting the lid sufficiently to permit a brief tantalising glimpse of the steaming pink flesh. 'And we have venison Arrandale to follow!' she promised proudly.

'What! No cuddies, bannocks, or crannachan?'

Alice looked horrified. She'd never heard of such things. 'Certainly not!' she replied indignantly. Whatever they were, they sounded absolutely repulsive!

She took her seat opposite and adjusted her napkin. 'You might like to pour her ladyship a glass of wine?' she suggested, looking hopefully at the crystal decanter which now contained a fine French claret from her father's cellar.

Filling both goblets to just below the rims, he touched glasses. '*Slàinte!*' he smiled, and she returned a 'Bon Appetit!' of her own.

The dinner was excellent and afterwards they retired to the drawing room to recover. Seeing the moonlight, she threw on a shawl, caught hold of his hand and led him out onto the veranda to look at the moon.

Out here the air was redolent with the spicy fragrance of honeysuckle where it scrambled up a wall nearby. She closed her eyes as the delicious scent wafted over them. She placed her hands on the stone balustrade, her fingers playing it like a piano. He placed a hand on top of them, stopping the melody. She looked up smiling, her bright eyes throwing back the moonlight. They were dilated now, liquid and enticing. He might fall in and drown there if he wasn't careful.

He stood looking down at her fragile beauty, unable to speak, feeling special that it was for him. Words seemed unnecessary between them at that moment, for another sense was at work; a silent secret language they both felt keenly.

There was a halo round the moon now and a dew was forming. She pulled her shawl against the cold. He came up behind her and rubbed her upper arms, warming her. She leaned back against him, inviting his arms to enfold her and he obliged, slipping his hands down to envelope her slim waist completely. She placed her hands on his, feeling their warmth, enjoying the security they gave her. She closed her eyes and murmured contentedly, drawing a long sigh of pleasure from him. They stood thus entwined, swaying to the rhythm of the moonlight, feeling its silent secret song that only they could hear.

She told him the story of the moon weavers; the fairy people who lived at the bottom of the garden and who weaved magic spells in the moonlight. And when young lovers looked up at the moon, they would be struck by the spell the fairy people had weaved for them. And from that day forward, they would be destined to remain forever in love . . .

An owl hooted in a nearby tree and she giggled at the sudden absurdity of its call 'Toowit Toowoo!' she echoed. He told her it was Gaelic and translated it into English for her. But she didn't believe a word of it! How could an owl she'd never met possibly know such intimate things about her? She squeezed his hands with delight for she loved it when he teased her; at that moment, he was hers completely. She looked up smiling and caught the gleam of mischief in his eyes, and the dark hair, falling in roguish disorder across his forehead, tickled her nose.

Suddenly it started to rain. Lightly at first, then heavier by the minute. She moaned disappointedly and the owl hooted again. He held his hand out to catch the raindrops and whispered in her ear, 'Too wet to woo!' Laughing, she pulled him back indoors before the heavens opened. Once inside, she removed her shawl, shook it free of rainwater, and closed the French windows behind her. 'Ross!' she said, turning suddenly serious. 'I am worried about Father. He has not been himself lately.'

He spun round on the spot, the laughter fading from his face as she spoke.

'I thought at first that it may have had something to do with you, or perhaps, out of some concern for me,' she shrugged her shoulders, looking perplexed. 'But now I'm not sure what to believe.'

He sat down on the edge of the chair in front of the fireplace, looking equally puzzled.

'He was all morning in Inverness, I think he had a rumpus with General Hawley and that horrid Provost Marshal!'

Ross lifted an inquiring eyebrow, for he knew little of the present goings-on in the Highland capital and even less of the military personnel who were now running the town's day-to-day affairs.

'A certain Captain Stratford Eyre!' she informed him. 'He processes the prisoners in the Tollbooth – a despicable man, Ross!' she said cuttingly. 'Father has crossed swords with him and Hawley frequently of late and I feel certain that he has succeeded only in drawing attention to himself!' She was pacing the floor now and wringing her hands in anguish.

Ross came over to her and caught hold of her hands, calming them between his own. 'Out of concern for me and my missing friends, he made enquiries of his own and came to me last night with his findings.' He glanced away as if searching the room for the reason. 'But there is no need for him to continue on my account. I cannot think why he should do so.' He wore such an expression of misgiving that Alice felt all the more concerned:

'Oh, Ross, please tell him to be careful!' she pleaded. 'He will listen to you, I know he will!'

Cupping her troubled face in his hands, he smiled down, his eyes filled with compassion. 'I will speak with him the moment he returns – I promise!'

His words calmed her considerably. She could feel the tension ooze all out of her as he spoke. She looked up smiling, and regarded him a long moment. No-one else could do to her what he could. With just a word, a smile, or a touch of the hand, sweep her cares so easily away. It was uncanny!

'You are a strange mixture of a man, Ross MacLean,' she told him, sweeping the shock of dark hair from his forehead. 'You play the inscrutable card so well with that devil-may-care manner of yours. And yet, your actions betray a very different man. Kind, considerate, loyal . . . '

He looked away, feeling exposed.

'I know that you sent Angus away on some wild goose chase so that he would be out of harm's way on that awful day. I saw the look in his eyes when he told father the incredible story of how he brought you here that night.' Her eyes were like two beams of light penetrating the dark veil of secrecy he had for so long concealed himself beneath. 'It takes a very special kind of man to evoke such loyalty in another. Even Father, who is no mean judge of character, has an uncommonly high regard for you.' She placed a hand on his arm, and went on:

'But it is your feelings towards *me* that I find confusing. You tease so outrageously and yet say nothing of your true feelings. And always you seem afraid somehow, as if being with me might in some way place my life in danger! Am I to deduce, therefore, that you feel only concern for me?'

Standing in front of the fireplace, he turned from her in silence and, with a hand resting on the mantel, gazed intensely at the glowing embers. It was easy for him out there in the moonlight when he teased her, but he could not bear to have his feelings so openly challenged. It was not the Highland way!

'Is it *concern* that you feel, Ross?' she entreated as she drew near, her eyes searching his for some flicker of response. She sensed his uneasiness, knowing instinctively that her question had struck a raw nerve.

His eyes narrowed and though he remained silent, it was a silence that spoke volumes of a deep, inner conflict.

'Is it *concern* that you feel?' she insisted now earnestly.

Suddenly he turned to face her, his blue eyes burning with an intensity she had not seen there before. 'My feelings for you run deeper than you will ever know!' he told her. 'But I can bring you only heartache and sorrow, and I would never wish you such pain!'

The unswerving resolve which had borne her along so confidently, all at once deserted her in that instant of confession. With tears filling her eyes, she threw her arms around him, squeezing him with every ounce of her strength. 'If you would deny your own feelings out of concern for mine, then it is truly love that you feel!' she cried, her face hidden now on his chest, to spare him the sight of her tears. 'Oh yes, it *is* love that you feel, Ross, and I have felt it too since that first moment!' She lifted her head, showing him the tears and caught the look of indescribable tenderness in his eyes as her own overflowed to see it.

'Yes . . . I do love you,' he whispered, his voice faltering with emotion. Tenderly he wiped the little rivulets of tears from her cheek. She pulled close against him, shuddering as he brought his mouth down on the nape of her neck. She rolled her head sideways then arched it backwards, offering more of her flesh to him. Covering the strong pulse with his lips, he followed the firm line of her jaw upwards. Lightly and gently he lowered his mouth down on hers. Her whole body trembled, anticipating that first touch of lips. There was an instant of hesitation, then, with an urgency that betrayed a long burning hunger they pressed hard together.

Everything fell suddenly silent, only the two of them alive in the world as their eyes closed, locking in the moment. That kiss was endless. It stopped the rain and brought the moon out for a look, but all too soon for Alice he broke free, looking ashamed, as though he had stolen something from her! She searched his eyes for the reason but again, that stubborn inscrutable Highland streak of his gave no clue. Did he think her still a child, too young for adult games? But she had waited too long for this moment and he would not deny her!

Fetching a candelabrum from the table, she grabbed his hand and led him down the hall to the foot of the stairs. Stealing a glance at his doubtful expression, she ascended the oak-panelled staircase with the candles lighting the way. Having no will of his own, he followed obediently, watching with silent fascination their two giant shadows leap and fall in the flickering candlelight.

In the corridor outside the guest room they hesitated, exchanging glances; that silent secret language at work again. Opening the door, she kissed him lightly on the cheek and left him in the doorway.

The room, as he glanced around, looked different from the sick-room he remembered. Perhaps the pain and the uncertainty of those early days had numbed his senses to its undeniable charm! A low fire burned in the grate and the bed was prepared. Someone had been expected! Strange that he should have the oddest feeling that the someone was him!

He crossed the floor to the bay window and gazed down at the garden grounds below. The moon was winking behind the swaying branches of the giant beech tree, everything bathed in a ghostly light. His thoughts were of Alice. She the enchantress and he the enchanted. He glanced from the fire to the bed suddenly feeling like the fly caught in the spider's web – total entrapment! The moon weavers had spun their magic well!

He placed his forehead against the cold glass of the window, suddenly aware of the odd stillness in the house; an eerie silence broken only by the sound of its creaking timbers and the wind sighing through its rooms. It was not difficult to imagine why she might fear its solitude.

The clock in the downstairs hall struck midnight, the last chime dying away in a long unearthly clang.

'The bewitching hour' seemed suddenly appropriate.

Outside the room a floorboard creaked. Candlelight flashed under the door and the handle clicked open. He turned startled, his body responding mechanically, that same absence of conscious movement. There, in the doorway, shimmering in a nightgown of whispering silk, stood Alice. The light from the single candle she was holding seemed superfluous in the strong moonlight that played upon her skin. Gone was the high, elaborate hair of evening, now cascading across her shoulders in golden profusion.

On naked feet she glided towards him with that dreamlike quality of movement.

'Captain, be careful down there!' Angus had warned, and even as Alice drew near, Ross could only stand and marvel at the young lad's uncanny powers.

'Damnation! If the boy hadn't seen it coming once again!'

'Alice, please!'

But his protests were snuffed out by a firm finger against his lips. Her steely glare allowed no argument. 'I love you, Ross!' she declared in a voice husky with desire. 'I have loved you from the first moment we spoke, right here in this very room!' She teased his hair with her fingers. 'Dearest Ross, how could it be otherwise? You are the kind of man every woman dreams of in the deepest, most secret recesses of her heart. Please don't deny your feelings, now that I know for certain that you love me.'

She reached up on tip-toes and kissed him softly on the cheek. 'I have waited all my life for this moment,' she whispered. 'And I can conceive of no other I would rather share it with . . . ' Her breasts came against him as she smothered his face with kisses. He closed his eyes, all resistance – if indeed, there had ever been any – simply ebbed away under that touch of lips.

Slipping an arm round her waist and the other behind her knees, he swept her gently off the floor.

'Be careful, Sir Knight!' she murmured. 'Remember your leg – it will give way and send us crashing through the floor!'

Ignoring the warning, he carried her from the window and placed her gently on the bed, watching her long strands of hair tumble across the white linen pillows in a tapestry of gold.

Sitting on the edge beside her, he took the candle from her hand and placed it in a holder by the bed. Feeling loving eyes upon him, he gazed down longingly, taking in the full sensual picture, filled with admiration that she had planned his seduction so cleverly. And with such innocence!

She pulled herself up from the pillows and whispered hot breath in his ear then fell back, looking suitably coy and demure again. His blue eyes flashed and with one last exchange of glances, he leaned forward and blew out the candle . . .

During the night rain had fallen, and with the returning light of dawn a gentle breeze rustled the dripping curtain of leaves. Blackbirds whistled their waking song among the branches as the tall Highlander on the dark stallion, slipped from the stables, through the labyrinth of trees, and out into the morning.

Many hours would pass before Alice stirred from sleep to find him gone . . .

7

Neil Cameron couldn't be certain which of his two senses had first detected the conflagration. In truth, the pall of black smoke hanging on the skyline had been visible for quite some time and distance. But the faint breeze from the west, which had borne the unmistakable smell of burning to him, had perhaps been the earlier messenger.

Leaping ashore with the mooring rope, Alasdair made fast the rowing boat to what appeared to be the only living tree on the island. Big Coll MacDonald, who was next to disembark, almost succeeded in tipping his men headfirst into the water when the sudden loss of his considerable ballast caused the flimsy craft to lurch violently to one side as he followed his kinsman over the edge.

It was an overcast evening in June on the little island of Rona, that rocky upthrust in the sea at the northern tip of Raasay, which lay between the island of Skye and the mainland. Local rumour had put the fugitive Prince on all three islands at one time or another and as the small group of grim-faced men neared the scene of devastation it was clear that the redcoats had heard these rumours too!

It seemed that everything combustible on the island had been torched. Food stores destroyed. And strewn across the hard land, the black carcasses of shaggy-haired Kyloes – the West Highland cattle, so named for their ability to swim the Kyles between islands and the mainland – lay butchered where hours earlier they had stood docile and trusting.

Coll's dander was up, and rising by the minute. But the sight of the little blind girl, who had been so cruelly used by the soldiers, put the giant Highlander into a seething rage, the like of which Neil Cameron had never seen before in man or beast, nor ever wished to see again.

Wielding his huge broadsword in the air, he took off down the beach like a charging bull and, with the plight of the wee lass fresh in his mind, he was clearly in a mood to slice off more than heads!

It was many hours later, after the sun had set on that terrible place, before they found him; sitting quietly on a rock and gazing far out to sea with what appeared to be the tracks of dried-out tears on his dark face.

His men, who knew his moods well, decided it safer to leave him alone with his thoughts. Only Neil, who knew him less, had the temerity to approach at close quarters. He sat down beside him in silence and looked out over the water as the tide came hissing and foaming its way up the beach towards them. A sideways glance at the big fellow confirmed the futility of conversation. He looked for all the world like a derelict house where all sign of human life and laughter had long since departed. Even the incoming tide, which had encroached so far up the beach now that it lapped against their feet, failed to snatch him back from that distant place where he had so deeply retreated.

After many long moments of silence, the big man moved to speak, though in a voice utterly drained of emotion:

'Some of the happiest days of my life I spent here . . . but so much of what used to pe hass gone now . . . ' He lapsed once more into silence until, feeling the cold waves against his bare legs, he regrouped his senses and rose very ponderously to his feet. 'When you get back to France, Meester Cameron – you and your precious Prince!' he said coldly, 'I would ask that you please remember what you saw here today . . . ' Then, splashing his way through the water, the big man made his way up the beach in search of his men, leaving a very pensive Neil Cameron to ponder his words in solitude.

Early next morning Neil awoke to the rousing cries of Ranald, the night lookout, pointing and urging the sleeping men to stir themselves into life. Although the young Cameron couldn't understand a word of the excited exchanges, it was clear from their reactions that some life-threatening danger was imminent. Following the frantic lookout's pointing finger, Neil's gaze fastened upon the white sails of a British man-of-war drifting towards them behind a flotilla of small rowing boats, rapidly closing with the shore. And already, red-uniformed soldiers were spilling on to the white sands and advancing up the beach towards them.

The smugglers, in their panic, abandoned everything they owned and took off at a hare's pace down the hill in search of their boat. Snatching up the little blind girl in his powerful arms, Coll MacDonald chased after his stampeding men with Neil following close on his heels. Behind them, as they ran, there came the sound of gunshots and an unlucky ball struck the giant Highlander on the shoulder, causing him to drop the unfortunate girl in the heather, where he himself tumbled head-over-heels down the hill towards the beach.

Neil, who had stopped on the brow of the hill to assist the fallen girl to her feet, was now quite some distance from the leaving boat, with the soldiers closing fast around him. The last he heard of the smugglers was the big fellow's booming voice calling frantically to him. Despairingly, he looked on as his departing friends pulled away; knowing that even now with one last desperate sprint he too might yet be safe. But in the heather beneath him, lay the cause of inertia; he could not abandon the poor sightless creature to the cruelty of the soldiers a second time. While the tearful lass clung trembling to him for protection, Neil, swallowing his courage, drew his sword as the redcoats gathered around him.

A semi-circle of steel bayonets bristled menacingly towards him now and a fresh-faced officer pushed forward, stopping as the sharp point of Neil's sword pricked his oncoming breast through the fabric of his smart red tunic.

'Lay a finger on her and, so help me God, I'll drop you where you stand!' warned Neil in a voice that surprised even himself with its threatening tone.

The redcoat officer stepped back gingerly as the row of bayonets levelled against the defiant young swordsman.

'Well now!' exclaimed the officer, rubbing his chest in amazement, 'You, sir, are a very foolish young man indeed, and you will pay most dearly for this show of impudence!' he snapped in his very English voice. Then, stepping aside out of harm's way, 'You have precisely five seconds to lower your sword, sir, before I order my men to fire!' he warned, with remarkable politeness.

But Neil stood yet defiant; his sword arm outstretched to its fullest extent.

'At you . . . and the girl!' the officer added coldly.

Staring down the barrels of the dozen or so muskets ranged against him and hearing the faint sobbing sounds of the frightened lass beneath him, all at once Neil's steadfast resolve ebbed rapidly away. Slowly, yet still reluctantly, he lowered his sword.

The last thing he would remember as the onrushing soldiers wrenched the sword from his grasp, was the instant of blinding pain when the heavy wooden butt of a musket crashed against his skull.

When next he came to his senses, in great pain, much confused, and shackled hand and foot in foul-smelling darkness, Neil wondered if he had, perhaps, made that final journey to the 'downward place', for hell itself could not be more unpleasant than where he now found himself to be.

After many moments spent collecting his thoughts, he gradually became aware of a rhythmic, rolling motion. There was the sound of creaking timber and a damp, musty odour. Somewhere above the darkness, there came the thundering of sail-canvas in the wind. All these things reminded him of his days aboard the 'Bellona'! Then, for sure, he must be on board a ship! And with only earth and stone ballast for company, he must be down in the hold somewhere.

Each fresh stab of pain brought back the memory of those last moments on the little island of Rona. And of the tragic blind girl – what fate had befallen her? he wondered. And what news of Coll and the others – had they escaped to safety?

Time dragged by on such heavy feet during those long hours aboard the ship, and all the more, it seemed, as the full impact of his sorry predicament hit home. But where they were taking him, and to what purpose, he could only guess. Down here in the darkness, deprived of all daylight, there was simply no way of knowing anything!

Sleep must have overtaken him, for when he next came to himself he soon became aware that the rolling motion of the ship had subsided. Voices above deck confirmed that they were dropping anchor and lowering the boats.

Presently, a hatch above his head creaked open and the sudden flood of daylight, streaming through the opening, blinded his vision of the descending visitors. Rough hands pulled him rudely to his feet and the leg-irons, which had secured him during the voyage, were unlocked. His hands, however, did not enjoy the same sense of freedom.

As he blinked painfully against the intrusive sunlight, a gruff voice ordered him up the wooden steps to the deck above, where a gleaming steel bayonet ushered him along the deck and over the side. Here he was directed to climb down a rope-ladder into the eager hands of uniformed soldiers who manhandled him into an open launch.

Only now, seated between two burly sentries, his eyes growing accustomed to the intense light, could he see the full picture of his surroundings. They appeared to be anchored in a sea loch some distance from the shore. In addition to their own ship, other sloops of war were lying at anchor further landward. On the mainland, the imposing structure of a great fortress was just visible beyond the forward ships. He remembered Coll and the others speak of a formidable fortress on the Linnhe Loch which the rebels had failed to capture during the Rebellion. The description seemed accurate enough and, looking up at the huge snow-capped mountain which dominated the backdrop of blue sky, soon confirmed it. So this was Fort William!

As the launch cast off and passed beneath the bowsprit, Neil glanced up and saw for the first time the name of the huge vessel in which he had endured so terrible a voyage. And, at that very moment, when every bone and muscle in his body seemed to cry out in pain, the mocking words 'Happy Janet' grinned down from the ship with a sickening irony.

Ashore, he was bundled out of the boat and urged forward at the point of a musket. An officer on a strutting grey gelding trotted by for a brief look at the prisoner, but, seemingly unimpressed, he rode on at a faster pace.

Everywhere Neil looked along the shore there was a hive of activity. A fleet of small rowing boats were ferrying fresh stores from the ships to be loaded on wagons and pack-horses. And all the while, above the lash of the whips and clatter of hooves, came the odd mixture of provincial dialects from the common foot-soldiers, contrasting richly with the occasional clipped, educated voices of the officers on horseback.

Presently, as their journey inland took them closer to the fort, Neil could see the daunting stone structure in stark reality for the first time. It was not difficult to imagine why Coll and his fellow besiegers had failed to take it. Fort William was a bastion-defended fortification whose walls were guarded by ditches, a bog, a river, and the Linnhe Loch itself. The line of the landward walls was swept by cannon mounted on the bastions. It was an impregnable giant for sure, and all the more imposing against this rugged mountain wilderness.

As they passed through the huge open gates, Neil was ordered to 'Halt!' at the behest of a mounted officer, approaching from behind his line of vision. Dismounting, this officer threw the reins to a gate sentry and marched over to where the prisoner was standing.

Examining the head wound where the musket had struck, he looked clearly displeased with his findings and even more so when he learned that Neil had neither eaten nor drunk fresh water since his arrest on the island three days earlier.

Fetching a canteen of drinking water from his saddle, he returned to offer the container to the prisoner's parched lips. The cold refreshing liquid was the very nectar of the gods; mere water had never before tasted this good, Neil was certain!

'Thank you,' he gasped weakly, and with all his heart in the words.

But this simple pleasure was cut all too short by the appearance of an older and evidently more senior officer who ordered his humane subordinate to remount his horse and return at once to his duties at the lochside.

This fellow Neil concluded to be of an altogether more brutal nature. The deep-set eyes and dark features betrayed it, and the short leather riding-crop, which he continually slapped the side of his boot with, confirmed it!

'Welcome to Fort William, Mister Cameron!' he sneered, knowingly, as the look of perplexity on his prisoner's face grew ever more obvious. Surely, thought Neil, he must have spoken his name whilst semi-conscious, for he was certain that he had informed no-one of his true identity since his arrest. Only Coll and his men knew the truth about him and the reason for his presence here.

'The original Inverlochy fort was commissioned by Oliver Cromwell!' the sneering officer informed him proudly. 'Built in 1654 with the purpose of sustaining an English strike force in the very heart of the Scottish Highlands!' he added, smiling in that same sardonic fashion his prisoner would come to know well in the weeks to follow.

The heel of the riding-crop, which had been thrashing the officer's leather boot continuously, was now very violently thrust under Neil's jaw, jerking his head backwards; the sneering face of its owner mere inches away.

'I've waited a long time for this little meeting! he revealed in a sinister whisper. 'Since the last day of April, if I'm not mistaken!' he informed Neil coldly. 'Don't look so surprised!' he grinned. 'You see, I've come to know quite a lot about you and your little exploits these past few weeks. I also happen to know the reason why you came to these islands!' he added with a cunning chuckle.

An icy finger ran down the length of Neil's spine. If this brute knew so much about him then, but for his unfortunate arrest on the island, he would almost certainly have led these monsters to the very one he had come so close to finding. The realisation appalled him.

For several long moments the dark-faced officer lapsed into silence, all the while thrashing his boot with the riding-crop in that same impatient manner. During this interlude of agonising silence, a heavily-built soldier in sergeant's stripes joined them on the quadrangle. The arrival of this ugly-looking villain seemed to stir the other into a state of yet higher excitement.

'This young gentleman,' he informed the newcomer, 'had the audacity to point a sword at an officer of the King! – Now, what do you make of that, Mr Sturrock?' he asked, surprised.

The muscle-bound sergeant, now standing a few feet from the prisoner, shook his bald head and 'tut-tutted!' disapprovingly.

'Perhaps our young friend requires a little lesson in manners, Mr Sturrock, so that he might know how to behave in future?'

The sergeant's hostile glare never wavered from the prisoner's face for a single second then, with a sudden malevolent grin and with no word of warning, he swung a huge fist into the pit of Neil's stomach; the impact of the blow dropped him to his knees, gasping for breath. Then a huge ammunition boot thumped into his ribs, spinning him over and over in the dirt. Waves of excruciating pain engulfed him as the daylight seemed to fade into darkness.

Hideous monsters sprawled across his vision, their blood-red eyes staring owlishly, then a rough hand gripped his clothing, shaking him violently to his senses and to the living nightmare of Sergeant Sturrock's grinning face above him. Somewhere off in the distance, a gravel voice urged him to his feet, but try as he might he could not move for pain.

Lying face down in the dirt, his manacled hands reached out for some imagined crumb of comfort – a mother's touch perhaps? Then, in that instant before all conscious thought and feeling ebbed away, the huge studded-boot crashed down upon his outstretched fingers with a sickening crunch.

In the weeks that followed, Neil Cameron would suffer many such beatings at the hands of the sadistic fort commander and his brutal henchman. But for the interventions of the impeccable young Lieutenant, who had shown some Christian kindness on that first day, he might well have perished without trace in that hellish place.

And during those long insufferable days Neil would learn of other whispered atrocities committed here within the walls of Fort William, and in the hills and glens – atrocities which were never officially reported. Rumours of beatings, shootings, and hangings were on every prisoner's lips. And the plight of the blind girl on Rona, he soon learned, was no isolated incident.

A wounded MacLeod, brought in some days after Neil, told of a raid on the island of Raasay which had left three hundred houses on fire, including the Laird's mansion. In the brutality that followed, some three hundred head of cattle, seven hundred sheep, and twenty horses were slaughtered where they stood. And standing tall in all these tales of woe, the prime mover, time and time again – their beloved fort commander, Captain Caroline Frederick Scott!

But another name too, would crop up with the same whispered dread; that of a certain sea captain, John Fergusson of H.M.S. 'Furness', whose job it was to ferry Scott and his henchmen from one unsuspecting island to another. On these sleepy islands off the west coast of Scotland, these two names in particular would leave bitter memories of death and destruction in their bloody wake.

But of all the horrors Neil Cameron would endure during those dark days in the mountain hell of Fort William – some sixty or so miles to the north-east, at the opposite end of the Great Glen, a yet more terrifying fate awaited . . .

8

July slipped into August that year of 1746 full of warm winds and late summer sun, but slowly and imperceptibly the lengthening shadows of autumn crept ever longer with each passing day.

It was upon one evening in the fourth week of this month that Charles Lamont came thundering through the gates of Arrandale House upon the spur; his sweat-lathered horse panting with exhaustion. With his face and clothes caked in dust and his manners lost somewhere on the journey, he barged past Molly in the hallway and swept into the study, slamming the door behind him. The old housekeeper lingered long enough to hear the sound of the cork being pulled from a bottle then, shaking her grey head disapprovingly, she turned down the corridor with more than a little concern, for she had not seen the master of the house look so deeply disturbed in many a long year.

The master's absence from the dinner table that evening caused a heavy atmosphere to settle on the old house as midnight drew near. Upstairs in the bay window of her bed-chamber, Alice sat at the dresser, her chin resting on her joined fingers. The brown eyes staring back from her looking-glass seemed distinctly melancholic.

Her father, who had fallen unusually silent of late, now appeared to have withdrawn completely into himself. And the closeness, which had been the touchstone of their relationship for as long as she could remember, seemed somehow distant now. How she longed for those halcyon days before the soldiers came — they were responsible for Papa's inexplicable behaviour — she was sure of it!

Picking up her pearl-handled hairbrush, she continued with her grooming, only to throw it back down again in a fit of frustration. She would go at once to her father and have it out with him or be damned!

Throwing her evening shawl across her shoulders, she followed the corridor down to her father's bedchamber. A soft knock on the door and a peek inside proved that it was empty. Downstairs, a search of the study found the room in darkness and the drinks cabinet emptied of the master's favourite malt whisky. But surely Molly had not carried out her threat? 'She wouldn't dare!' thought Alice aloud. Back upstairs, she was startled to find a light under the door of the locked room. But nobody had gone in there for years; not even Molly with her feather duster would venture in there.

Trying the handle, she found the door locked in the usual way. Tentatively, she knocked softly. 'Papa – are you in there?' she enquired, but her words were greeted by an eerie silence. With growing concern, she tried again. 'Papa, please open the door – you're frightening me!' she pleaded. But again, the same silent reply. Frantic now, she hammered on the door, repeating the same urgent demand.

But still nothing!

The commotion brought Molly down the hall with a worried face. But even her valiant attempts failed to rouse the silent occupant. 'That does it, Molly!' cried Alice, now on the point of tears. 'First thing tomorrow, I'm going to see Ross – he'll know what to do! Father will listen to him, I know he will!' she gushed, then fell sobbing into the old housekeeper's comforting arms.

Early the next morning Ross MacLean was riding fast through the gates of the old house in response to Alice's frantic pleas for help. Though she had wanted to ride back with him, he insisted that she remain at the croft with Angus until his return. Secretly he was more than a little afraid of what he might find in the locked room, and he didn't want Alice there in case his suspicions proved correct. Smiling reassuringly at Molly in the doorway, he took the stairs with anxious steps and followed the east wing corridor to the offending room.

Stopping outside the door, he thumped loudly with his fist, but to no avail. His deep, strident command brought no more success.

Stepping three paces backwards from the door, his stomach a knot of apprehension, the Highlander drew a deep breath and charged. There came a resounding crack of splintered wood as the lock yielded under his broad shoulder and the heavy door burst open, the impetus of the assault sending him careering into the centre of the darkened room. Recovering his equilibrium, he crossed over to the window and wrenched back the curtains. The sunlight streaming through the glass picked out the chaos of 'dead' whisky bottles, the overturned chair, and the scorched hearth-rug where the candelabra had fallen. The room reeked with the smell of stale whisky.

Seated behind a dust-covered writing desk, half-hidden by the wings of an armchair, Charles Lamont sat bolt upright; his face a mask of concentration. His eyes, red-rimmed from lack of sleep and the fire of whisky, stared trance-like at the wall opposite. Gone was the powdered periwig he always wore. The unruly hair, bearded stubble, and general dishabille told the story of a man who had lost all interest in maintaining even the semblance of respectable appearance.

After a profound silence, the visitor ventured to speak:

'What's this all about, Charles?' he demanded; his voice sounding strangely hollow in the sparsely furnished room. The man in the armchair offered no reply but continued to stare, unblinking, at the wall behind his visitor.

Seeing that his words had proved ineffectual, Ross turned to look at the object of the other's attention. On the wall above the empty fireplace his gaze fell upon the portrait of an exceptionally beautiful young woman. She was the image of Alice, and yet – she was not. Shielding his eyes against the bright morning sunlight, he stepped forward for closer inspection.

'*Memories are all that's left me now,*
'*Pressed between the pages of my mind,*
'*Words and feelings, laughter and tears;*
'*All my treasured moments . . .* '

Ross had spun round, startled by those words, for the voice emanating from the armchair had come so sudden and unexpected that it caught him completely off guard.

'Elizabeth — my wife!' the voice informed him. 'It was painted on her twenty-first birthday. The year before she died.' The lawyer's bleary eyes glazed over. 'Twenty years ago, yesterday, as it happens.'

The Highlander drew a deep sigh of comprehension as the veil of mystery lifted.

'I hung it on the wall the day we moved in, then I locked the door.' The storyteller's head lolled forward, he clasped his hands tight together and stared down in surprise at their uncontrollable behaviour.

'I haven't had the courage to come back here until now,' he mumbled.

In the confines of that sad and lonely room, surrounded by the debris of drunkenness, Ross MacLean stood silent. Now was not the time for condemnation; he would listen and try to understand.

Through a sea of alcohol and sleepless fatigue, the dishevelled lawyer lifted his gaze and focused on the young man he had come to trust.

'I killed her, you see!' he said in a cracked whisper.

But the Highlander shook his head against the notion.

'Oh yes!' confirmed the other, nodding his head emphatically. 'She was much younger than I, of course, but a childhood illness had left the legacy of a weak heart.' He reacquainted his gaze with the portrait on the wall. 'She wanted, so much, to give me a child . . . but we were warned that it would be dangerous . . . ' He broke off momentarily, then resumed with the smile of memory on his face:

'When Alice was born, it was the happiest day of my life!' Then that smile, all too quickly, faded. 'But it was a happiness that came with too high a price.' His head fell forward. 'A week later, Elizabeth was dead!'

Ross tried to speak, but words would have been intrusive at such a moment. After a long silence, he picked up the overturned chair and sat down opposite his wretched friend, and said:

'Far be it for me to lecture a much older and wiser man,

Charles, but if this unfortunate business is due to some twisted sense of guilt, then it is sadly misplaced,' he informed the unhappy man. 'There is no blame here! In your heart of hearts you must know that.' The Highlander fastened his intense blue eyes on the listener. 'Do you blame Alice for her mother's death?' he asked.

Charles Lamont shook his head vigorously.

'Then you cannot blame yourself, either, for the one cannot exist without the other!' Ross stated assuredly.

The older man looked up; his face a picture of torment.

'This is not about guilt, Ross,' he said in a sinister undertone, 'but betrayal!'

The young man moved closer to the other's face so that he might read it more clearly. 'Betrayal! — I don't understand. Who has been betrayed?'

The man opposite nodded at the painting. '*She* has been betrayed,' he answered, 'and Alice!'

Ross sat back in his chair, sighing deeply. Nothing was making sense at all. His tormentor was now just sitting there, head cradled in his trembling hands, fighting against the waves of sleep which were threatening to drown his conscious thoughts completely. Then suddenly he looked up, pushed himself back into his chair, and with a stubborn effort of will, focused his attention once more on his young visitor:

'My whole life has been a sham; a charade of pious duplicity,' he said in a voice that startled his visitor with its harsh tone of savage self-condemnation.

Ross sat in silence, wondering what was coming; now, perhaps, he would learn the reason for his friend's inexplicable behaviour.

'After Elizabeth died,' he began, 'I was distraught, inconsolable. The city firm I worked for decided in their wisdom that it would be best for me to get away for a while — lose myself in work. Oh, they meant well enough at the time, I know. But, with hindsight, it was really not a wise decision,' he muttered regretfully.

'A well-to-do client had recently died, leaving a Highland

property of some consequence to the care of his bereaved widow. My brief was to travel up there and sort out the business of the estate . . . ,' he paused a moment, then that little smile of memory again:

'From the first instant I saw her, I was struck by the resemblance to my Elizabeth.' His eyes widened, recalling the moment. 'The hair, those eyes – they would have been almost the same age, even!' he explained excitedly, his words coming faster now as the memories flooded back. He glanced from his visitor to the painting. 'Just as you thought it was Alice up there on the wall!' he reminded Ross pointedly. 'Oh yes, she was beautiful, but like me, lonely and vulnerable.' He clasped his hands together as if preparing himself for the painful part:

'To save time, she invited me to stay over while I sorted through her affairs . . . but as the days went by, we found ourselves spending more time talking about personal things than we ever did on the business of her estate.' He broke off, then that little smile again. 'She was so easy to talk to. We found that we had much in common. In truth, we grew very fond of each other as time went by.' The smile gradually faded; his eyes closed. When they reopened, there was a haunted look:

'One night after dinner – perhaps it was the wine, some delayed grief maybe? I'll never really know – but in the fire's flickering light,' his eyes wide now, the memory poignant. 'As God is my witness, Ross, she was suddenly my Elizabeth again! – for the life of me, I couldn't distinguish one from the other!' He was shaking his head and on the edge of tears now with the realisation. 'We were in each other's arms before I had time to think . . . to stop!' he looked up, a flicker of shame in his eyes. 'When I came to my senses, it was too late . . . ' He was closing his eyes now and clasping his hands tighter together. 'Too late!' he repeated, his words barely audible.

A moment later, he was sitting upright in his chair again with that same stubborn effort of will, gazing at the portrait of his beloved Elizabeth, seeking forgiveness, or was it condemnation?

Ross had listened in silence. Another time, another place, another man, and he could almost have smiled at the innocence of it all. Yet, there was no laughter here. Only the torment of a principled man haunted by the perceived betrayal of a dead wife's memory. It was almost pitiful.

'Charles – is it a crime now to be human?' he asked in a pleading voice. 'And if it be so, then do we not all stand accused?'

The self-condemned man did not answer but, from his impassive features, it was clear that the Highlander's wisdom had fallen on deaf ears.

After many moments of silent fascination with his wife's image on the wall, the eyes of the implacable lawyer suddenly flickered:

'Two years later, my duties took me north again,' he continued. 'I decided to call on her unexpectedly. That's when I discovered the truth she had been keeping from me.' He looked directly into the blue eyes of the young man opposite, his own burning now with an intensity Ross had not seen there before; his spine tingled with anticipation.

'There was a child! A son!' He paused, looking incredulous. '*My* son!'

The revelation hit Ross MacLean like a thunderbolt:

'You – have a son? – You, and this woman?' His eyes wandered the room seeking confirmation of what he had just heard. 'But Alice made no mention of a brother!' he reminded himself aloud.

Charles looked away. 'She doesn't know!' came his tortured reply.

The Highlander's face – a picture of disbelief, suddenly hardened as he looked accusingly at the other. But Charles reached over and caught hold of his accuser's sleeve.

'Try to understand!' he said imploringly. 'When Alice was old enough to know I wanted so much to tell her, and a million times I almost did!' He looked away, tortured by the dilemma. 'But I had given my parole of honour that I would keep the secret – even from her.' He laughed; a little choking sound in the stillness. 'I even offered the lady my hand in marriage, that the boy might know his father . . . his half-sister,' he gazed over intently, returning that look of accusation. 'Oh, but you Highlanders, you are so proud – so stubborn! She would have none of it. Only my promise to keep safe the secret!' The lawyer's face drained of expression as the other looked on disapprovingly.

A long, awkward silence descended.

'I love my daughter very much, Ross,' said the distraught man after some moments, his words warm now with affection. 'It has not been easy bringing her up alone all these years. I'm not sure if I have been a good father, far less a mother to her . . . I wasn't always there when I was needed . . . ' his words trailed off as his heart sank with regret.

The Highlander leaned forward, his intense blue eyes burning with a desperate desire to understand. 'So why all this now?' he demanded. 'Now, after all these years?'

Behind the grey stubble, Charles Lamont returned a little fractured smile. 'Ghosts of the past!' he whispered. 'Remember?' His eyes wide, conveying the memory:

'I warned you about them – they always come back . . . '

A cold shiver ran down the Highlander's spine; that same feeling Alice had provoked at the mere mention of the supernatural; that sense of remembered dread.

'He's a young man now . . . all grown up,' the voice opposite informed him. 'Handsome, like his father!' That stifled laugh again. 'Educated by some of the finest tutors in Europe. Quite the young gentleman, his mother tells me.' He lowered his gaze, his eyes filling. 'It could have been a promising life.'

Ross, still struggling to understand, narrowed his eyes with a growing sense of unease at the lawyer's sinister words.

'Your Prince, he has much to answer!' the other continued. 'How many more lives will be destroyed – how many is enough?'

The Highlander looked back with uncertainty. 'What are you trying to say, Charles?' he asked, almost fearing the answer.

The man opposite took a deep breath, fighting to suppress some inner rage:

'It would appear that my son, too, has been touched by the Stuart Curse!' he answered; the words spat out like sour wine. 'After the debacle of Culloden, he came over from France to take the Royal fugitive home to safety. But, as luck would have it, before he could discharge his duty, he was seized by the soldiers and taken prisoner.

The Highlander's eyes were wide now. At last the other's rambling trail of words had touched his understanding. Rising ponderously to his feet, he paced the floor, rubbing his chin in that pensive way of his:

'Charles – this is unbelievable!'

The man in the wing-chair sat staring impassively at his interlocked fingers. 'Yes, it is, isn't it!' he agreed, nodding vigorously then glanced up with that little ironic smile again. 'Unfortunately, however, it also just happens to be true!'

Stunned by this new revelation, Ross sat back down on the chair looking at the dejected lawyer through very different eyes. 'But why did you not tell me this sooner?' he asked, his words softened by sympathy.

Charles shook his head. 'I only learned of it myself three days ago when the boy's mother sent a message asking me to call. I knew from the hurried scrawl that something was wrong.' He shrugged his shoulders. 'She had hoped that there might be something I could do, professionally – some strings that I could pull.' He shook his head against the idea. 'Perhaps, if the young fool had not nailed his colours to the mast with such a show of impudent defiance, there might have been some defence; some mitigating circumstances.' He spread his hands in a helpless gesture, leaving Ross in no doubt that all hope had already gone.

'The boy knows nothing about me, of course,' he said, shaking his head. 'He assumes his father to be his mother's dead husband.' He looked across at the Highlander's deepening frown lines.

'It's all rather complicated, I know,' he admitted with an

understanding grin. Then, reaching over, he caught hold of his visitor's wrist. 'Strange as it may sound,' he whispered with a heartfelt intonation. 'your arrival here, that terrible night, brought him so vividly to mind. Suddenly, I came to realise how much I had wanted a son of my own; how much I had been missing . . . I went to her then, pleading that she would release me from my vow of silence . . . ,' he shook his head dejected. 'But, alas, she would not . . . ' He looked away dumbfounded by a sudden realisation:

'Little did I know . . . how soon I would have my wish . . . '

In the dark aura of that unfortunate room, the Highlander could feel that sense of indescribable dread returning.

Pulling himself upright in his chair, the man opposite turned his attention once more on his young confidant; his eyes filled now with a look of utter despair:

'On the castle esplanade . . . on Friday next . . . my little Neil—' he broke off, looking incredulous. '—My own flesh and blood is . . . is to be executed.'

9

On the landing outside the frowsty room, Kate MacPhee took a sharp intake of breath, adjusted her unruly hair, and popped a secret bundle down the valley of her ample bosom. She descended the spiral staircase in the dim light, clutching the polished handrail as she went, then stepped blinking into the strong evening sunshine.

The road outside lay silent. No wagons rumbled by. No clatter of horses' hooves. The heavy tramp of soldiers' boots had long since died away. Only the scorched and flattened earth, where the tented village had once stood, bore testament to the Royal Army's recent occupation of the little town.

Kate pulled her coat against the evening chill and proceeded down the tree-lined avenue that fringed the green meadow of the Crown. And even as she walked, the late summer leaves of burning red and golden yellow that interlaced above her head, were already falling. Autumn, it seemed, was just around the corner; she could feel it in the air and there was sadness in the feeling. She remembered all the young Highlanders she had known before the soldiers came. Bonnie lads every one; the flower of the glens cut down in the springtime of their lives. Fleeing from the dark thoughts in her mind, Kate hitched her skirts and set off across the lush meadows, stopping at the cusp of the hill where Barnhill Vennel fell sharply to the cobbled street below.

Here lay a precarious footpath of impacted earth. The steep gradient was a notorious short-cut with a wicked reputation for playing tricks on shoe-leather. Even sensible shoes often came to grief here. But for a lady, dressed as she was in the height of fashion, such audacious boots would be tempting fate to the limit! Hitching her skirts once more, she started down the slope, half running, half sliding, and whooping all the way like a Red Indian on the warpath. And when she had done descending, she looked back, counting her blessings that she had alighted safely from such a treacherous downward journey. Someday someone should build steps, she thought. And the sooner the better!

Here at the end of the narrow passage behind a dingy doorway, she passed the lodgings of Brevet-Major James Wolfe, one of General Hawley's staff officers. He was destined to remain in the town for almost a year following the Battle of Culloden before fate would take him across the Atlantic to Canada, where he would win his immortality as the victorious General Wolfe of Quebec.

Kate was on Doomsdale Street now, the cobbled road to the gallows, which sloped gently upward to the Castle Hill above. Across the way stood the plain rubble building of the Town House. This stolid, unpretentious seat of local government was now very much the hub of military administration. Round the corner stood the former town residence of Lord Forbes of Culloden, now the Horns Hotel used exclusively by Cumberland's staff officers.

At the Tollbooth, on the Exchange, where the three principal roads converged, local merchants plied their trade. Here could be bought, sold, and exchanged the commodities and essentials of the day: malt and meal, beef and wool. Half-a-crown would buy a Galloway pony and, on a good day, the buyer might receive a 'luck-penny' from the trader by way of a discount on the price.

Half-buried in the earth, near the market cross, lay the huge Clach-na-cuddain stone where the women rested their wash-tubs on their return from the river, and whereupon their menfolk would hammer out the business and the politics of the day. But lately there could be heard no dissenting voices.

Kate was on Kirk Street now, with its baronial towers, crow-stepped gables, and turnpike stairs. On her left, opposite St John's chapel, stood the town house of Lady MacKintosh of Moy – where Bonnie Prince Charlie had lived in the weeks before Culloden. And where, until recently, the Duke of Cumberland had taken up residence during his stay of occupation.

The Lady MacKintosh had remained suitably unimpressed

by both of her illustrious visitors. 'I've had two King's bairns living under my roof in my time, and to tell you the truth I wish I may never have another,' she had said. Kate was sure in her own mind, that the good lady and the town were well rid of them both!

Turning left at the end of the street, she took a cobbled alleyway through a row of ramshackle houses and came out on to a broad open square where women in shawls were busy thrashing and wringing clothes on flat rocks by the river's edge. Upstream, the seven arches of the stone bridge spanned the turbulent water, now in full spate from the recent inclement weather. The old wooden structure, that once had stood on the spot, had collapsed in 1664 and was replaced by the present stone toll bridge. A crossing cost a bodle (one sixth of a penny) but was free to the MacLeods and Frasers, whose clan chiefs had contributed to its building from their own private sporrans.

Across the river lay the pebble beach at Friars' Shott, where often of an evening townsfolk would gather to watch the salmon netting. In 1240 the mendicant friars of St Dominic were awarded by Royal charter from King Alexander the Second, the 'whole water and fishings from Friars' Road as far as Scurry.'

But the pebbles were barely visible below the water-line now, and only a coble boat bobbed there in the strong current, tugging at its moorings.

Across the Maggot Green the long-fingered shadows of evening pointed eastward and Kate duly followed, her heart quickening with her step at the sight of the tall mast, rising above the distant rooftops. Captain Rudi Van Halen's Dutchman lay at anchor in the firth; her next port of call. She felt for the letter in her coat pocket and smiled at the message it contained; hand-delivered that same afternoon by a chubby-cheeked cabin-boy with a knowing smile.

Between Kate and the harbour lay a warren of narrow passages and the dark corners of a dubious neighbourhood. Drunks and vagrants and other creatures of the night lurked in the shadowy interior. A not-to-be recommended walkway for those of a nervous disposition. But it was a short-cut to her destination and she was already running late. Heart in mouth, she stepped through the pend only to jump back smartly as the cry of 'Gardyloo!' from above sent the contents of a chamber pot splashing on to the cobble path below. Kate, whose nose was by no means delicate, found the mixture of odious odours suffocating. Waving the offending air aside with a busy hand, she soldiered onward. Dampness seeped through her clothes and the drips from overfilled gutters splashed against her upturned face as she passed beneath them.

The winding passage, surrounded by so foul a locality, took some wicked twists and bends along its length, and in the dim light sinister shadows chased one another down the dark way; the whole place was gripped by a peculiar silence. With only the heavy thud of her heart for company she moved through the hideous labyrinth, her mind suddenly filled with a sense of impending evil. Just when she thought to turn and run for her life, faintly through the gloom she could see daylight ahead. Like a breath of fresh air, the tang of the sea wafted above the stench, sending a shiver of excitement down her spine. She thought of the waiting launch that would carry her to the ship – and the welcoming arms of Captain Rudi Van Halen.

She was almost out now – just a few more steps would do it. As she made for the opening, a flight of pigeons broke from the rooftops. Startled, she looked up. At the same instant an unseen hand shot out from a darkened doorway; her scream of terror stifled under another which clamped tight against her lips. Under the vice-like grip which possessed her, she struggled valiantly, but to no avail. Any second now, she would faint or die, she was sure of it.

'Hello, Kate!' came the familiar voice in her ear. For an instant the blood froze in her veins. The soft, Highland lilt was unmistakable.

And yet, how could it be? As the strong hands slackened about her, she rounded on her abductor and stared up through

terrified eyes at the handsome smiling face of the tall Highlander, Ross MacLean.

'But . . . but you're dead!?' she exclaimed in a hushed
whisper, the blood draining from her cheeks as she said it.
Tremulous fingers reached out and touched the skin of his face
to confirm it. She pulled back thunderstruck. 'Bless my flannel
drawers, but we heard you were all dead!' she told him, still
unwilling to accept the evidence of her own eyes and fingers.

Though his smile remained undiminished, looking up into
his deep blue eyes she could see in them little of the sparkling
humour she had come to remember. Where once there had
been so much laughter, now she could see only pain and
an overwhelming sadness. She reached up and cupped his
cheek in her still trembling hand. 'You men — when will you
ever learn?'

For a brief moment he held her hand there under his own.
Then, turning it over, he pressed his lips against her palm,
kissing it tenderly.

In his eyes, the look of remembered hurt tugged at her
heart-strings. She could help him forget, if only he would let
her . . .

'Forgive me if I frightened you,' he said softly, 'but I had to
see you.'

When the affection of that moment had passed she looked at
him with renewed concern. 'But it cannot be safe for the likes
of you here, now — surely?' she reminded him. 'Even in those
fine city clothes!' she remarked, clearly amused by his very
un-Highland appearance.

He looked at her with a kind of earnestness. 'I have a
favour to ask, Kate,' he said, and saw her green eyes flash
like emeralds in a jeweller's window.

Reaching out, she touched his arm, squeezing it gently.
'You, bonnie lad, can have it for free,' she told him in a
seductive whisper.

The Highlander's eyes flickered with amusement and, for a
wonderful moment, she could see that the haunted look had
gone from his gaze.

'Not that kind of favour, Kate!' he said, laughing.

Puzzled, she wrinkled her nose. 'What, then?' she asked, a little deflated.

'I need a uniform – an officer's uniform!' he told her, looking suddenly serious again.

She stared back, frowning. 'An officer's uniform?' she repeated, sounding astonished, this being a strange request, even by her standards. 'But why on earth would you want such a thing?' she asked him, her eyes bright now with curiosity.

'The less you know about that, dearest Kate, the better!' he answered evasively. 'But it's important – life and death important!'

Kate scratched her luxuriant red hair.

'It would need to be my size – or as near as doesn't matter,' he added hopefully.

She looked him up and down, her frown lines deepening, then a gleam of an answer brightened her eyes.

'An old Major comes calling once a week at my lodgings, regular as clockwork,' she told him, staring back rather suspiciously. 'It is just the uniform you want? I wouldn't want him damaged. He's a harmless old soul.'

The Highlander spread his hands in innocence:

'Just the uniform, Kate – I promise!' he assured her, crossing his heart solemnly.

She held his gaze a long moment, testing his sincerity then sighing resignedly. 'I need my head examined,' she said as he caught hold of her hand, kissing it gratefully.

'You do remember the address?' she enquired, challenging his memory.

'How could I forget!' he replied, shame-faced.

'Aye,' she said, smiling wistfully. 'If my memory serves me well, your lads were seldom strangers!' She looked at him quizzically. 'But never you? I never could tempt you Ross – could I?'

The steeple bell struck eight of the clock. Kate gave a look of lateness, gathered her skirts, and made ready to leave:

'Seven o'clock! Tuesday evening! I will leave the door unlocked,' she informed him in a rush.

The Highlander removed his three-cornered hat and gave his fellow conspirator an exuberant sweeping bow. 'Until Tuesday, then,' he said, smiling. 'Give my regards to Rudi!' he added with a grin.

Kate offered no reply but stood, skirts hitched, staring back coquettishly, at the devil-may-care grin of the rogue Highlander. With a final sweeping glare, she took off across the Citadel Quay in search of the boat that would carry her beyond the harbour to the strange horizontal adventures that beckoned out there on the ship.

That Ross had watched the Dutchman come in from Rotterdam, that same afternoon, was unbeknown to Kate. And, knowing the sea captain's shore routine from past experience, it was not difficult to determine where the lovely lass would be headed that fine evening. In the little Highland town, Kate's bountiful charms – known locally as 'Ben MacPhee' – were legend. And Holland, as Rudi himself had often complained, was a dull, flat landscape. The Highlander's wicked grin broadened as he turned to walk away. For he knew that tonight, for certain, the Dutchman would have himself a mountain or two to climb . . .

Moonlight sparkled his eyes as he corked the empty wine bottle and tossed it in the river. It hit the water with a soft splash and was immediately caught by the vicious current and off downstream at a rate of knots. He sprang to his feet, watching its progress intently and, running along the riverbank, soon found that the object of his attention, now bobbing and glinting in the moonlight a long way off, had easily outpaced him.

He repeated the experiment with a large empty ale barrel which he had found abandoned in the Ness Islands. Rolling it into the water, he pushed the heavy container clear of the bank and watched it, too, drift rapidly away.

It was an interesting exercise and proved, if nothing else, that the River Ness, now in spate after the recent heavy rainfall, was indeed one of the fastest-flowing rivers in the Kingdom. Only the River Spey, some miles further to the South, had the reputation of a swifter course to the sea.

Earlier that day, while standing on the high ground at Barnhill, he had looked down, with more than a passing interest, on the castle esplanade, where the military carpenters were hammering the last nails into the awful wooden structure of the scaffold.

The usual summary execution by hanging from the nearest available tree (an all-too-common fate for many unfortunate rebels) would be a wasted opportunity for the Redcoats. This Neil – French spy/friend of the Prince – Cameron was something of a celebrity; the man who had threatened an officer of the Crown at point of sword! Such audacity was deserving of a more public departure. And, so that other misguided souls might be dissuaded from similar treasonable behaviour, the site of execution was well chosen to set the example.

The castle, which had been partially blown up by the Rebels, stood yet proud on a grassy eminence on the south bank of the river.

The red sandstone rubble had been largely removed by local builders but much of what was left of the structure was still in use by the present occupying forces:

The esplanade where sentinels stood ever watchful; the dungeon where the prisoner, Neil Cameron, now languished in chains; and a small chapel of worship, whose Godly connection had saved it from the gunpowder that killed the French explosives 'expert' who set the charges. Fortunately, his pet dog was blown clear across the river by the explosion, only to land safely on the opposite bank, minus its wagging tail.

All this, of course, was old hat to Captain Ross MacLean. Indeed, he had been personally responsible for much of the activity involving the enemy's 'Fort George' during those heady days of Rebel occupation. The castle's intimate secrets were well known to him. But the object of his fascination, as he stood in the warm August sunshine of that fine afternoon, was the high scaffold platform, towering above the castle perimeter wall . . . and at no great distance from it! Such an odd juxtaposition had interesting possibilities and he would explore them further in the days and nights that remained.

Later that evening, he went to see Angus at his grand-mother's house in the Maggot.

'Kate MacPhee!' you could almost touch the disbelief in the young lad's voice. 'Hell, Captain – she's killed more redcoats than you have!' he sniggered cheekily.

'Now you just mind your mouth!' returned the other, point-ing irritably. 'Kate MacPhee has a heart of gold, and don't you forget it!'

Angus choked down a laugh. 'Aye!' he wholeheartedly agreed. 'But I'm thinking t'would be another part of her anatomy that earns it!'

Ross shook his head in open frustration:

'You have a gey cynical tongue in your head for one so young,' he said disappointedly. 'But you'll learn, soon enough, the ways of the world!'

Angus was having none of this and drew himself up defi-antly. 'You'll no catch me paying for it – and I can tell you that for nothing!' he countered indignantly.

'Oh, is that a fact now?' exclaimed Ross, surprised. 'Then I must see this endless queue of lassies, pining at the garden gate for your favours!' he said, yanking the door open and scanning the empty road outside. He closed the door, looking distinctly perplexed.

'Now that's odd!' he said frowning. 'There doesn't appear to be anyone there! Do you think they got fed up waiting, maybe?'

The boy's face remained resolutely unmoved and his tor-mentor could see from the obstinate pout that there would be no winning of this particular argument. At last relenting, Ross came over and ruffled the boy's red hair playfully. 'All men pay for it, Angus – one way or another,' he grinned, then gave vent to a deep sigh of worldly weariness:

'If not with their gold, then yet more dearly with their hearts!

Kate and lassies like her are perhaps a little more honest than the others . . . that's the only difference.'

He retrieved his three-cornered hat from the rocking-chair, jammed it down rather forcefully on his head, and pulled open the door to leave. 'Now, will you help me or no?' he asked the boy bluntly.

Angus gazed out through the scullery window before answering. He would do anything for this Captain of his. But this particular request had sinister implications.

Away beyond the boulevard and the dreary thatch-roofed houses, the castle's dark silhouette loomed above the smoky haze. And below it the river, like a long silver ribbon under the moon, flowed ever onward to eternity.

The young lad looked up at his friend's doubtful expression. 'Aye, Captain,' he said, turning suddenly serious, 'I'll help you!'

10

Charles Lamont dropped the letter he was reading and looked up at his daughter. It always gave him pleasure to look at Alice and particularly that morning as she stood in the study doorway with her glowing complexion, graceful figure, and brown eyes alight with expectation. She seemed more beautiful, more vital than usual. He was so proud of her.

'Good morning, my dear. You look wonderful!'

Alice dropped a curtsy. 'Why, Papa, a compliment! Then it is indeed a good morning! I was beginning to wonder if you would ever notice me again?' she complained, looking and sounding suitably neglected.

Her father spread his hands, inviting an embrace. 'Yes, I know. Please forgive me, my dear. My recent behaviour has been abominable!'

Alice gave him a look of delayed forgiveness then beamed one of her favoured smiles before embracing him warmly. 'I know that something has been bothering you, Papa. Please don't shut me out again. I cannot bear to see you so unhappy.'

Her father patted her reassuringly. 'Perhaps I'm getting old, my dear? Sometimes I forget that you are no longer a child!'

'Getting old, indeed!' she scolded, stroking his cheek affectionately. 'What nonsense!'

Picking up the letter from his writing desk, he handed it to her with a rather painful smile. 'We have received an invitation to a Grand Celebration Ball at Culloden House next week!' he announced in a trying-to-sound-enthusiastic tone of voice.

Alice showed him a puzzled frown as she unrolled the very formal-looking parchment scroll and read it with little interest.

'Tradition dictates that the accession of the Hanoverian dynasty is celebrated by the British Army on the first of August,' explained her father, 'but this year, in particular, the great victory over the Young Pretender and his Rebels is to be a singularly ostentatious affair!'

Alice dropped the letter of invitation on the desk as though it were contaminated by some vile plague.

'But we cannot possibly accept!' she exclaimed. 'The place will be crawling with blood-red uniforms!'

Her father nodded and shook his head simultaneously. 'But I have no choice in the matter – I must accept!' He winced visibly at the thought and flopped into his chair, giving vent to a deep sigh of frustration.

'When the Lord President of the Court of Session – Scotland's premier judge! – sends an invitation, believe me, my dear, you accept! Bowing all the way there and all the way back!' He glanced up with pleading eyes. 'Every Big Wig of the judiciary will be there! It's supposed to be an honour! Only death would excuse me!'

Alice looked down at his anguished face; he had appeared so depressed of late that she did not wish to be the cause of any further unhappiness.

'Although you would be expected to accompany me, I quite understand your disinclination to attend – in deference to Ross and his dead comrades.'

She turned her face away from him then, biting her lip at the dilemma.

Her father sat patiently behind his desk waiting for her answer. A moment ago he had seemed so happy to see her; how could she refuse him this otherwise harmless request?

'Well then,' she sighed finally and with a great effort of contrived enthusiasm, 'I had better look out my best hoop and powder; we mustn't disappoint the good gentleman.'

Coming slowly to his feet, her father gathered her up in his arms and embraced her again, this time more in sympathy than gratitude.

'Bless you, my dear! I promise that I will have a miserable time also.'

Alice smiled back encouragingly. She was sure she had made the right decision but, in her heart of hearts, she wished that a certain young Highlander could be there to lead her on the floor of the dance. Alas, that would not be possible.

A familiar soft double-knock on the door brought Molly into the room with a polite half-bob and an apologetic smile. 'A young gentleman, name of Angus MacLean, wishes most urgently to see you, sir!' the old housekeeper announced brightly.

'Angus – here?' Alice looked suddenly apprehensive, and her father equally perplexed.

'Well, well, show him in, Molly – good heavens!'

'It's Ross – something's happened to him!' cried the girl in alarm.

'Now, now. Let's not jump to conclusions. We will learn soon enough. It's more likely a social call!' soothed her father.

A moment later the hesitant figure of young Angus MacLean came in holding the brim of his cocked hat, rather coyly, between his fidgeting fingers. He bowed politely as Alice came rushing over to him.

'Is it Ross? Has something happened to him?'

'No, miss. Captain MacLean is well. I spoke with him only last evening,' Angus assured her.

'There now – what did I tell you,' interrupted her father. 'You and your jumping to conclusions!' But the wily old lawyer could see from his visitor's doubtful demeanour that the news he was carrying was not fit for his daughter's ears. 'Now, my dear, we mustn't forget our manners,' he smiled, guiding her towards the door. 'Why don't you go and find Molly and see if she will be kind enough to prepare some refreshment for our guest.'

Alice smiled back dutifully; she knew a dismissal when she heard one, and went with much reluctance to convey her father's wishes to the old housekeeper.

Making certain that his daughter was safely away, the master of the house closed the door firmly behind her and came over to his anxious-looking visitor.

'Now then, Angus – what's this all about?' he asked, inviting the boy to sit. 'And you can give me that hat before you strangle it to death!'

'It's Captain MacLean, sir!' confessed the boy in a rush. 'I think he may be planning an escape for the prisoner in the castle.' He shook his red thatch in an obvious quandary. 'In fact I'm sure of it!'

'What?' Charles Lamont was thunderstruck. 'Has he taken leave of his senses?'

Leaning over the desk, Angus clasped his hands tight together in front of his chin, as though the conveyance of his friend's conversation with him on the previous night, required some extra-firm hold on reality.

'When the castle was in our possession – we blew it up!' said the boy proudly.

'Indeed!' replied the lawyer, 'And a right pig's ear you made of it too, as anyone within a mile of the place at the time can testify!'

'Well, anyway,' continued the boy, 'when the stables went up, all the straw bedding was strewn across the castle hill, and what was left of it we simply dumped over the wall – there's heaps of it up there still!'

The lawyer sat listening intently as the boy's explanation unfolded:

'Yesterday, Captain MacLean noticed a gang of street urchins playing with the straw on the castle hill – making hay stacks of it, that sort of thing – and the soldiers never turned a hair!' Angus glanced over his shoulder for eavesdroppers, lowering his voice. 'That's why he came to see me with the suggestion that I join the gang of ragamuffins on the hill so that I might arrange for a great heap of the hay to be piled up at the foot of the castle wall.'

The lawyer's eyebrows went up and a moment later he was on his feet, pacing the floor, his professional brain running ahead of him.

'I remember some of us younger ones used to jump down from the wall into the hay stacks below,' Angus informed him with the glint of memory in his eyes. 'It's some height, I can tell you, but a safer landing you couldn't wish!'

But Charles Lamont hardly heard a word; so lost was

he in his own private thoughts. A moment later he was back in his chair again looking more worried now than confused.

Then Angus got up and made to leave. 'I shouldn't be here at all, Mr Lamont,' he grumbled. 'I'm betraying a confidence and I don't feel very proud of myself for doing it,' he admitted, shaking his red head ashamedly.

'Now, now, Angus, just you sit yourself down, for goodness' sake! If Molly sees you sneaking out like that, and her off preparing you a refreshment, she'll be none too pleased, I can tell you!'

Remembering his manners, the boy retook his seat, but all the while, as he sat on the edge of the chair in silence, his face remained a vivid portrait of self-disappointment.

'Now you see here, Angus MacLean!' commanded the older man, now leaning purposefully towards his disconsolate visitor. 'You did the right thing coming here today, and for all the best reasons! And if that man had an ounce of common sense in his stubborn head, he'd thank you for it!' Seeing the nod of acquiescence, the lawyer sat back in his chair and, holding his hands prayer-like in front of his lips, he eyed the boy with a growing admiration. That couthie face and clumsy manner concealed a complex personality; a deep sensitivity not often encountered in one so young.

'You are very fond of this Captain of yours, I think, Angus?'

The young lad looked up from his pre-occupation, a little taken aback by the other's sudden observation.

'Aye,' he admitted after some deliberation, 'I suppose I must be?'

'You risked your neck for him once before, and I suspect you would do it again for the asking.'

Angus fell pensive again. 'He was, as we say, our *Ceann-cinnidh*,' explained the boy.

But his listener's furrowed brows required an English translation.

'The Head of the Clan, Mr Lamont. As his father was before

131

him. He is the splinter of an ancient dynasty, and though there are many scions of the clan chieftain, none has the blood as strong as Captain Ross MacLean.'

The master of the house was now leaning forward on his desk again, his hands clasped tightly in front of him, absorbing every word of the boy's explanation.

'But now,' sighed Angus mournfully, 'without his little *clanna*, with nobody to protect and care for, he is lost!' The boy glanced over at the older man, smiling at his obvious lack of understanding. 'It is the Highland way, Mr Lamont,' he explained. 'Only this time, it is *he* who is in need of protecting – and from *himself*, I think?'

Charles Lamont eased himself back into the chair again, looking thoroughly thoughtful.

'You are a remarkably wise young man, Angus MacLean.'

The boy smiled back appreciatively. 'My old granny always said that I had an old head on my shoulders and that one day when I grow into it, I'll be a force to reckon with!'

'I think that day has arrived, my boy – and no mistake!'

But Angus scarcely heard this glowing tribute to his coming of age, for Molly had intervened with a tray of tea and a selection of her home baking for the guest's pleasure. And all the while, as the young lad tucked in with relish, Mr Lamont sat silently in his chair opposite, staring at the ceiling with a singular intensity.

Then, suddenly, as if stabbed by some invisible sword, he sat bolt upright in the chair, pulled the writing quill from the inkstand, and hurriedly scribbled something on a sheet of notepaper.

Angus, having finished his tea and scones, sat watching in silent fascination.

'Now then!' said the lawyer, folding the sheet of notepaper and handing it across the desk to the bemused boy. 'Take this message to Captain MacLean! Tell him that I wish to speak with him most urgently; the time and the place, I have written there for him!' Then, getting to his feet, he pushed out Angus's hat and conducted him to the study door. 'Urgent, mind,

Angus – not a moment's delay!' were the lawyer's parting words . . .

Perhaps it was the look on the young girl's face that caught Molly's attention. She had seen that look many times in recent days and the reason was all too obvious.

'You wouldn't happen to be thinking about a certain young man with dark curls, blue, blue eyes, and an easy smile . . . by any chance?' she ventured mischievously.

Alice's face drained of its dreamy expression and took on a look of haughty indignation. 'I don't know what you're talking about, Molly!' she retorted, her face reddening by the second.

'Och, away you go, dearie!' argued the old housekeeper. 'Your face is an open book and I've read the story a hundred times already this week!'

Alice came away from the window, pulled out a chair, and sat at the table opposite her tormentor.

But Molly's eyes, so keen and knowing, had gone back down to the potatoes she was so diligently peeling. 'I've worn that look a few times myself when I was your age,' admitted the older woman. 'I wasn't always a wrinkled old biddy, you know. I've had my moments!'

Alice clasped her hands in front of her lips to conceal the smile of surprise. 'Tell me more!' she challenged wickedly.

But the housekeeper's potato-knife had taken a sudden burst of energy and it was several potatoes later before she answered. 'I was considered quite a looker in my day, I'll have you know!' she proclaimed proudly. 'Many a lad in the village where I grew up had his eye on me! And, I don't mind telling you, I led them all a merry dance just for the fun of it!'

Alice clapped a hand against her mouth.

'Aye, you can laugh if you like – but that's no lie!'

Alice's face was a picture and she shook her head at the very idea.

Molly, having recovered her composure, put the potato-knife

down with a clatter and looked across the table with a determined eye. 'We lived for Sundays back then!' she explained. 'All the lassies of the village would pretty themselves up for their visit to the kirk!' The old woman's eyes were alight with the memories. 'Everyone for miles around would be there in their best kirk claes; it was the high spot of the week, dearie! Aye, and many a fruitful courtship was launched on the Sabbath day from the kirk pews!'

Alice could only shake her head at the wonder of it all; church-going in her own experience was an all-too-sombre affair.

Seeing her listener's look of scepticism, Molly tut-tutted disarmingly. 'Och, nobody paid much heed to the minister; he may as well have gone home for all we cared!' Sensing a shadow of a smile, the old housekeeper took the bull by the horns, 'My mother had a wee poem – would you like to hear it?'

Alice nodded, curiously, as Molly checked her memory for the words:

> The Sabbath is a special day
> When people go to church to pray
> Some may go to gain a lover
> Or perhaps some guilt or fault to cover
> Still others wish their face to show
> Or neighbour's indiscretions know
> And some just go to sit and nod
> But few go there to worship God . . .

Molly's eyes were misty now. 'Aye, they were grand days, Alice. And fine people too . . . ' Feeling the nostalgia a little too sharp, she smiled anew and, reaching, over, claimed the girl's hands firmly between her own. 'Och, but you have your whole life ahead of you, dearie. And a fine handsome lad too,' she reminded the other, encouragingly.

But Alice's gaze held a distant, troubled look and it was some moments before she answered:

'That day on the moor, when the good Captain lost his entire command,' she said chillingly, 'I fear he may have lost his reason to live also . . . '

Molly pulled her hands away, a little taken aback. But the girl's eyes had a glare of determination now. 'If it's the last thing I ever do on this earth, Molly,' she said steadfastly, 'I will prove him wrong on that score!'

11

Charles Lamont opened his eyes to the fire of sunset on the walls and ceiling. Through the open window he could hear the sound of waves lapping against the shore and the urgent call of an oyster-catcher on the wing. Yawning, he stretched his arms aloft in the wing-chair where he was seated, pulled his gold watch from the fob-pocket of his waistcoat, and checked the time. It was nine o'clock precisely, and the last musical chime had all but died away. He must have fallen asleep for he was certain that a good half hour had elapsed since he had first sat down. Pulling out his tobacco pouch from his coat pocket, he made ready to smoke when the sound of a stifled cough stopped his fingers in their tracks.

'Good evening to you, Mr Lamont – I trust you slept well!' came the wry greeting from the far corner of the room.

'Ross! Is that you?' enquired the man in the chair, peering through the gloom. 'How long have you been there?' he asked surprised.

'Long enough,' came the laconic reply from the darkness. 'You'd make a bonnie sentry – and I don't think!' the disembodied voice informed him. 'Could have lifted your gold watch and your precious tobacco pouch. Aye, and your breeches, too, if I had a mind – and still you'd be sleepin' like a bairn!'

The lawyer stood up from the chair, pushed his tobacco pouch back into his pocket, and brushed off the dust from his clothes.

'So, the wee clipe came to see you then – singing like a lintie!' the voice continued. 'Would have been as well telling it to the town crier!'

'If you are referring to Angus,' replied Charles Lamont bristling somewhat, 'then yes, he did come to see me, as it happens, and not "singing like a lintie" – as you put it – but through unswerving loyalty and a genuine concern for your

136

welfare – if you only had the eyes to see it!' He raised his finger and jabbed it into the darkness:

'He saved your skin once before, but God only knows why he bothered!?' raged the lawyer as he kicked a piece of broken glass aside in anger and watched it skid across the floor to smash against the skirting-board quite some distance away.

'Why don't you give the lad some credit – he's only a boy after all!'

'Aye,' chuckled the other. 'I've known many a redcoat make that mistake!'

Charles Lamont shook his head, exasperated.

'Och well,' conceded the Highlander. 'I suppose subordination was never his strong point.'

The older man gave a deep sigh of satisfaction, having just scored a point in the argument.

'Well – what was it you wanted to see me about?' demanded the Highlander, taking up the cudgels once more. 'You said half past eight, and it's gone nine!'

'You know perfectly well why I'm here!' returned the other angrily. 'And if you knew me at all, then you would understand why I cannot allow myself to sit idly by while you contemplate suicide on my account!'

The Highlander suppressed an ironic laugh. 'The last time I saw you,' he said scornfully, 'you couldn't sit straight in your own chair. Why should I listen to anything you have to say?'

The lawyer drew a deep breath to calm himself. 'That's all in the past!' he snapped.

'Is it?' The Highlander was not so sure.

'Let's stop playing games, Ross. We both know why we're here. But for my careless confession, you would be blissfully ignorant of my son's very existence! And now, out of some twisted sense of duty to me, you set your life against the boy's freedom!' he broke off, enraged. 'It's insane! And I will not allow it!'

The Highlander glared back, rubbing his forehead in open frustration.

'I have come to the conclusion,' continued the lawyer in a

measured tone of controlled temper, 'that Neil has been largely the author of his own misfortune and there is nothing that you or I, and certainly not Angus, can do to prevent the inevitable!' he glared daggers at Ross. 'Now, let that be an end of it!'

The Highlander looked askance then turned back frowning. 'You've changed your tune all of a sudden,' he noted suspiciously. 'The distraught father I remember would do anything for his son,' he reminded the older man.

'I've had time to think since then,' answered the lawyer firmly. 'Sometimes the fog of intoxication brings its own clarity of purpose.'

The Highlander laughed mockingly. 'Oh, you would make a grand actor, Charles – strutting your stuff in one of those English plays – but you don't fool me for a second! You can rant and rave till the cows come home, but it won't change the fact that in here . . . ' he said, thumping his heart with the heel of his fist, 'you're still the same wretched father from that pathetic room who would stop at nothing to help his own flesh and blood in his hour of most need . . . ' The Highlander's strident voice suddenly softened. 'You wouldn't be the man I've come to know and respect if you were not . . . ' He looked directly into the lawyer's troubled eyes, his expression growing all the while less hostile. 'Why don't you admit it, if not to me, then to yourself?'

Charles Lamont pushed his hands deep into his coat pockets and, stepping backwards with his head bowed low, he sank into the wing-chair, still warm from his recent repose. His whole manner was that of surrender and defeat.

After a prolonged silence he looked up at his adversary and grinned, rather in the way of a little boy caught stealing biscuits by his mother. 'That obvious, eh?' he murmured softly, then lowered his gaze once more. 'Angus was right about you,' he said, to some imaginary listener in the floor. 'I'm beginning to suspect that the boy has a better understanding of life's little problems than either of us.' He glanced up, smiling at the other's puzzled expression. 'Some people need protecting . . . from themselves,' he said equivocally.

'What is that supposed to mean?' the Highlander wanted to know.

But the lawyer, seeing the unsmiling, unyielding face, shook his head disappointedly. 'Ah, never mind,' he said thoughtfully. 'You wouldn't understand.'

Heaving himself up out of the armchair, he crunched his way through the shards of broken glass, walked over to the opening in the wall, where the window used to be, and peered out. In the twilight of sunset there had fallen an extraordinary silence; an odd stillness which had a sound all of its own and like no other. It was almost tangible.

'Do you want to hear something amusing?' the man at the window enquired, turning suddenly and glancing over his shoulder to be sure that his listener had not deserted him. 'Today I received an invitation to a Grand Ball at Culloden House. All the top brass from the military will be there!' he gave an ironic laugh. 'The soldiers are preparing to murder my son and they send me an invitation to their celebration ball!' He looked off into the distance. 'Just about sums up this whole sorry affair, don't you think?'

The Highlander regarded his friend a long time in silence before answering, the aggressive demeanour of argument now replaced by a more human face:

'It doesn't have to be that way, Charles,' he said, with what sounded, to the man at the window, like rather forced optimism.

'You do realise, of course, that what you are proposing is lunacy in the first degree?' the lawyer reminded him coldly.

Ross did not answer but stared back blankly, biting his lip.

'Nevertheless, right now, I'm so bereft of hope that I'm willing to consider anything,' the lawyer yielded.

The Highlander pricked up his ears. 'You are willing to consider *any*thing?' he repeated disbelieving.

'If the sword of Damocles falls, Ross, then I too should be under it,' said the older man resolutely and, leaving the window, he came over to where the younger man was standing, caught hold of him by the arm and led him out through the open doorway.

'Whatever it is that you are planning,' he said in a purposeful voice, 'then you will need horses and somewhere to conceal them. I can provide both. And perhaps most important of all, a safe refuge for the fugitive . . . ' he looked at the other hopefully. 'In the unlikely event that it might be needed . . . '

On the driveway outside the derelict ruin, the full extent of the devastation was still all too painfully visible in the fading light.

'Why choose this ramshackle old place for a rendezvous, Charles?' the Highlander wanted to know.

'The original owners . . . ' answered his friend as a flight of squealing bats broke from an upstairs window, 'were clients of mine, and good friends too, as it happens. One day in April – the eighteenth, to be precise – a patrol of dragoons came riding by, and it was they who ransacked the house!'

His walking companion stopped dead in his tracks, looking bewildered.

'Over there in the field,' Charles explained, indicating with a finger, an area of scorched earth and charred timber, 'there stood an old barn where six rebels had taken refuge on their flight from Culloden. The soldiers barricaded the doors . . . and torched the place to the ground,' he broke off, watching the impact of his words building on the young man's face, whose piercing blue eyes glazed over and snapped shut against the horrific image.

'They say that the screams could be heard over a mile away.'

The Highlander stood on the edge of that darkness for a timeless moment, struggling with the twin evils of rage and vengeance that screamed somewhere deep inside of him.

Then the lawyer cleared his throat:

'I learned some time later that my friend Kenneth had tried to stop them but was, unfortunately, killed in the confusion,' he hesitated, looking doubtful. 'Or that's how it was officially reported.' He shrugged his shoulders, feeling suddenly desolate. 'Fiona and the children moved away . . . I never did manage to find out where . . . ' He looked up at his companion's stunned face. 'Whenever I feel sorry for myself, I come here,' he added with the shadow of a smile. 'It helps to put things in perspective!' Then, taking the Highlander's arm as they walked on, he steered the conversation once more to the task ahead.

Coming to the end of the drive, they saw the clump of yew trees with the little brook running through, which gave the district of Alt-na-hurich its name. Here stood the black horse with the distinctive white blaze, pawing the earth, impatient to be off.

Charles Lamont pulled out his pocket-watch and flicked open the hunter case as Ross made ready to leave. 'Ten o'clock!' declared the older man, surprised, then tucked the heavy timepiece back into its pocket.

'It's still not too late to change your mind about this foolish enterprise, Ross!' he reminded the other. 'No good can come of it!'

But the Highlander shook his head, resolutely. 'I'm not doing this just for Neil!' he answered solemnly. 'These past weeks living up there on the hill like a wounded deer! Jumping at every sound! Running from my own shadow!' he shook his head disappointedly. 'My men used to think me courageous . . . what would they make of me now, I wonder?' He looked long and hard at the older man. 'Surely you must see it, Charles?' he entreated with an imploring smile on his dark face. 'I don't know who I am any more. Perhaps I need to do this thing to find myself again,' he speculated. Then, gathering the reins, he placed his foot in the stirrup and swung into the saddle.

Looking down, the Highlander gave his lawyer friend a leaving smile. 'Until tomorrow then!' he said in that taciturn way of his. And, like a man too pressed for time, he threw his cloak over his left shoulder and urged his horse onwards down the dirt road.

Charles watched him go as the moon burst through the clouds, spilling its mercurial light over the dark water of the loch. His young friend, his daughter's future happiness, was riding to certain disaster and it was all he could do to stand helplessly aside and watch the tragedy unfold . . .

12

Slowly and persistently, the bell in the ancient clock tower pealed out its doleful monotone; each dreadful 'clang' sounding against the nondescript buildings, studded doors, and shuttered windows of the sleepy little town on the river.

Huddled in the gloom, faceless, nameless people held their breath as the hanging hour drew near. For when the death bell tolls, superstition stalks the streets like a hungry wolf. And woe betide anyone touched by the dark shadow of the Grim Reaper as he treads his sinister way to harvest the departing soul.

Ross MacLean, resplendent in his scarlet and gold officer's uniform, took the salute from the castle guard, strolled smartly across the broad esplanade and, with a furtive sweeping glance, descended the narrow flight of steps to the little chapel below. Once inside, he concealed himself in a dark corner near the altar, removed his gold-braided tricorn, unbuckled his sword, pulled the crescent-shaped gilt gorget over his head and, laying all three neatly on the floor, settled in to wait . . .

Meanwhile, across the river on the north side, some five hundred yards downstream, Charles Lamont and young Angus MacLean dismounted at the pebble beach where the direction of the river dog-legged sharply to the right. Here at Friars' Shott, the current, unusually swift for the time of year, washed everything ashore at this point along its journey. Here, too, Charles showed Angus where he was to conceal himself and the horses from the prying eyes of passing patrols. The livery stable was a communal affair for the convenience of working townsfolk on the north side. Charles and his firm of solicitors occupied an office on the upper floor of a building overlooking the river and, when he had climbed the stairway to the top landing, he looked down from the narrow side window to ensure that Angus and the horses were in position.

Outside his office door the lawyer hesitated, breathing deeply. The butterflies had taken flight and his stomach was protesting angrily. A turn of the key and the lettering on the door-pane, *Charles Lamont & Partners, Solicitors and Notaries*, swung away as the door yawned open. Inside, the room was filled with shelves of large, mostly leather-bound reference books, an old pedestal writing desk, some chairs, a hat stand, and a few oddments of furniture. The dingy interior was noticeably silent save for the monotonous ticking of an ebony-cased bracket clock on the fireplace mantel. The whole atmosphere was heavy with the musty smell of the leather-clad library within.

Flipping open the lid of his gold pocket-watch, he observed that the time concurred precisely with the clock on the mantel-piece opposite. Trembling, he selected two books from the shelves and opened them randomly on the desk. Sitting briefly in the chair, he arranged the books, inkstand, and quill in a manner consistent with his usual habit of working. If, for whatever reason, the soldiers were to pay him an unexpected visit tonight, then he must make certain that everything in the room should appear normal and above suspicion. He had come too far down the road of complicity to be complacent now!

Heart in mouth, he walked over to the window and opened it, leaving it slightly ajar. From here he had a perfect view upstream to the stone-arched bridge and the castle dominating the hill above. Sitting by the window in the half light, his attention was drawn to a sudden movement on the bridge. He pulled the small telescope, borrowed from Angus, from his coat pocket and, as he focused the lens on the source of the commotion, he could feel his skin creep as the glass picked out a large force of soldiers marching in line across the entire span of the bridge.

Presently, an officer riding a strutting grey came into his field of view. Charles watched him traverse the full length of the bridge from the north side, inspecting, meticulously, the assembled line of red uniforms, now standing rigidly to attention. There came a deep sigh of relief when the thin red line fell in behind the rider and marched off in the direction of the castle gate. Was this some high ranking officer come to enjoy the evening's 'entertainment'? The lawyer's blood ran cold at the very idea.

Another flick at the pocket-watch and a glance at the mantel clock confirmed the time at twenty minutes to eight. He glanced nervously around, ensuring everything in the room to be in order. He peered through the window again, satisfying himself that the level of bridge security had returned to normal. Then he checked his watch again.

And again.

And then once more, just to be sure!

He undid the top button of his ruffled shirt and, pulling a handkerchief from his waistcoat pocket, proceeded to mop the perspiration from his fevered brow. The clammy sensation under his collar was becoming increasingly unbearable and the beating of his heart raced alarmingly. It was fear and apprehension of the worst kind.

And yet, there came a strange excitement with the danger. He felt suddenly more alive at this moment than he had felt in years. His part in the unfolding drama was minimal; a mere spectator in the amphitheatre. But, what of the young gladiators in the arena, he wondered?

A narrow shaft of evening sunlight found Neil Cameron through the single slit window of his dark dungeon cell. Deep in the bowels of the castle rock, he had endured the last hours of life with remarkable self-possession. The young adventurer had come a long way since that April night at Loch Nan Uamh. Indeed, his whole life had taken a rather long and convoluted journey. And how strange that it should come full circle to this final destination?

Even as that infernal bell struck away his last moments, his thoughts returned to the young Prince he had come so full of hope to rescue. How forlorn that foolish enterprise seemed now!

Footsteps in the stone passage outside, spun him round. The key turned in the lock and the heavy iron door screeched open.

'Prisoner – it's time!' the officer of the guard proclaimed in his clipped English voice.

Neil Cameron's eyes closed against the words. Those dreaded words. Like a cold sharp icicle through the heart! He opened his eyes to the two granite-faced sentries standing to attention either side of the open door. A priest came in and administered last rites to the condemned man.

But not a word of it registered. The officer of the guard bound his wrists behind his back with a stout rope and clamped a set of leg-irons round his ankles, locking them securely. Then, smiling a little apologetically, the officer placed a firm hand on his prisoner's shoulder before bending him out through the open door.

The rapid beating of drums signalled the approach of the prison guard: a large force of heavily armed sentries marching forward at the double. Half of this body traversed the castle esplanade to the foot of the wooden scaffold, where they formed a tight cordon, encircling the structure completely and standing to attention with their muskets set in the shoulder-arms position. The remainder made a secure corridor from the castle courtyard to the site of execution, through which passed the aforementioned priest, clutching a bible to his breast, an officer with a proclamation to hand, and the hooded figure of the executioner himself.

With the heavy leg-irons mocking his progress, Neil Cameron stepped, blinking, into the bright evening sunshine, his ears suddenly deafened by the tremendous crescendo of drums.

'Keep moving, prisoner!' the officer of the guard yelled above the din, and a firm hand on his shoulder urged him forward. His feet, blistered from the want of shoes, stung painfully against the rough stone esplanade as he shuffled his way through the corridor of red uniforms. Ahead, down the avenue of grim-faced sentries, the hideous instrument of death beckoned.

At the foot of the wooden structure, the firm hand on his shoulder stopped him rudely. Here, so that the prisoner might enjoy the freedom to climb the steep steps to the raised platform, the officer of the guard knelt down to unlock and remove the cumbersome leg restraints.

The young Jacobite, unbowed and defiant to the end, climbed that devil's staircase with all the courage he could muster. And, when he had reached the top, it was through rather incredulous eyes that he received the gaze of the execution party, already assembled and waiting.

The crowd, as he gazed down, seemed to perceive him with a great outpouring of sympathy. It was clear from those watching faces, that there would be no entertainment here!

Neil, took in the scene around him as though he, too, were a spectator. Surely, it was all just a bad dream; a nightmare from which he would at any moment awaken – wouldn't he?

Taking hold of him by the upper arms, the executioner's firm hands led him to a position directly beneath the wooden gibbet, where the length of stout rope, ending in a thick noose, dangled inches from his face. With rapidly diminishing disbelief, Neil bit down hard against his lip, for to his horror, he could feel his eyes begin to fill, and since he could not move his hands, all that was left for him to do was to close his eyes tight against the tears and pray God the soldiers would fail to see the sudden flight of his courage.

As the minute hand on the face of the steeple clock strained for the hour, Neil opened his eyes to that west-bound glen from whence the warm August sun upon his face was soon to sleep.

Yes, these southern intruders might take his life and dreams, but not this golden sunset; such things were not theirs to take! And yet could he smile, for his heart was Highland, and the dying embers of this Highland summer evening were his alone to keep . . .

The loud rolling of drums gradually subsided to a soft rallentando as the proclamation of the death sentence was read out. Then the priest recited a perfunctory verse from scripture. This done, the drummers picked up the beat once more; the tempo and the volume increasing to a terrific thunder which filled the air with an almost tactile vibration. So loud was the awful sound that the many townsfolk who were absent from the scene could hear the woeful din from a long way off.

Charles Lamont too could hear that terrible sound. Standing by the open window of that lonely room, his back pressed against the wall, he sank sobbing pitifully to the floor. The insufferable days of torment. The hopeful self-deception. All would be over soon. Crouched in the gloom, head in hands, the unfortunate man surrendered totally to his feelings.

Then all at once, on the castle esplanade, the drums fell suddenly silent.

'Do exactly as I do and you may live! Friends and horses are waiting! Nod your head when you are ready!'

Trembling with fear on that desolate spot, Neil Cameron could scarcely believe the words he had just heard whispered in his ear. Stupefied, he nodded. Almost immediately his hands fell free behind his back as the razor-sharp blade of a *skean dubh* sliced through his bonds. Turning sharply he saw the hangman's hood in the air and the 'executioner' leaping from the edge of the scaffold. Without a second's hesitation, Neil followed; both men sailing over the heads of the astonished sentries, standing statue-like beneath them.

Down and down they fell the full height of the castle wall, yelling as they went with the sheer frightening exhilaration of the drop. Then, with the enveloping safety net of deep straw bedding breaking the impact of their fall, they were pitched violently forward into an uncontrollable head-over-heels tumble down the long sweep of the castle hill. Over and over they rolled, in a blur of green and blue as grass and sky merged into one. Ross was only vaguely aware of another body falling somewhere close behind him then, all at once, they encountered the dirt road with a painful arresting thump!

Amid a cloud of dust, Ross sprang instantly to his feet, turning full circle for the direction of the river. His head spun dizzily and his legs buckled beneath him. Neil was experiencing similar difficulties.

'This way!' Ross yelled, grabbing Neil by the arm and charging headlong for the river. At that same instant the first bullet zipped through the air and struck a tree, splintering the bark in all directions. Another ricochetted off the road in a puff of dust and a third hit the water ahead of them with a muffled *sploosh*.

The air was filled now with angry gunfire from the castle above as the two fugitives crashed through the bushes and into the raging torrent.

Gasping in the freezing water, they surfaced as the strong current took hold, pulling them outwards from the bank and swiftly towards the bridge. The bridge sentries, alerted by the sound of gunfire from the castle high above them, tried desperately to draw aim at the two heads bobbing in the water towards them. But the rapidly moving targets hindered accurate marksmanship on the upstream side of the bridge so they ran to the opposite parapet and waited for a better opportunity. Ross, anticipating the move, plunged Neil's head downwards below the water-line as the stone arches loomed above them. At the last possible moment, he dived for the riverbed at the same instant a bullet ripped through the water in a trail of deadly bubbles, inches from his head. And yet another tore the skin from his wrist in an instant of stinging pain.

Gulping for air, Neil broke to the surface in time to hear the last stroke of the bell in the clock-tower toll the fateful hour. Turning in the water, he could see the menacing bridge, and the sentries, waving and yelling frantically, now at a safe distance. Carried swiftly onward by the strong current, everything seemed to fly past him in a blur. To the right, the thatched roof of a riverside cottage and beyond, a horse-drawn carriage parked by the roadside. And here to the left, the spiky skyline of church steeples, and a dog on the embankment barking furiously; as he drifted hurriedly by.

Presently, he could feel stones against his feet as he came upon the shallow waters of the pebble beach. But Ross, having surfaced some way off in deeper water, could not free himself from the river's vicious clutches, now dragging him inexorably further and further from the safety of the shore. He was aware of the two shadowy figures running on to the stones and pulling

Neil bodily from the water. He could see beyond them, the horses saddled and waiting . . .

Thrashing vigorously in the water, he made one last desperate lunge for the bank. But to his horror, the men waving their arms wildly above their heads on that pebble beach seemed to be shrinking in size; everything fleeing rapidly from his outstretched fingers. Then, all at once, he was round the dog-leg and gone from sight . . .

Above the castle esplanade, the air was filled with the smoky residue of burnt powder as the soldiers looked on in numbed disbelief at the sudden, unexpected turn of events. The assembled gathering of townsfolk stood similarly struck; some openly horrified at the escape of a detestable rebel and his daring accomplice. And yet still more, secretly delighted at the naked embarrassment of the King's finest!

By nightfall the escapee and his two companions were passing through the gates of Balblair House, where Lady Elaine Cameron waited anxiously for news. The sound of approaching horses brought her running from the house. Slipping down from the saddle, Neil ran to his mother's waiting arms. Sinking together with the embrace, she cradled his head tenderly against her breast a long moment, pouring little words of comfort upon him. And through eyes filled with tears, she could see that he was once more, her little lost boy come home . . .

Charles and Angus witnessed the scene rather hazily from their saddles, for in truth, they could not see clearly for the moisture in their own eyes.

13

Later that night, as young Angus MacLean languished mournfully in an armchair, Charles Lamont paced the floor in front of a blazing log fire like a man possessed. His boots, still damp from wading in the river, were now steaming so alarmingly from the intense heat that the boy could not be sure if the older man's feet had ignited, spontaneously, from his continual to-ing and fro-ing across the fireside rug.

'Now see here, Angus!' he argued, in the manner of an angry father to a wayward son. 'You can forget saddling a fresh horse and riding back there tonight!' He stopped dead in his tracks and pulled out his pocket-watch to check the time. 'It's gone midnight, for pity's sake!' He flopped into a chair and looked across at his dejected listener. 'Why don't you get some sleep? I will return to Inverness at first light to see what I can learn.'

Drained of argument, Angus smiled back something of an agreement.

'Come now – to bed with you!' ordered the other in a tone of quiet firmness and coming over to the boy, helped him out of the chair.

'I was proud of you tonight, Angus. Damned proud!' he said, with all his sincerity in the words.

Exhausted by the night's events, Angus went without further ado upstairs to the bedchamber prepared for him. Holding high the candelabrum to light him up, Charles was joined at the foot of the stairs by the lady of the house, smiling encouragingly. When they were satisfied that the young lad was safely abed, they walked together into the drawing room.

Closing the door quietly behind her, Lady Cameron came over to her hero, her eyes filled with a new admiration. 'Oh, Charles, how can I ever thank you,' she quavered, claiming his hands ardently between her own, 'for the life of my . . . ' she broke off, looking suddenly ashamed. 'For the life of *our* son!' she said firmly.

Charles looked back, hardly daring to believe the evidence of his own ears. That little word of self-correction had monumental significance. In all the long years that passed since Neil was born, she had jealously claimed the boy as her own and belonging to no other.

Smiling, he kissed her on the hands. 'How is he?' he asked, concerned.

'Sleeping like a bairn,' she beamed, with the mist of memory in her eyes.

'I will have Ronald MacTavish look him over in the morning,' he promised. Then he walked over to the fire and, leaning on the mantel, he gazed rather forlornly into the flickering light. 'Fortune has indeed smiled upon us this night, with the safe return of our precious son, but I fear that we may have paid most dearly for it!' he said chillingly.

'How so, dearest – what terrible thing has happened?' With growing concern she came over to him, seeking the reason for his fretful behaviour.

Feeling worried eyes upon him, Charles turned to face her and, touching her cheek tenderly with his fingertips, he gazed down upon the timeless beauty that had so bewitched him all those years ago. Her dark ebony hair had strands of silver in it now, but the brightness of those eyes still burned with the same fierce intensity of old.

'Charles, what is it! Why do you hurt so?'

For an instant his eyes fell from her gaze and when they reopened, there was despair in them. 'My young and loyal friend, the man upon whom my little girl has built her dreams may already be dead! Or worse – captured by the very demons who contrived with such relish to snuff out the life of our own flesh and blood!'

Lady Cameron froze at his words. 'Oh, dear God! Let it not be so . . . ' she gasped, clamping her hand instantly to her mouth in the way that women do when something unspeakable slips out.

'Then you must go to her at once! She will need you now more than ever!'

He broke from her embrace, shaking his head against the suggestion.

'I fear, Elaine, that I cannot!' and he turned from her so that his face was hidden from her searching gaze.

'My love for Alice knows no bounds. There is nothing I would not do to ensure her complete happiness. Yet my love for Neil, albeit from a distance, is equally profound! But I fear that my connivance in securing the boy's freedom has brought about a most tragic paradox. For in the success of the one, I have succeeded also in the failure of the other!' Resting his elbow on the mantel, he bit down, despairingly, into his clenched fist.

'Don't you see?' he implored. 'I cannot go to her now and tell her that I have conspired to kill her sweetheart in order that my child might live – a child she doesn't even know exists!'

Elaine Cameron caught hold of him firmly by the arms. 'Charles, you talk in riddles! You have conspired to kill no-one! You are distraught and talking foolishly!'

But he would have none of it. 'No, Elaine!' he argued, breaking from her. 'I stand accused, and will be judged guilty! I used that foolish Highland loyalty of his so cruelly for my own ends – I can see it now!' His hand was on his forehead, rubbing furiously. 'As surely as though I had plunged a sword into his breast with my own hand, I have killed him!' Sitting now on the edge of the fireside chair shaking his head incredulously, 'I have killed him!' he repeated.

She went quickly to him then and sitting on the arm of the chair, took hold of his head and held it gently against her bosom, stroking his hair with soothing fingers. 'You must not torture yourself like this, dearest Charles. You must not!'

And there they remained together, a long time in silence, the tormented man nodding drowsily in her arms until, with all conscious resistance gone, he fell into a deep and dreamless sleep.

Elaine Cameron watched him drift away and from her position on the arm of the chair, she gazed at him a long moment. He looked so peaceful sleeping that she could see, behind the lines that time had etched upon his noble face, the young and handsome man she remembered. Many times she had wished, and never more than in recent days, for all that had been done to be undone. Yet here, sleeping not inches from her beating heart, was the man who many years ago had given to her the most precious gift a woman could ever know. And yet again tonight, had returned it to her.

'Oh, Charles,' she whispered softly, 'you have been the soul of discretion throughout these long years, guarding our secret so jealously, and yet at what price to you, dearest? Watching helplessly from a distance, your own flesh and blood grow to manhood, never knowing the joy of those early years; the first faltering steps, the endearing little baby words, the sheer pride you so richly deserved in the achievements of your own unique child.' Growing more and more disturbed by her own part in all this unhappiness, she stood up carefully from the chair, lest she wake him from his sound slumber and, wringing her hands in silent agony, she gazed up at the ceiling, seeking forgiveness:

'Dear God, how could I have been so selfish?' Turning now to look once more at the sleeping man, she spoke again to him in the same whispered voice:

'After all the hurt that you dearest, gentle Charles have so selflessly endured; tonight it would seem, your pain has only just begun . . . '

The east coast haar, which had condensed during the night, now rolled in from the firth to cloak the town with its impenetrable vapour. Yet high on Leachkin Hill, where the sun shone brightly, already those dreaded red uniforms were emerging from the cold, grey blanket of mist. With the glint of sunlight on their steel bayonets, the relentless search had begun.

Every building, outhouse, and barn; every nook and cranny large enough to conceal a human form would be suspect and diligently examined at point of steel, and woe betide anyone found giving succour to the fugitives.

Charles Lamont knew only too well the dangers, and while

Neil was outwith their reach for now, it was only a matter of time before the ruthless red fingers of death touched the House of Balblair itself. Neil would need to be moved on before then, of that he was certain.

But it was thoughts of Ross MacLean that lay heavy on his mind this sombre morning as he remounted his docile old mare to be waved through the brigade of searching soldiers by an enquiring officer. When he had reached his destination by the pebble beach which had witnessed the drama of the previous night, he quickly set about scanning the riverbanks for any visible sign of his missing friend.

By now news of the daring escape was on everyone's lips and the little town's reputation for embroidering the truth was already hard at work:

Arthur Strickland, the executioner, was a devout Christian gentleman and his solitary visits to the castle's English chapel, immediately preceding a hanging, was common knowledge in the Highland capital. His habit of never revealing his face to the public gaze, for fear of reprisals, was yet another interesting piece of essential gossip to delight the townsfolk in their whispered conversations.

Captain Ross MacLean, too, had heard these same whispers; indeed his whole plan depended upon them. It should have come as no great surprise then to the redcoats when they found the stripped body of Arthur Strickland sprawled across the chapel altar. The discovery of the officer's uniform, neatly folded in a dark corner would, perhaps, be less easily explained!

Yet not one whisper of a body washed ashore, nor any suspect arrested. Charles would take solace in those small mercies – for now, at least.

The enquiring lawyer spoke to everyone he knew for news of the fugitives, but heard not so much as a rumour. He went to see Kate MacPhee at her lodgings, but she had not set eyes on the Highlander since that night at the harbour when he had scared the life our of her.

All day he searched, until the lateness of the hour and the

strict curfew bell, enforced by martial law, persuaded him to abandon all hope of finding his missing friend.

It was a long ride back to Balblair that evening. Charles knew that soon Alice would have to be told the truth about Ross, and about Neil; he could not put off the inevitable for much longer.

Riding through the gates of the old house some hours later, he could see Lady Cameron's carriage parked by the front entrance and she coming out to greet him as he dismounted.

'What news dearest?' she enquired anxiously.

He did not answer, but gave her a look that said it better.

'Your friend Doctor MacTavish dropped by,' she informed him brightly, but his enquiring eyebrow did not receive an immediate reply, rather more of an evasive smile.

'It will take a long time, Charles, before our son is restored to health,' she told him, 'but he is alive and he is free,' she added, rubbing his arm in shared anguish. Smiling a little encouragingly she followed his gaze to the horse-drawn carriage.

'We have a visitor!' she answered. 'I have sent for Alice. She is here now!'

Charles looked thunderstruck.

'I sent my carriage to fetch her, she knows nothing yet. Only that I am a friend of her father and that you are here assisting me with a most delicate matter.'

'Delicate!' he echoed.

'I have done a great deal of soul-searching this day, Charles, and I have resolved once and for always that the truth must finally be told.'

He shook his head at first, then nodded.

'Neil has all day been asking the reason why three complete strangers should risk their lives for him. We owe him an explanation!'

'Yes, yes, of course! I have thought about little else all day,' he admitted finally.

'You, dear Charles, have suffered long enough for my foolish pride, and I have no intention of letting you shoulder that burden any longer.'

She took possession of his hand determinedly. 'We will face this together!' she said firmly. 'Neil is walking by the loch with Angus. I will go fetch him. Alice is in the drawing room awaiting your return. We will join you presently.' With these words, she hurried off across the lawn in search of their son, leaving Charles to speak alone with his daughter.

Outside the drawing-room door, he took time to compose himself for, to his horror, his hands began to tremble. He had endured many nerve-racking moments in his time, but this would be the hardest thing he would ever do in his life.

Alice sprang instantly to her feet, rushing to embrace him as he entered. 'Papa – where on earth have you been? I have been worried sick for your safety,' she scolded.

'Forgive me, my dear, I should have let you know that I was here, but so much has happened since I saw you last,' he smiled, patting her comfortingly.

'Have you heard the news?' she inquired excitedly. 'The rebel prisoner has escaped – everyone is talking about it.'

'Yes, I had heard,' he nodded, inviting her to retake her seat in the armchair near the fire. Sitting opposite, he gazed across at the brown eyes, glowing with expectation. Reaching over, he gathered her hands tenderly in his own.

'Papa, what is it?' she asked, growing apprehensive, for his manner was subdued and she knew his moods well enough to know that this one suggested something was wrong.

'Do you remember when you were a little girl, and how you used to ask me questions about your mother, what she was like and did you remind me of her?'

Alice nodded positively that she did remember.

'Once you asked me if I was ever lonely and would I, perhaps, consider marrying again? I do believe that you even suggested that I should.'

His daughter smiled at the memory of it. 'Yes – and to *me*, as I recall!' she replied, laughing.

'Would you be surprised to learn that I had wished it once, many years ago.'

Alice looked surprised. 'But you made no mention of this before!' she answered, frowning.

'Because there was no need, for the lady in question would not agree to it. She believed it was for the wrong reasons I asked.' Her father's face turned suddenly anxious. 'Alice, please forgive me for not telling you this years ago, but I was sworn to secrecy and could not. It began soon after your mother died, it was a mistake and should never have happened.'

His daughter returned a look of complete equanimity. 'There is no need to apologise, Papa. I am no longer a child. I understand these things.'

But when her father stood up from his chair, the troubled expression remained. 'If only it were that simple,' he sighed, despairingly.

Alice, sensing some dark secret, sprang from her chair to comfort him. 'What papa! – what could be so terrible?'

He turned away a moment, then back suddenly to face her, his eyes pleading forgiveness. 'There was a child, Alice – a son!'

There fell a moment of utter silence. Some huge sledge-hammer, she felt, had come down crushing her life beneath it.

'You, you have a son? You and . . . this woman?' She shook her head, denying all possibility. 'No – it cannot be true!'

Her father, now on his knees before her, looking up through begging eyes. 'You must believe me, I wanted so many times to tell you!'

She pulled her hands from his grasping fingers, turning from him, all the while shaking her head in disbelief. 'All these years, and never a word!'

A moment later when the door opened to admit the lady of the house and the very gaunt young man, all at once for Alice, the penny dropped.

'You? . . . Lady Cameron . . . it is you!' she stammered.

'Yes, Alice. It is I!' the pretty dark-haired woman replied in a remarkably composed voice. Reaching out for Charles to come forward, and turning to Neil, who was fully as shocked as his half-sister. 'Neil – this is your father!' she proclaimed boldly.

Neil stepped forward, limping somewhat from his ordeal of the previous night and, though his eyes remained fastened to the man, it was to his mother he spoke:

'But my father is dead! – you told me.'

Elaine Cameron shook her head. 'No, Neil!' she stated steadfastly. 'My husband is dead, but this gentleman is your father!'

'But why did you say nothing of this last night?' asked Neil, turning his attention now to a very wounded-looking Charles Lamont.

'Your father', interrupted Lady Cameron, addressing both Neil and Alice, 'kept his silence in order to protect me. He offered very graciously, at the time, to marry me – but I refused.' Turning now to Charles, whose hand she was gripping tightly. 'It was not one of my wisest decisions,' she admitted, 'and one I have since come to regret.' She looked at him longingly. 'I believed that he had made the offer out of duty rather than love, but now, I suspect I may have been wrong about that also?'

Charles Lamont smiled back something of a confirmation.

'Alice, you must not blame your father for his secrecy. I begged him not to tell a living soul and demanded his parole of honour on it,' she paused, looking at him for forgiveness. 'I now realise that it was much too heavy a burden to ask of anyone.' Turning now to all three of them:

'Please try to understand,' she begged. 'I was young, frightened, and confused, but time has taught its lesson well.'

Alice, who had stood listening in stunned silence, could suffer to hear no more. Clapping her hands firmly to her ears, she fled the room in distress.

'Have you told her yet about Ross?' Lady Cameron enquired anxiously, but the lawyer's wretched demeanour answered her question. 'There wasn't the time,' he sighed, sinking into an armchair. 'And in any event, I'm no longer sure if I would know what to say,' he admitted dispiritedly.

Neil came over and placed an understanding hand on his father's shoulder. Under different circumstances it should have been a time for rejoicing, but the young man knew instinctively what the unhappy girl was feeling.

'I will speak with her,' he said, and bowing politely he left the room to search for his sister.

It was not difficult to find Alice down by the lochside. Through the veil of overhanging branches, her turquoise gown shone bright against the dark waters of the loch.

Neil caught sight of her long before she became aware of his shambling approach. She was sitting on a flat rock some yards from the shore and pitching pebbles into the calm water. Across the wide sweeping lawn and down the heather path he came at last, to sit next to her in silence. Gathering a handful of pebbles from the shingle beach, he began to disturb the surface of the water with a salvo of his own. Stealing little sideways glances, still he could not believe it; this beautiful creature, his sister!'

Presently, after many moments of silent self-congratulation, he ventured to speak. 'Yesterday,' he admitted bravely, 'I was more alone than I have ever been in my life! Today, I am reunited with a mother I have not seen in years, introduced to a father I believed long since dead, and now,' he paused, looking amazed, 'I discover that I have a sister I never knew existed!' He shook his head at the wonder of it all. 'Yesterday, I would never have believed that I could know such happiness again.'

Alice stopped her hand in mid swing and looked at the emaciated young man with a quizzical expression. 'You are very thin. Have you been ill?' she asked.

Neil smiled at her directness. 'Yes, in a manner of speaking, I suppose I have.'

'Then you should eat more and build up your strength,' she told him with a slight scolding.

He laughed, in spite of himself, at the innocent remark.

'Have I said something amusing?' she demanded.

'Forgive me,' he smiled, trying to sound serious. 'Only the people who have been looking after me of late are not known for their hospitality,' he explained.

'Then you should choose your company with more care,' she advised.

Neil grinned again. 'You may depend on it!' he assured her.

'Just look at your hands – what on earth?' she exclaimed, suddenly seeing their very crippled appearance.

Neil pulled them from view. 'Our father is a very brave man,' he said evasively. 'You should be proud of him.'

This glowing tribute caused her next pebble to fly with such force that she achieved a distance Neil would never have deemed possible from a woman's hand.

'It could not have been easy for him bringing up a child on his own without the help of its mother,' he reaffirmed.

But this new suggestion only resulted in yet another pebble gaining a distance even greater than the last.

'You had better take care or you will hit Angus on the far shore,' he warned, pointing now to the tiny red-haired figure across the loch.

'Angus – here?' she exclaimed, surprised.

'Why, yes, he is sitting where I left him earlier. See? Over there under the tree!'

'Is Ross with him?' she enquired, now on her feet and scanning the distant shore for a sight of him.

'No, he is not here!' Neil informed her.

'Then I will go at once to Angus to find out where he is – I have not seen him in days!' And she took off round the edge of the loch with Neil, fearful of what Angus might unwittingly tell her, following in hot pursuit. But his sister had set a blistering pace and he was in no fit state to follow.

'Alice, please wait. I have something to tell you. Alice, please! . . . ' Neil's frantic appeals stopped abruptly when he tripped, plunging headlong into the heather with a cry of pain. Turning on her heel, Alice hurried back to the spot where her brother had fallen, breathless and in obvious distress.

'My, my, you really are in a bad way, aren't you?' she told him with a trace of sympathy. 'Is it your ankle?' she enquired, now kneeling beside him and examining the foot, which was already badly swollen.

'Alice, you must listen to me!' he pleaded urgently between breaths as Angus, alerted by the commotion, came running round the shore towards them.

'Ross – Angus . . . and your father helped me to escape. But Ross is missing . . . Father has all day been searching!'

Alice, her brown eyes wide now with bewilderment, sat back on her heels as the words seeped in. 'Escape?' the hairs on the nape of her neck bristled as she said the word.

Neil caught hold of her hands, a frantic, urgent grasp as Angus loomed above them. 'The fugitive!' he almost shouted. 'Last night! . . . from the castle! . . . Alice – it was me!'

Half an hour later, with Neil safely indoors, Angus returned to the lochside, to find Alice sitting with her head resting on her updrawn knee, in the heather where they had left her.

'Why don't you come back to the house?' he pleaded. 'They are asking after you.'

Blinking back the tears, Alice looked up dreamily from her repose and regarded the uncomplicated boy a long moment. His ever-friendly face mirrored concern.

Like a safe harbour for a storm-bound ship, the young lad stood head and shoulders above all the madness that had broken over her world this day. Brushing away the tears, she patted the earth beside her, inviting him to sit:

'Tell me what happened last night, Angus. The truth, please, and not some watered-down version for female consumption.'

Shielding his eyes against the late evening sun, now striking them at a low angle through the pines, the boy sat down beside her as he was bid, but his reticence was plain to see.

'Please, Angus! You are the only one I can trust now to tell me the truth.'

After a long silence, Angus relented and told her, albeit reluctantly, the whole sad story of the escape, the days leading up to it, and everything that had transpired since. When he had finished his rather graphic monologue, Alice stood up, thanked him for his honesty and returned at once to the house.

She found Neil alone in the drawing room, sitting in a

chair by the bay window, his now bandaged ankle resting on a padded footstool.

From his elevated position overlooking the loch, he had watched the two distant figures huddled by the shore. It was not difficult to guess the subject of conversation. 'You must hate me!' he told her without turning to look in her direction. 'I am beginning to wish that I had never been born. Too many people have been hurt already by my dangerous existence. All day, I have been asking Angus questions about the man who risked his life for me. I couldn't help but notice a distinct feeling of resentment towards me. He has good reason to condemn the man responsible for the loss of his friend!' His crippled fingers rippled through his hair in anguish. 'God only knows what you must think of me.' Not looking, he pointed a finger at the bureau against the far wall. 'There's a loaded pistol in the top drawer,' he informed her. 'Use it on me if you will. It's all I deserve!'

Alice, who had stood in the doorway listening in silence, chose to ignore that last remark; it was, after all, just the confused ramblings of a troubled mind.

Neil, sitting motionless in his chair, fell silent. He neither knew, nor particularly cared, whether or not Alice was still in the room behind him. He half expected to hear the drawer slide open and the sound of a shot ring out at any moment. He almost wished that it might. But none came. He felt only the warmth of loving arms around his shoulders, and the sweetness of a gentle kiss upon his cheek.

14

The sky was ablaze with every conceivable shade of red, orange and yellow as the four-horse team clattered through the leafy environs of Culloden House, and the sun, which had burned steadily throughout that long, hot afternoon, now lingered on the horizon like a warm memory.

From the sanctuary of their woodland enclosure, a herd of fallow deer watched the coach's dusty progress with nervous glances as proud, ring-necked pheasants scattered in squawking confusion from the thundering hooves. Down a shady boulevard, white fan-tailed pigeons broke from the round tower dovecot as the coach rumbled past the stone-walled stables and onward up the drive.

Under the watchful eye of her father, who sat impassively with his hands resting on the heel of his evening cane, Alice peered out through the coach window as the high chimneys and round towers of the great house reared into view above the treetops. On the wide curving driveway horse-drawn carriages were parking, awaiting the despatch of their passengers. From the front entrance immaculate footmen came rushing to open the carriage doors for the arriving guests to disembark with the dignity this pompous occasion demanded.

Alice took in the scene with a peculiar feeling of unreality as she alighted from the coach on her father's arm to be flamboyantly welcomed through the entrance by bowing doormen. A fuss of servants preceded them down the hall to the long gallery where the stately music of violins came sweetly to them. Here they were ushered into line behind the many guests awaiting formal admittance.

Of their announcement, Alice heard nothing, nor indeed did she detect the flat note dropped by the musicians at the sight of her stunning arrival.

In a state of numbed detachment she accompanied her father to the huddle of guests who were now greeting their hosts with cordial salutations. When her turn came she dropped a polite curtsy of introduction and smiled back, dutifully, to each and every one.

Time was not long in passing before a detachment of young officers had surrounded her place of neutrality, pressing her father for an introduction to the most beautiful creature they had ever seen.

For in truth she was beyond compare that evening. Her pale pink gown of whispering silk co-ordinated perfectly with the delicate pallor of her skin, and the long tendrils of her powdered coiffure, dangling as they did so teasingly about her neck, completed a picture of wistful enchantment so attractive and bewitching to men.

But Alice had eyes for no-one that evening, for lost was her heart to another, and that she might die of love would be for her a welcome release from an otherwise desolate future. Like a perfect autumn rose, struck by an untimely frost, her little-girl-lost demeanour served only to heighten the irresistible charm she so unwittingly conveyed.

Charles Lamont, who had fought valiantly to fend off the pack of young wolves howling for his daughter's favours, was on the very point of capitulation when a much older and evidently more senior ranking officer intervened.

'Come now, gentlemen!' he scolded. 'Call off your siege and give these good people some air.'

Like a gang of unruly children called indoors by their father, the group of young men bowed to a higher rank and obediently withdrew from the scene.

Charles drew a sigh of relief and thanked the newcomer for his timely intervention.

'If I may be so bold, Mr Lamont, please permit me to present myself,' smiled the gallant officer with a polite bow of the head. 'Your humble servant, sir. Major John Harding.'

Shaking the major warmly by the hand, Charles turned to Alice, who was now fanning herself furiously. 'Allow me to present my daughter, Alice,' he said proudly, bringing her gently forward to meet the uniformed gentleman.

Alice favoured him with one of her sweetest smiles and dropped a half-bob as the bowing major planted an obligatory kiss on the back of her outstretched hand.

'I have seen many breathtaking sights on my journeys round Scotland, Miss Lamont,' said the redcoat officer, gleaming behind a bushy moustache. 'But none that could compare with the beauty I now behold.'

Alice could feel her flesh creep from head to toe. Having just narrowly escaped the wolf-pack, she was now in the snake-pit with the king viper!

Smiling back coyly from behind her busy fan, she could only look on helplessly, as the grinning major imprisoned her recently kissed hand securely between his own.

Charles, feeling his daughter's dilemma, coughed diplomatically for its release as Major Harding smiled obligingly with a show of absent-minded clumsiness, and Alice in return sweetened her smile in the joy of liberty.

The violins had struck up a fast and merry tune and now one of the former wolf-pack, doubtless egged on by the others, returned to try his luck afresh. Alice, seeing that the persistent young man looked considerably less objectionable than the present company, finally relented.

Her father watched her glide away like a fairy princess while her partner winked triumphantly at his onlooking friends, now elbowing each other in a frenzy of delight.

Smoothing the gold braid of his tunic, Major Harding fingered his considerable moustache in a display of irritation.

'It would appear that one of your subordinates has just outflanked . . . if not outranked you, Major,' observed the amused lawyer, struggling desperately to contain an outburst of laughter that was threatening to erupt in the other's inflamed visage.

Spying a passing waiter with a generous tray, Charles secured two glasses of the house punch and offered one to his crestfallen companion. 'Come now, Major, time to drown our sorrows,' he sympathised. 'Let the youngsters have their moment of fun. They'll know soon enough the disappointments of advancing years!'

Major Harding smiled respectfully and raised his glass. 'Indeed, sir. Indeed,' he agreed in impotent surrender.

There followed a long interlude during which the two men enjoyed the spectacle of the dancing couples, now strutting the stately measure of a harpsichord minuet.

Alice, as before, was centre of attention, much to her partner's delight, as he too now fell under watching eyes for having picked the sweetest cherry in the orchard.

Alice's face, however, was a touch too demure for her father's liking, and though she smiled in all the right places, he knew from painful experience that lurking beneath that cool exterior a two-headed serpent lay poised and ready to strike!

He had agonised about bringing her to the ball in her present grief-stricken condition, but, as usual, no amount of persuasion – or, indeed, forbidding – would alter her determined course. Even her new brother, who seemed to exert a singularly positive influence upon her of late, could make little impression on her decision to attend. Like a loose cannon, rolling on the deck, she might go off at any moment and send a fatal shot through the hull of the good ship Lamont, sinking it to the depths of despair and ruin!

Closing his mind to that horrifying prospect, Charles scanned the room for a friendly face when, all at once, his gaze came to rest on a familiar figure.

He appeared to be standing in a state of splendid isolation, distinctly apart from the others. Charles recognised the man as one of General Hawley's former staff officers, now seconded to Lord Albemarle who, since the middle of July, had taken over as the Commander-in-Chief of the King's Army in Scotland. The man was, oddly enough, dressed in a suit of civilian clothes, unlike his fellow officers who stood resplendent in their immaculate dress uniforms.

The puzzled lawyer touched his companion's arm for an explanation. 'Is that Major Pendleton over by the fireplace?' he enquired.

Major Harding craned his neck for a sight of him then pulled a look of disapproval. 'Ah, Mr Lamont, therein lies a rather sad tale,' he confided woefully and, drawing closer to the other's ear, lest he be overheard, set about explaining the reasons for his comrade's sorry predicament.

'It would seem that lady luck has dealt our solitary friend a most unfortunate hand, sir.'

Charles widened his eyes in anticipation.

'He apparently returned from an evening stroll . . . ' The storyteller paused a moment, to heighten the suspense, then glanced round for eavesdroppers, 'Wearing only his private undergarments!'

Charles looked suitably aghast. 'Well, bless my soul!' he exclaimed.

The major raised an eyebrow knowingly. 'He was set upon by a gang of ruffians who, after a ferocious struggle, overpowered the good major and made off with his complete attire – boots and all!' Tapping the tip of his prominent nose, the storyteller impressed upon his confidant the need for the utmost discretion. 'I, of course, have my own suspicions! As indeed did Lord Albemarle, who expressly ordered our misguided friend to appear this evening in civilian clothing as a stark reminder to others who might be tempted to mislay the King's uniform!'

Suddenly remembering how Ross had cunningly purloined an officer's uniform in preparation for Neil's escape, Charles could suffer to hear no more. 'Please excuse me, Major,' he quavered, in an octave higher than usual. 'I think I need some air.'

Alice, meanwhile, growing weary of the dance and more especially her tiresome partner, dropped a dismissive curtsy and quit the floor in a flurry of discomfort – leaving her deflated escort to the mercy of his onlooking friends.

Taking advantage of her father's absence, the viper grinned lasciviously at the vulnerable girl as she returned.

'Growing tired of the little boys, Miss Lamont?' he enquired sardonically. 'A girl of your obvious spirit needs the firm handling of a mature man!'

Alice's eye kindled. 'Indeed, sir!' she agreed, smiling

sweetly. 'But unfortunately there doesn't appear to be one present!'

The viper's eyes narrowed. 'Then perhaps you should join Mr Bush over in the dunce's corner!' he hissed menacingly. 'See!' he pointed. 'The nice young lieutenant all on his own.' He gave the flustered girl a look of utter contempt. 'Junior officers become outcasts when they are disrespectful to their superiors – you two should get on famously!' Stupefied with rage, the loathsome major stomped off into the crowd.

Fanning herself with relief, Alice peered over at the solitary young officer in question. Neil had spoken of a certain Lieutenant Bush at Fort William who had shown much kindness to the captive rebels in his care. Could this be one and the same? she wondered.

Nettled by Major Harding's prickly remarks and intrigued by the plight of the errant young Lieutenant, Alice threw protocol to the winds. Drawing admiring glances from scarlet and gold, and some envious ones from hoop and powder, she pushed her way through the convivial huddle of guests to the place where the forlorn young officer was standing. He looked so pitiful as she approached that she could only wonder at the warped mentality that would demand the presence of a young man at such a prestigious social event, in order that he might be castigated in the full glare of his peers. Then she recalled Neil's broken fingers and emaciated condition and wondered no more.

'Hello!' she smiled charmingly. 'Lieutenant Bush, Fort William, is it not?'

The young man looked at first too surprised to answer. Then, relenting, he smiled back nervously and nodded. 'Yes, miss. I have that unhappy distinction,' he replied.

'Then please allow me to introduce myself,' she said with a proffered hand, 'Alice Lamont!'

For an instant, he seemed hesitant to take it.

'We have a mutual friend,' she informed him.

At this the impeccable young officer bowed politely and, taking possession of her delicate hand, kissed it gently. 'May

I be permitted to know the name of our mutual friend, Miss Lamont?'

'You may not!' replied Alice boldly.

The nice Lieutenant looked both surprised and amused by her directness.

'Suffice it to say that he speaks highly of you as an officer and a gentleman,' she told him admiringly.

Smiling, a little embarrassed, the young man bowed his head appreciatively. 'Then he should speak in my defence at the court martial,' he replied deprecatingly.

'Court martial?' Alice looked dumbfounded.

'I suspect it may come to that one day,' he answered blandly, 'unless I resign my commission first and save the army's blushes.'

Alice shook her head, disconcertedly.

Seeing the young lady's obvious confusion, the Lieutenant explained further. 'It would seem that I have committed the cardinal sin of showing undue care and attention to prisoners in my custody,' he said, smiling a little at her furrowed brows. 'It is not the behaviour expected of an officer in the King's army.'

Alice was appalled. 'Then perhaps you are in the wrong army, Lieutenant?'

'My Christian faith led me to believe that we were all in the same army, Miss Lamont,' he replied obliquely. 'When I took the King's shilling, I honestly believed them to be one and the same.' He lowered his gaze in disappointment. 'It would appear, however, that I have been proved very much mistaken . . . '

Alice murmured compassionately then, throwing off the black mood which had descended on them both, she lifted her chin and beamed him one of her encouraging smiles. 'Tell me, Lieutenant,' she ventured with a challenging eye, 'how did you feel when you learned that the prisoner, Neil Cameron, had escaped?' For one horrible moment she wondered if her question had overstepped the mark, for the face of the pleasant young officer looked suddenly subdued. Then, glancing to either side, lest he be overheard, he leaned towards her ear. 'If the powers that be heard my answer to that, dear lady,' he whispered, with a twinkle in his eye, 'I can tell you for certain that they would more dearly wish to hang me instead!'

His reply amused Alice immensely and earned him a tap from her fan.

The violins were now playing the introduction to a popular waltz and Alice touched her ear invitingly. 'This is one of my favourites, Lieutenant!' she said hopefully. 'But I appear to be in need of a partner!'

'Nothing would give me greater pleasure, miss,' he replied in an urgent undertone, 'but I would not wish for the shadow of my shame to fall upon you.'

Alice smiled back, imperviously, and pinning a confident smirk on her face, she linked arms with the bashful Mr Bush.

'Then we will let the shame fall upon *them*,' she said, leading her obedient escort out on to the very centre of the ballroom floor.

Her partner proved an accomplished dancer but, feeling disapproving eyes upon him as they glided elegantly together, his movements became unduly tense.

Alice, feeling the anguish, squeezed his hand encouragingly and he responded with a brief nervous smile.

'You cut a fine figure on a ballroom floor, Lieutenant!' she said admiringly. 'You should give lessons.'

There was a flash of perfect teeth as a quick smile came and went. 'I have sisters, Miss Lamont. A brigade of them,' he answered. 'A brother with two left feet would die of shame!'

Alice giggled in spite of herself at this explanation. 'But I thought brothers were supposed to be horrid to their darling sisters, Lieutenant,' she smiled. 'It's nice to know that they come in useful for something.'

It was the young man's turn to laugh. 'Then am I to deduce from your reply, Miss Lamont, that you have never known the joy of a brother's love?'

Alice returned an indignant look. 'If you mean have I ever had my pigtails tied together, spiders in my shoes, or frogs in my bed, then I would have to say a definite *No*, Lieutenant, and thank goodness for it!'

It would be difficult to imagine a more changeable human face or, indeed, mood than that witnessed by Alice at the precise moment her dancing partner erupted in laughter, and it was a laughter perpetuated all the more by her continued look of vile disgust. It was a happy, carefree moment and she was pleased to see that the sad young man of earlier had, at last, caught the intended mood of the occasion.

But even as they laughed, already a dark eye and heart had fastened their attention on the unsuspecting couple.

Overfilled with the social juices, the human malevolence barged brusquely out to the middle of the ballroom floor and, stopping behind the laughing Lieutenant, tapped him rudely on the shoulder:

'You're a bloody disgrace to the uniform, rebel-lover!'

The rough edge of the voice cut like a blunt razor through that light-hearted moment and, with a sinking heart, the young officer turned to see the grim features of his fort commander, Captain Caroline Frederick Scott, sneering in that loathsome way of his.

In that awful instant, the harmony of music and movement died completely with those rasping words, and the whole room fell suddenly silent.

'You've obviously had too much to drink, Captain. Perhaps a breath of fresh air would be wise?' suggested the young Lieutenant with remarkable composure.

Swaying unsteadily on his feet, a loaded glass of whisky in his fist, the deep-set dark eyes of the brutal officer turned now upon Alice:

'And is this little tease one of your rebel whores, Lieutenant?'

In a flash, the invisible cord of self-control, which had been stretched to the limit all evening, finally snapped. With one swift movement Alice snatched the whisky glass from the obnoxious man and threw the contents into that offensive sneering face.

There came a loud unified gasp of horror from the onlooking guests, as though the air from every corner of the room had been sucked in by the lungs of a giant.

Charles Lamont, who had returned from his constitutional stroll just in time to witness the spectacle, and from no great distance, could only stand in impotent shock as the unfortunate scene unfolded. Somewhere in the recess of his mind, he heard the distant thunder of a loose cannon. The good ship Lamont was going down with all hands and there wasn't a thing the Captain could do to prevent it!

To the despairing lawyer, the entire action seemed to move at sleepwalk speed, everything caught in a nightmare slowness. The distance was but a few feet, though it may as well have been a hundred miles away and a thousand years too late! With his feet stuck in leaden shoes, he moved towards his daughter just as the hapless girl was forming the very words that would surely tear their fragile veil of deception forever. But another figure, too, was moving towards her, and on yet more nimble feet.

Alice, at the same instant her lips moved to speak, caught the full glare of the oncomer's intense gaze even as her own eyes popped open with her mouth, choking the fatal words in her throat. Swaying and speechless, her trembling hand came up to her forehead, her knees buckled beneath her and, in a great swirling blossom of silk, she swooned to the floor in a dead faint.

The onrushing stranger was first to react, gathering up the delicate bundle in his arms as her distraught father retrieved her fan and reticule from the ballroom floor.

'The lady is clearly unwell!' he explained to the horri-fied onlookers. 'Please give us space to take her outside for some air!'

Pushing through the corridor of anxious faces, the two men carried the unconscious girl out on to the balcony, where she was laid out, ever so gently, on a seat of wicker wood. Here, the good samaritan removed his coat of soft satin and folded it under her head for a pillow, while her father fussed over his fallen angel.

So caught up in the drama of the moment was he that Charles Lamont had failed to observe, with any close attention, the helpful stranger now kneeling beside him and though he thanked him profusely for his kindness, still he did not remark his identity until the man spoke directly to him:

'Don't you know me Charles?' he asked, surprised.

Those innocent words, or more especially, the familiar voice that spoke them, sent an icy tingle down the lawyer's spine. Looking hard now at the stranger's powdered wig and face paint for the first time, Charles could see behind the disguise, those unmistakable blue eyes of his missing friend, Ross MacLean, twinkling back at him in the darkness. Charles fell back on his heels in a state of utter stupor as the Highlander addressed him in an urgent whisper.

'Charles, I must go now before I am discovered! Tomorrow morning I will call on you at the home of Lady Cameron.'

As the Highlander moved to leave, Charles, coming to his senses, caught hold of his friend's sleeve. 'For pity's sake, Ross! Where the devil have you been?' he demanded to know.

But Ross merely smiled back disarmingly. 'A friendly sea captain has been showing me the sights of Rotterdam,' he answered matter-of-factly. 'It seemed the wisest thing to do in the circumstances.'

But the befuddled lawyer was still unconvinced by his friend's resurrection. 'But, but, that wig . . . and, and, these fine clothes?' he protested.

Anxious to depart, the Highlander removed his friend's grasp from his sleeve. 'The same place I acquired the uniform, Charles,' he whispered impatiently. 'Why, it's the best tailor in town!'

'Ross? Ross?' Alice's soft moaning sounds brought the Highlander abruptly to his feet and, without so much as a by-your-leave, he was off down the stone steps to the garden grounds below.

Charles, still reeling from the shock of it all, leaned over the balcony wall:

'What do I tell *Alice?*' he whispered after him.

But like some fleeting shadow in the night, the Highlander had already vanished into the darkness.

'Ross?' Alice's voice had the intonation of urgency now, awareness returning quickly. An instant later, she opened her eyes to the disappointment of her father's face. Feeling the softness of the folded coat under her head, she sat up and looked searchingly around.

'What is it, my dear?' he asked, concerned.

'Oh, Papa, I don't like this place!' she said complaining. 'I think it might be haunted!'

She gazed at him with uncertainty, all the hostility of those last few days gone now from her eyes. 'Take me home!' she pleaded, in that little-girl-lost way of hers.

Patting the delicate hand, her father smiled back:

'As you wish, my dear. As you wish.'

Back in the ballroom the music had restarted. People were dancing again; the awkward moment was already forgotten. Evidently the good ship Lamont was still afloat and sailing, 'Steady as she goes!'

As his daughter repeated her pleas to leave, the wily old lawyer allowed himself a little wry smile. 'Now isn't that typical!' he whispered under his breath. 'And just when I was beginning to enjoy myself!'

15

Early next morning Alice awoke with a suffocating sense of disappointment. Fool that she was – to believe, even for an instant, that the flash of blue eyes, which had struck her like a bullet from a gun last night, could be anything other than a figment of her grief-stricken imagination!

Wishing to escape from that dip into despair and desolation, she skipped breakfast and headed down to the loch to walk the shore. Down here, in the hour before dawn, the wild scents of bog-myrtle and thyme gave out an overpowering fragrance and the song of the moor, as it sprang into life under the veil of lifting darkness, had a poignant kind of magic no city-dweller could ever hope to know.

She must have been gone a long time, for when she rounded the far side of the loch on the homeward leg of her journey the sun was already a good height above the dwindling heather hills behind her. In the distance, as she picked her way through the pines, she could see the full splendour of Balblair's baronial mansion, standing proud at the end of its broad sweeping lawn, and coming down from the house now she could just make out the tiny figures of her father, Neil, and Angus, tied together in a knot of conversation.

'Come on, Alice!' cried her suddenly ebullient brother as she drew near. 'We're going to play a game of blind man's buff and we've decided that you're it!'

Despite her protestations to the contrary, the hapless girl soon found herself, as on the previous night, the centre of some very unwanted attention.

Quickly encircled by all three, she was blindfolded by a silk scarf and spun playfully round in the customary manner. Now suitably teased and disorientated, and clawing the air frantically after her tormentors, Alice was totally unaware of the black stallion's silent approach, nor could she see the tall figure dismounting and advancing across the lawn to stand, smiling, a few short feet from her outstretched fingers.

A moment later she had caught her first victim. Now she must identify her captive by name. It was a simple enough task, for the individual characteristics of the three were quite distinct. She very quickly eliminated Angus from her mind, for this fellow was much taller! Nor could it be her father, for unless her sense of smell had deserted her completely, that ever present aroma of pipe tobacco was most definitely absent!

Then it could only be Neil!

But wait, surely Neil was thinner, much thinner!

As her searching fingers travelled along her captive's shoulders and tip-toed across his cheek, the light brush of long eyelashes sent a sudden shiver down the length of her spine. Those same fingers, trembling now, reached up under the hairline, where the unmistakable ridge of a healed wound lay clearly visible to the touch. She pulled back sharply, fearful to believe what her heart was racing to tell her. An instant later, she had slipped the knot, dropping the blindfold from her eyes. 'Ross!'

From a discreet distance, Charles Lamont heard the disbelieving whisper and witnessed the heart-rending embrace that followed, with more than a little tear in his eye and, somewhere in the distant back of his mind, there came a tingle of memory too.

'Oh, I could die of happiness for them!' quavered Elaine Cameron, coming up behind the emotional man and placing a casual arm around his waist. 'I can scarcely believe it,' she sighed, choking back the tears. 'Neil home safe, Ross alive and well, and Alice restored to happiness.' Placing her head against his shoulder, she squeezed him tightly with the sheer joy of the moment.

'And it's all thanks to you, Charles!' she smiled admiringly.

'Oh, come now! Hardly my doing,' he countered. 'Had things remained as they were, I would have been remembered as the villain of the piece for evermore.'

'Not by me!' she claimed emphatically, then, gazing long-ingly at the still blissfully entwined couple, she whispered softly in his ear:

'It must be wonderful to be so young and in love,' and smiling up at him now with a twinkle in her eye, 'Does love favour only the young?' she asked.

Charles met that smile with another, for the innocent question held inviting implications.

'I think I might be persuaded to put that particular theory to the test,' he chuckled, and yet another little squeeze round his waist only confirmed his suspicions.

'Oh, Charles!' she murmured. 'I feared so much that you had grown to hate me for what I had done to you in the past, that you could never find it in your heart to forgive me.'

His arm around her shoulder dispelled those fears completely and his eyes upon her were filled now with understanding and forgiveness. Then all at once they were in each other's arms in a long ardent embrace, much to the surprise of the others, who whooped their delight and applauded rapturously.

That evening at dinner there was much to celebrate. Charles proposed a toast to Ross's safe return and to his daughter's future happiness. Ross in turn, toasted:

'The young couple, Charles and Elaine!' much to the amusement of them all.

And of course young Angus MacLean had his little moment, toasting everyone in sight, including Lady Cameron's West Highland terrier, and a grim old stand of harness, whose frowning occupation of the far corner of the room, returned a most ominous presence.

But the laughter had scarcely died away before the dark clouds of uncertainty were gathering to spoil the sunshine of the moment. And when Charles rose to his feet with a toast to Neil's future prosperity in the bosom of his family, the look of discomfort on the young man's face was impossible to ignore.

'Neil, what is it? Are you unwell?' his mother enquired anxiously.

His father, sensing it too, put his glass back down on

the table with a thump. 'Neil!' he entreated, but the young Cameron's answer was not forthcoming; only that he shifted rather uneasily in his chair, until his father's steely glare drew out the truth. With a deep sigh of resignation, Neil gazed up at both his parents; a painful, apologetic look.

'The ostensible reason why I came to Scotland', he explained, hesitantly, 'was to deliver the cargo, in my trust, safely to its destination. So far as I am given to believe, that particular part of my mission has been successfully completed.' He broke off, glancing at the faces studying him with a shared look of intense curiosity.

'However, due to unfortunate circumstances, the main reason for my being here remains yet unresolved.'

His father's raised eyebrows only reflected the curiosity of them all as Neil crossed his fingers in preparation for the painful part:

'I arrived here in April,' he explained, 'with express orders to locate the Prince and shadow his safe return to France, if and when all hope of the Rebellion had passed.' He paused, looking at Ross for some semblance of understanding. But there was none.

'There is a ship due in Loch Nan Uamh this month of September. I would be failing in my duty if I was not there to see that my charge is safely aboard.'

There fell a deafening silence at this most unexpected bolt from the blue. Neil, never one to suffer disapprobation gladly, pushed back the chair and rose to his feet, dropping his napkin on the table.

' . . . Nor can I rest easy in my mind, when the lives of those I love the most are in danger for keeping me safe.' Wishing to hear no argument, he bowed politely and left the room in silence.

Snapping shut her eyes against the appalling prospect of losing her son again so soon, Lady Cameron rose to her feet; anger showing in her every movement.

'Men and their duty!' she exclaimed, the hot flush of temper flooding through her slight frame as she struggled to keep her voice from breaking. 'What is it about you men and your absurd sense of duty?' Throwing her napkin on the table, she put a despairing hand to her face and stormed out of the dining room in distress.

Charles, Ross, and Angus sat stone-faced in their chairs under the watchful eye of Alice, who, by her withering look of disapproval, seemed all too eager to applaud the good lady's emotional outburst.

Presently, after a long, oppressive silence, Ross was seen to clasp his fingers tight together and mumble something incoherent – a signal Angus recognised from past experience as the harbinger of some unpleasant announcement.

'If Neil is determined upon this foolish course of action,' he uttered hesitantly, 'then I can see no alternative but for me to go with him.'

'Oh, dear God, no!' It was Alice now disappearing behind anguished hands.

'But Alice!' pleaded Ross, seeking her understanding. 'Neil is clearly unwell and would never survive a hazardous journey alone through such demanding country.' Looking at her father for some moral support, 'Lord knows, it's a difficult enough journey at the best of times – but now!'

Charles, who had hitherto lost all power of speech, finally stirred into life as the realisation came to him too. Pulling himself up, rather stupefied, from the table, he crossed the room in silence, all the while shaking his powdered periwig in disbelief. Hesitating in the doorway, he turned to look back at the remaining guests; his eyes upon Ross were blank with incomprehension.

'After all that has happened,' he muttered incredulously, 'still it goes on and on and all because of your precious Stuart Prince and his beglamouring . . . '

Alice, who could suffer the stifled atmosphere no longer, mumbled some excuse and left the table, following her father from the room.

Angus, who had remained totally tight-lipped during the

whole awkward scene, now came suddenly to life, in that irrepressible way of his.

Reaching across the table for the wine bottle, he made a great show of studying the label with the intensity of a connoisseur selecting only the finest for his own private cellar. Then, replenishing his Captain's glass, he proceeded to pour more than a generous measure for himself. Leaning back in his chair, he raised his goblet to some imagined truth that only he could understand.

'Do you know something, Captain?' he crooned, smiling at the other's downcast expression. 'It's at times like this that I realise how lucky I am to be an orphan!'

Elaine Cameron found her son in the rose garden at the rear of the house. Hands deep in pockets, he stood gazing westward, where soon his foolish heart must take him. Lost to the dangers of that journey, he failed to hear his mother's approaching footsteps until she had all but come upon him. Startled, he turned, smiling apologetically for his recent unsociable behaviour at the dinner table. He opened his mouth to say as much, but she waved his words away, wishing to hear no more on the matter.

Gathering his hands instead, she looked down at their very crippled appearance and tut-tutted reproachfully.

'You really must take more care of yourself, Neil,' she scolded and, fussing now with his coat buttons, she fastened them, each and every one, all the way up to the neck.

'This is not France, you know!' she reminded him. 'It gets cold here in Scotland at night – even in summer!'

He couldn't help but laugh. 'Mothers!' he teased, kissing her on the forehead as she fussed. 'Always worrying about their little boys.'

Seeing the truth of it in her own fingers, she could only smile, in spite of herself, even though her heart was breaking.

Charles came at last to join them. But, wishing no more tears, she bid them talk alone in peace while she took herself and her sadness away.

There was much to say between father and son, but so little

time to say it. Standing alone together, overlooking the loch, in that garden of many climbing roses, Charles turned to Neil, a little curl of amusement on his lips.

'Have you the time, my boy?' he asked. It was an innocent enough question, but it brought a bemused look to the young man's face. His shrugged shoulders only confirmed what his father already knew.

Smiling now a little self-indulgently, Charles Lamont pulled the trusty pocket-watch from its home and, flicking at the gold case, he held the heavy timepiece open in the palm of his hand, showing his son the fine detail of its *champlevé* dial.

'Time – it's a strange thing,' he said, reflectively. 'We can't see it, we can't touch it, and yet it changes everything. You young people live always for the future, we old folk dwell – perhaps too much – in the past . . . ' He paused, sighing, a little world-weary. 'If only we could see that all we ever really have is the present. It's a pity that we don't make more use of it when we have the chance . . . '

Snapping shut the hunter case for the last time, he unfastened the gold-link chain from its buttonhole anchorage. Taking Neil gently by the wrist, he lowered the heavy bundle into his son's open hand. 'A young gentleman should have a watch!' he declared, closing the lad's fingers around it. 'It has served me well over many years; as it did my father before me . . . '

Suddenly struck by the significance of the gesture, Neil embraced his father warmly.

Sundown filled the sky with enchantment as Ross walked the shore with Alice, lachrymose and silent by his side. Under the veil of falling darkness, a sandpiper called, hauntingly, across the dark water as the brooding stillness of the moor gave way, at last, to the little loch's nocturnal waking.

Seeing the many white fluffs of bog-cotton, nodding among the purple bell-heather, Ross pulled a handful of the downy plant and showed it to the tearful girl.

'CANACH!' he smiled, remembering. 'Folk in the west use its softness for pillows,' he told her. 'And it makes a fine wick for the fish-oil lamps too.' His dark eyes probed every corner, admiring the rugged landscape in the fading light.

'Peats for the fire, water for the whisky, and the kind of scenery artists dream of. We are fortunate, indeed, to have so much of nature's kindness. I think the good Lord must be a Highlander.'

Alice wiped her eyes. 'The heather is beautiful,' she croaked, her voice husky with tears. 'I have seldom seen it look so fine.'

'Aye,' he sighed wistfully. 'And to think there was a time, not so long ago, when I thought never to see it bloom again . . . '

Alice, sensing the hurt, reached out for his hand and squeezed it, reassuringly, in that way of hers. He smiled down at her touch and, though no words passed between them, he knew instinctively that she always understood what he was feeling during those quiet moments.

A short breeze whipped the water, causing her long strands of hair to lift and flow back off her shoulders. Catching her breath, she pulled her shawl against the unwelcome intrusion; inviting his arm to enfold her with his warmth, his protection. She loved that feeling. And gripped now by the sudden dread of losing him again, she placed her head against his shoulder so as not to show him too much of her sorrow.

'Are we destined always to say goodbye?' she quivered after the silence. 'Will there ever be a time for us?'

Halting her languid progress along the sand, he placed a tender hand under her drooping chin, lifting her moist brown eyes to his own intense blue.

'When I have delivered Neil safely to his destination,' he soothed her, and with all his heart and soul in the words. 'No power on earth will keep me from you!'

'Oh, Ross,' she murmured, fighting back the tears. 'If only I could believe it . . . '

Pulling her slender beauty against him, he buried his face in her clouds of golden hair, seeking the sweet curve of her mouth, only to find her lips sighing for his own.

'And when I return,' he crooned softly, 'we will share the rest of our lives together. I promise!'

16

There was an odd stillness in this midnight hour, broken only by the soft, rhythmic splash of the oars on the water's surface as Neil Cameron, his heart heavy with leaving tears, sat in silence, watching the dark shoreline of Lochend slip inexorably away.

In the little boat beside him, Ross MacLean sat similarly preoccupied. But with thoughts of a more immediate kind! The journey ahead – difficult enough in peacetime – seemed now, in the wake of the Rebellion, so daunting a task that he fancied a leap from the top of Ben Nevis to be an infinitely more sensible proposition!

With the main road west denied to all but the military, and those with legitimate reason and the necessary papers for travel, the MacLean Highlander had enlisted the help of his kinsmen at Dochgarroch to supply a boat and an oarsman to transport them the twenty-three long miles of Loch Ness. And it was to this particular that Neil now turned his attention, for by his reckoning the man pulling on the oars looked at least a generation too old to be so laboriously employed.

Neil touched his companion's arm for an explanation. 'It's a mortal sin,' he whispered, nodding in the oarsman's direction. 'An old man like that rowing us two youngsters such a distance – it's downright embarrassing!'

The oarsman, overhearing the remark, shot his appraiser a daggered glance before delivering a tirade in the Gaelic to his namesake.

Neil, ever eager to engage in conversation, urged his fellow passenger for a translation, and Ross, clearly amused at something, was only too eager to oblige.

'He said that he's been rowing this loch since his father was a bairn, and if you don't like it, then you can always get out and walk!'

Leaning back in the boat's wooden seat, Neil folded his arms in a fit of pique and thought no more on the matter.

Hugging the rugged north shore of the loch, as far removed from the heavily patrolled southern side as possible, the little boat ploughed steadily onwards through the darkness. Holding their breath, all three sat in silence lest a careless whisper should carry above the stillness and betray their movements to hostile ears.

Suddenly, in a heart-stopping moment, the moon broke through the clouds, flooding the entire landscape in a ghostly light. As he gazed up at the towering cliffs and steep wooded hills, Neil Cameron's childhood readings of giant castles and foreboding forests came back to him in the moonlight with frightening reality. The sheer vastness of this deep mountain glen, so graphically exposed, served only to remind the young adventurer of the constant dangers that stalked the dark way ahead.

During these tense moments, the old man stopped rowing, pulled in the oars, and allowed the boat to drift under the lee of an overhanging rock. Frozen by fear, they remained motionless for many long moments until the danger had passed. Only when Ross was sure that the moon was once more tucked safely out of sight, beneath the thick cloud cover, did he give the signal to proceed. Relocating the oars, the boatman pulled with renewed vigour against the little craft's inertia in the water until he had, once again, fallen into that same steady rhythm as before.

Presently the wide sweep of Urquhart Bay came into view, then the dark, brooding ruins of the castle on the shore – the stronghold of the Grants in earlier times – slipped silently by above them.

The moon threatened again just as they passed under the shadow of the great red sandstone hump of Mealfuarvonie; that helmet of a hill which loomed like a sentinel between the glens of Urquhart and Moriston. But as they scrambled for the shore, the heavy clouds locked out the unwelcome intruder and the danger passed.

Despite the company of his two companions, not since he had stood on the very threshold of execution that terrible evening had Neil Cameron felt so utterly desolate. The eeriness of this water wilderness gripped his imagination so powerfully that, to his eternal dismay, he heard the sound of his own teeth chattering in the silence and could only look on, helplessly, as his two curious companions hunted around the vicinity of the boat for the cause of the irritating disturbance.

Fort Augustus, with its present occupying forces, must be avoided at all costs. It had been decided that a position on the south shore of the loch, below the Braes of Borlum, would present the best opportunity for a landing. And it was to this purpose that the old boatman now pulled hard on his right oar, turning the little boat away from the comparative safety of the north side, towards the more dangerous southern waters.

Neil sat tight-lipped and crossed himself in the Catholic way, for if the moon were to break through now, at this most critical moment, there would be no hiding place!

Fortunately the moon remained hidden behind the dense blanket of cloud for the rest of the journey and, in the early hours of the morning, the travellers were more than happy to be setting foot, once more, on firm ground.

Stepping ashore with the rope, Neil searched ahead for a hitching point, while Ross attended to their provisions on the beach. The knapsack containing oatcakes, bannocks, and some 'medicinal' brandy, had taken quite an immersing during the long journey. But, fortunately, as far as he could tell in the darkness, everything looked to be still in palatable condition.

Neil very soon located a suitable anchorage for the boat, but was amazed to see the mooring rope snatched rudely from his grasp as he bent down to secure it. Turning, he saw that the old boatman was already hunched over the oars, pulling away merrily!

'Where in the . . . ?' Neil exclaimed incredulously.

But Ross merely glanced up from his preoccupation with the food rations, showing no great surprise.

'Off back to Dochgarroch, I shouldn't wonder!' he informed his companion, rather nonchalantly.

'And not so much as a by-your-leave!' mumbled Neil.

Heaving the knapsack on his shoulder, Ross came over to

stand next to Neil, both now watching the little rowing boat pull away from the shore.

'Aye, that's old Murdo for you,' grinned his namesake. 'He was never very sociable at the best of times.' Then, pressing a finger against his lips, he left his companion in no doubt that from here on the utmost silence was paramount.

Scrambling up the hill, they topped the rise and crawled into a juniper bush by the side of the road.

General Wade's military road ran south-west out of Inverness, and tracking the loch's southern shore, it dropped down from the Farigaig hills to turn north-east here at Borlum.

This particular stretch of road, lying as it did on the extreme western tip of Loch Ness and close to Fort Augustus, was always vigilantly patrolled, and tonight was no exception.

Waiting impatiently in their place of concealment, the travellers very soon heard the heavy thud of approaching horses as a mounted patrol drew near. Hidden from sight, they held their breath in the junipers as the heavily armed troopers trotted by unsuspecting, the conversation between riders clearly audible in the still mountain air.

Satisfied that the way ahead was now clear of danger, Ross scurried across the road. Searching carefully around, he signalled for Neil to follow. For once the moon, peeping through the clouds, proved a welcome friend as its insinuating light showed clearly the direction they must follow.

Clambering down the steep incline on the opposite side of the road, they pushed on in the moonlight, fording the River Tarff and pressing onward down Glen More. Here they followed the river upstream where it poured from Loch Oich into the deeper waters of Loch Ness behind them.

Running at speed, it was not long before Neil's poor physical condition started to give cause for concern. And it soon became incumbent upon Ross to make frequent stops to allow his companion the opportunity to catch up. But, with the grey light of dawn fast approaching, the MacLean Highlander knew that they must put as much distance as possible behind them before daybreak.

Neil, to his eternal credit, never once complained at the hot pace set by his companion. Even though he stumbled and fell several times in the darkness, his pride would not allow him to betray any sign of discomfort to his pacemaker ahead.

Applying themselves assiduously to the task, and despite the frequent stops, they gained the southern tip of Loch Oich in time to see the sun come up over the Corrieyairack Hills.

During the day they lay up in Laggan woods, recovering their strength. Here they took the food provisions, a fortifying swig of brandy, and a good sleep. Ross, in common with others of his blood, demonstrated the uncanny knack of sleeping with one eye open, which proved in the circumstances to be a most fortunate trick.

Neil Cameron, by contrast, showed himself an exceedingly poor sentry, frequently giving way to slumber at the drop of a hat and with unpredictable ease.

Dusk was falling fast and Ross was growing ever more restless. Repeatedly, he would walk to the edge of the wood, peer out a little, then return to sit under the same pine tree. Neil watched this little ritual with a kind of amused fascination until his companion took off without a word, leaving Neil to scratch his head in wonder.

He returned a good hour later in the company of a rather hunched old man, not dissimilar to the Murdo of earlier. Neil was not in the least surprised to learn that this fellow too was a boatman. He was introduced as Archie, an old friend of Ross MacLean's late father.

Under cloud of darkness the boatman took the two adventurers across the Lochy, from one end to the other, landing at a spot where the River Arkaig poured in. During that uneventful journey Neil came to the conclusion that all boatmen must be struck from one and the same mould. Not once did Archie speak, smile, or exchange pleasantries even at the last; much in the way of old Murdo the previous night.

Stepping ashore in silence, they made all haste along the isthmus between Loch Lochy and Loch Arkaig. And all the while, as they proceeded along at pace, Ross made a great show of tipping his bonnet, bowing respectfully, and generally acting foolish.

For this, Neil discovered, was Cameron country – home of his clan chief – the gentle Lochiel. But the display of light-hearted banter ended abruptly when the said gentleman's great house at Achnacarry reared above them; a black, frowning ruin in the moonlight.

Clutching his bonnet reverently between his hands, the MacLean Highlander picked his way, rather disbelieving, among the charred remains of the once great house of Lochiel. It was a singularly poignant moment for both men, and it served only to remind them of the bitter legacy their Stuart Prince had left his gallant Highlanders.

Silenced by the stark evidence of their own eyes, they took the road round the north shore of Loch Arkaig, with its dark water on their left and a fine wood of thick cover to their right. And it was here on the banks of this Cameron Loch that they encountered an old shepherd, muttering away to himself and wringing his hands in sore perplexity.

Ross was obliged to give the poor old soul a good shake in order to extract any coherent conversation from his aimless rambling. Presently they fell in length to talking in the Gaelic. All the while, the old man pointing this way and that with his crooked stick and shouting in English, 'Bang! Bang!' And while Neil couldn't understand a word of the conversation, the main thrust of the narrative was evident enough in the story-teller's troubled demeanour.

When they had done talking the old shepherd slouched away, shaking his head continually, and stopping now and then to turn back, crying 'Bang! Bang!' in the same troubled manner as before. And when he was at last gone from sight, Ross flopped down on the grass verge, pulled his bonnet from his head and cast it aside despondently.

Neil, now thoroughly bemused, sat down beside him. 'So what was that all about?' he enquired. 'Something about guns – that much I gathered.'

'Aye,' groaned Ross. 'The way ahead gets tough from here

on, Neil. We'll need to keep our wits about us, and a sharp eye open.'

Neil's raised eyebrows required an explanation.

'According to yon old shepherd there's a redcoat behind every tree, bush, and sprig of heather between Loch Shiel and Loch Hourn!'

Neil shook his head, astonished, for it was a distance of some thirty miles.

'Our friend there disturbed a nest of them about an hour since and was put down the hill with a musket volley from all sides!' Ross tut-tutted disapprovingly. 'Aye, and him that never said boo to a goose in his life.' Ross glanced up, shaking his head. 'It's a sad day, Neil, when a harmless old *bodach* can't go about his business in his own country without a bunch of foreigners trying to make a grouse of him!'

Neil couldn't help but smile at the description. But Ross wasn't smiling; his mouth had a grim tuck to it now.

'I had a feeling things were going too sweet to be whole-some,' he grunted. 'We'll need to sit here awhile and rethink our position.' Then all at once he straightened his shoulders, swept up his bonnet, and sprang to his feet, pulling Neil up with him. 'Now then!' he said with a determined eye. 'If you were to conceal yourself in yonder wood and I was to scout ahead awhile . . . '

Neil got the general idea but was more than a little put out at being summarily dismissed from possible danger. His face must have said as much.

'Now look, Neil, there's no point in us both risking our necks — you've been down that particular road,' Ross reminded him. 'Or have you forgotten already?'

Shrugging his shoulders resignedly, Neil crept off into the wood, leaving his companion to whisper after him:

'If I'm not back by midnight, get yourself down to Archie's house at the far end of the Lochy — and stay there!'

Scrugging his bonnet down low on his brows, Ross set off down the road. Within the hour he had reached the head of Loch Arkaig, where a strange red glow in the sky stopped him in his tracks. Leaving the road, he clambered up the side of a hill and, following a bridle-path, he advanced with all caution towards the source of the light. Just below the summit, he dropped into a wood of birches which clung to a craggy shoulder of rock overlooking the loch, which was now quite some distance below.

Ahead, there was a panoramic view of Glen Dessarry with a river running through; the moonlight showing its westward course to the mountains and the Atlantic beyond. A line of innumerable fires, lit at regular intervals, straddled the glen in a north-south direction. The glow of each fire blended with that of its neighbour so that a continuous stream of light illuminated a vast area of the glen.

Directly below his point of observation, he could see the bright red uniform of an armed sentinel standing watchfully by his blazing fire. The soldier's Brown Bess musket was clearly visible in the firelight, with its cold steel bayonet glinting in the moonlight.

And so it continued, down the glen and over the hill, it seemed the entire landscape bristling with guns! But to what purpose? With the prime movers in the Rebellion already exiled, imprisoned, or dead, there seemed no good reason for such vigilance. But then another thought struck the Highlander and it sent a shiver down his spine. 'You would think I was Thearlaich himself!' the old shepherd had said. Could this then be the reason? he wondered.

He sat for a long time watching the movements of the soldiers below. Sometimes standing smartly to attention. Sometimes marching and countermarching. Sometimes meeting their opposite number in the middle, then turning on their heel to march back.

Forcing the line looked an impossible task. Yet the alternative was unthinkable: to double back to the Lochy and strike south for Loch Eil. Even assuming that his kinsmen in Ardgour could supply a boat to cross the Shiel – a dangerous proposition in the present climate of high tension – the whole journey would mean a long and hazardous detour that would see them arrive at their destination very probably too late!

During this period of observation, the smell of wood smoke came to him quite strong, and he was suddenly aware that the breeze had stiffened considerably. The flames from the fires were licking higher now and fanning outward in all directions; the intensity of the light rising and falling in the wind.

He looked up, wondering! The moon had gone and the sky was growing darker. Rain began to patter against his face. When he lowered his head it made a rapid drumming noise on his bonnet. Then all at once the heavens opened and a torrential downpour flooded everything in sight.

Water gushed like a fountain from every nook and cranny, cascading down the hill. Pretty soon, loose slates and fragments of shattered rock began to slip downward with the deluge; all tumbling together into the deep waters of the loch below.

The Atlantic storm broke over the Rough Bounds of Moidart to the southwest. Lightning flashed its deadly forks in all directions. And it was drawing ever nearer by the minute.

Ross felt suddenly exposed; both to the elements and to the watchful eyes of the soldiers below. Somewhere in the back of his mind he remembered Neil and the lateness of the hour. It was time to leave, and not a moment too soon!

Retracing his footsteps, he found the bridle-path and followed it down to the dirt road. But the descent of the hill was more difficult now in the absence of moonlight. And the slippery surface underfoot caused him to fall and tumble more of a distance than he could walk.

Returning with all speed, he arrived at the rendezvous an hour later. In that same instant the full force of the storm exploded above him. Fortunately, Neil was still in the wood where he had left him; his eyes peering through the darkness for a sign of his returning companion.

The storm was still raging an hour after it had begun, though the worst of the lightning had passed over. After much discussion, it was decided that they should press on and take what advantage they could from the tempest.

And so, an hour later, the travellers found themselves at the head of Loch Arkaig, where Ross had first seen the mysterious red glow in the sky. But that same glow had diminished noticeably now. And outwith the line of illumination, it was pitch black!

Crawling one in front of the other through the heather, they were now some hundred paces from the line of sentries and lying at right-angles to a deep, narrow trench which ran through the line for quite some distance. The ditch was filled with peat-water and fragments of rock. But it was deep enough for a man to crawl through if he had a reason.

Ross pondered the way ahead, carefully. The sudden down-pour had caught the soldiers completely unaware. Most of the camp-fires had died down to a peep with the soaking, and the timber fuel, lying in neat piles all around was now worse than useless. His experience with the fickle nature of flintlocks told him that the flash-pans of the muskets would be hard pressed to raise a spark after the dousing. And what state the powder? There would never be a better time. And pretty soon now, daybreak would rob them of the chance!

Sliding into the ditch, Ross bid Neil to follow. Smearing his hands and face with the peat-mud, he motioned for Neil to do likewise. Alice had laughed at their sombre choice of clothes. 'Like two mourners at a funeral,' she had said. But how sensible that choice proved now.

Heart in mouth, Ross dropped to his belly and slithered like a snake towards the line of soldiers, with Neil following close behind. Mercifully, the wind was howling across the moor above their heads, drowning the sound of their movements as they crawled on through the darkness. They had no way of knowing how far they had travelled, only that the faint glow of firelight appeared to be at its brightest now.

The gruff voice of a sentry shouting above the wind to his neighbour, across the line of the ditch, sounded close. But there could be no turning back now. Another shout sounded even closer. But what was this? Unable to hear his comrade's words in the teeth of the gale, the sentry was approaching directly above them! Ross stopped dead in his tracks, the soles of his boots hitting Neil on the head as he came on, both men now face-down in the peat-water, discovery just a heartbeat away!

Ross turned his cheek in the mud so that he could breathe more easily. In the same moment a pair of huge black toecaps peeped over the very brink of the ditch above their heads.

'Oi wouldn't send a duck out 'ere in a noight loike this, 'Arry!' came the gruff voice in the darkness above them.

During that heart-stopping moment Neil Cameron saw his short life flash before his eyes. Any second now, and the point of a bayonet would find his vitals for sure and end that life for ever!

'A roight bloody waste of toime if you ask me!' his comrade bellowed back.

One at a time and with excruciating slowness, the black toe-caps pulled back from the edge. There was a fleeting glimpse of a studded heel, then the heavy thud of ammunition boots marching away.

Tapping Neil on the head with the toe of his boot, Ross took off like a lizard, slithering at speed down the length of the ditch. He stopped briefly for Neil to catch up, then scurried away again through the gurgling mud.

The long line of the trench cut through a clump of pine trees. Once there, Ross peeked out over the top to look back at the chain of camp fires, now at a safe distance behind. Clambering out over the edge, he collapsed full-length on the bare earth under the trees, panting with exhaustion. A moment later Neil surfaced and rolled out beside him.

Looking at each other with a shared feeling of deliverance, Neil crossed himself and said a quick prayer of thanksgiving. 'If you get any more bright ideas,' he gasped between breaths, 'then I would ask that you kindly keep them to yourself!'

But his companion was already shaking his head at another affront. Schooled in the Inverness way of proper English, the Highlander's ears were still smarting.

'Och, Neil, I've heard some queer tongues in my day,' he

jeered, scornfully. 'But never in my life have I heard the King's English so cruelly treated as I did back there!'

When the worst of the storm had blown over, Ross went to the fringe of the pine wood and scanned the way ahead. Satisfied that the coast was clear, he signalled to Neil that it was time to press on while darkness prevailed. Keeping the clump of trees between themselves and the soldiers, the two men set off on a crouching run, following the line of the ditch so that they might drop into it for cover if danger threatened.

After ten breathless minutes of this cowering retreat, they stopped at a solitary birch tree and looked back at the faint red glow in the sky. Another bout of swift running took the travellers to the foot of an exceedingly steep hill. Here, the ditch they had been following ended abruptly and, looking back, they could see that the red glow in the darkness had, mercifully, gone!

Sucking in deep gulps of air, Neil threw himself down on a rock to rest. But his companion had other ideas — for already the darkness was lifting and his instincts warned him that they were not yet clear of danger. Surrounded on all sides by dark, lofty hills, he gleaned from his knowledge of the area that their headlong dash had taken them to the watershed between Glen Dessarry and Glen Pean, with the river of the name lying southwest of their present location. Focusing on the grim peaks of Sgurr Thuilm and Streap, he pulled Neil to his feet and struck out for the mountains.

It was hard broken moorland all the way, where rainwater issued from every hill, trickling and gushing into the myriad burns, rivulets, and streams that traversed the face of this undulating heather wilderness. It was the devil's own country; lonely and inhospitable, which Neil Cameron thought not fit for two Christian gentlemen to be abroad in.

They reached the foaming river as the dawn was breaking and, following its northern bank, came presently to a deep wooded gorge in the glen. Here fell a great waterfall, cascading over a sheer precipice; the terrific spill of water crashing into a deep pool far below. Standing now on a jutting rock, high above the pool, the two men could feel the tremendous vibration of rushing water under their feet as their ears rang to the deafening thunder of the falls.

Wiping the fine mist spray from their faces, the weary travellers glanced up, wondrously, at the sudden appearance of a perfect rainbow in miniature which had formed above them. And beyond the line of trees, they could see, the sun had at last broken through the clouds.

Scrambling down the high bank of the river, Neil very soon located a good spot to take water. But seeing again their dirty clothes and faces, and knowing too that they could not be wetter if they tried, all at once and with a single thought, they plunged in!

The water was bitter cold and a shock to the system. But yet, so refreshing in this warm sun that, whether by numbness of the body, or more likely the brain, the cold seemed after a time to matter no more!

The pool was teeming with trout and Ross, remembering his guddling skills, promptly proceeded to tickle one of the slippery inhabitants from its place of concealment. Neil, catching the idea with a surge of enthusiasm, had a try of his own but with woeful lack of success; all of which caused his companion no end of amusement.

But that carefree interlude of fun and frolic ended all too quickly with Neil's pointing finger:

'*Mon Dieu!*' he cried.

Turning, Ross could only stand and stare in stark horror at the sudden appearance of a bright red uniform floating towards them, face down in the water.

During that stagnant moment even the deafening thunder of the falls seemed to retreat into the stunned silence that followed this grotesque intrusion. Recovering his senses, Ross reached a hand into the deep pool and lifted the head clear of the water, only to see his companion stagger back against the rocks; his face a picture of revulsion!

'Good God! It's Sturrock!'

Despite the swollen face of deathly white, the bald head

and the blunt features of the brutal sergeant were yet unmistakable.

Frozen to the spot, Neil stood in the pool of dark water, gripped by the terror of remembered evil. But Ross's jaw had tightened and, seizing his companion by the wide lapels, he shook him rudely to his senses.

Then, all at once, an excited cry of *'Greas ort! Greas ort!'* came to them from the high embankment opposite. Looking up, they could see the figure of a kilted Highlander signalling for them to follow.

Awaiting no explanation, Ross dragged Neil bodily from the water and urged him up the steep slope of the bank, both now in hot pursuit of the stranger. Gaining the top, they spied the man running through the bracken at speed. Hesitating at the fringe of a birchwood, he turned on his heel and, looking sharply behind him, beckoned again to his pursuers before at last disappearing into the thicket.

Reckless of their own safety, Ross and Neil tore off after the mysterious stranger and plunged headlong into the wood. Stumbling in the darkness, a gruff voice urged them to *Wheesht!* At the same instant, many firm hands against their mouths silenced all words of protest.

Presently, the thud of heavy hooves sounded close by and, peering out through the trees, they could see a red line of dragoons go riding by with their sabres drawn at the ready. Pausing a moment, the troopers fanned out around the perimeter of the birch wood and, encircling it completely, they proceeded to stab away at the undergrowth with the points of their yard-long blades.

Tension showed in the fingers against Neil's lips, as the faint swishing sound of dirks being drawn from their sheaths only added to the high drama of that heart-stopping moment. Then, mercifully, the mounted officer ordered his men back into line before at last leading them off in the direction of the falls.

Only when this danger had past, did the many strong hands slacken their grip, and the travellers were once more restored to freedom.

'You ken fine it's no time to go fishing, with a redcoat pehind efery tree!' came the rasping tongue in their ears.

Neil, recognising the voice instantly, turned sharply. 'Coll?' he cried out in amazement, only to see the huge hand of the giant MacDonald come clamping across his lips again.

'Hud your wheesht! Pefore you get uss all kill't!' hissed the big man between clenched teeth, while Ross MacLean could only sit back on his heels and whisper his own astonishment at the sight of his former Jacobite comrade . . .

17

Warmed by the glow of a blazing log fire, cocooned in a snug tartan plaid, and with a large measure of the *uisge-beatha* coursing through his veins, Neil Cameron was ineffably at peace.

Ross MacLean, sitting similarly wrapped and fortified, was feeling equally blessed, the gleam of a wayward smile in his dark eyes betraying some imagined pleasure that was clearly not of this time or place.

Coll and his men had spirited the travellers, wet and weary, away from the drama of the falls to the comparative safety of the 'Lair' – a scooped-out hollow in the hills above Loch Beoraid. Here, sheltered from the buffeting Atlantic gales, and as far removed from redcoat patrols as it was possible to be, the smugglers had scrubbed out a more than comfortable habitat in this remote glen of pine forest.

Many such hidey-holes dotted the length and breadth of the Garbh-chriochan; that savage tract of country – known in English as the 'Rough Bounds' – which straddled the Western Highlands between Loch Suinart in the south and Loch Hourn to the north.

Presently, the giant Highlander reappeared before his two guests. 'A MacLean and a Cameron in the house of MacDonald!' he bellowed. 'So, it's a gathering of the clans, iss it?' The blade of the formidable broadsword he was holding, burnished bright from its long years in the scabbard, and the huge basket-hilt showed that it was clearly made to measure the considerable fist of the Highland Hercules who now carried it.

'The Rising in Lochaber!' His blood went up with the sword. 'Aye, there's peen much talk of it, and petter late than nefer, I'm thinking!' He looked keenly at the long blade, glinting in the firelight. 'Cridhe here iss honed to a fine edge and my pistols are primed for the word!'

Ross sat bolt upright from the tree trunk he was leaning

against and shot a glance at Neil. The big man's eyes switched from one to the other suspiciously.

'A strike at the Campbell's then?' he guessed again. 'Aye, that'll pe it right enough. Lord knows they've peen feeding on the dripping roast of rebellion for too long already!'

But the eyes of his two guests had averted rather sheepishly, and it was a look not lost on the giant Highlander.

'All thiss way from Inbhirnis . . . through yon plague o'red-coats . . . ?' The big fellow cocked a black eyebrow, pondering the significance of such a hazardous journey.

Ross, never one to make mealy-mouthed excuses for others, patted the earth beside him and smiled up at his perplexed host:

'Why don't you sit yourself down here a minute, Coll, while young Mister Cameron there explains the reason why we're here.'

'Weel!?' boomed the big man, suddenly switching his gaze to Neil.

Neil leaned back against the tree, his eyes half-closed, wondering at his own reasons for being here. But he had no adequate answer to offer and certainly none that the big Highlander, with his simple views of life, could ever hope to understand.

He opened his mouth to speak, but no words came.

'I came back because . . . because I gave my word!' he said at last, his voice soft and uncertain.

But Coll's beetling brows were dissatisfied, his dark eyes burning to understand.

'The Prince . . . I told you . . . that night on the beach.' Neil's eyes were roving now, his voice growing irritable. 'I have to find him . . . to take him home!' he blurted out finally.

Coll's massive frame leaned forward across the flames, his look of incomprehension total. Lifting up the huge *Cridhe* sword, he plunged it deep into the earth where it stuck almost to the hilt. Dumbstruck, the big fellow sank down on the gnarled trunk of a fallen pine tree, staring into the fire. He must have sat there for quite a time in silence, his mind lost somewhere, the firelight dancing in the pupils of his eyes.

Finding no meaningful answer, he was suddenly talking again, his voice flat and unfeeling:

'Yon baldie-headed fermine in the watter,' he said, his eyes still riveted to the fire. 'He had it coming a long time, I'm thinking!'

Ross sat up again, his curiosity aroused:

'Who was he?'

'Scott's number one cut-throat!' said Neil rejoining.

But Ross knew nothing of the dark deeds at Fort William, and even less of its perpetrators.

'And who is this Scott when he's at home?' he wanted to know.

Coll grinned a little sadistic grin behind his great ebony beard. 'Captain Caroline Frederick Scott!' he chimed, giving the man his full title and with a spit into the fire that almost extinguished it completely.

Ross shifted his gaze to Neil.

But the big man wasn't finished yet:

'If God made man ass the good book says, then Captain Caroline Frederick Scott iss the lifing proof that efen the Almighty can haf an off day!'

Ross and Neil exchanged a little half smile.

'We haf peen tracking Sturrock for some time now,' continued the MacDonald. 'A few old scores to settle, you might say . . . '

He broke off grinning, then stood up and turned his attention once more on Neil, the stare so penetrating that it seemed to scorch into his very soul.

'Aye, yon bonnie Prince of yours – I thocht ass much!' The big man shook his black mane of hair and walked away disappointedly.

But Neil's dander was pricked a little by the big man's nettling words. 'I wouldn't expect a man like that to understand,' he jabbed, turning again to Ross. 'He is a savage, tribal warrior from an ancient past! No loyalty . . . no compassion.'

Ross was too taken aback to answer this stinging indictment of his fellow Highlander.

A minute later, the MacDonald reappeared with a visitor.

'I haf someone here to see you, Meester Cameron!'

Getting to his feet, Neil turned to see that the big man was now holding a young lass by the hand. She was looking in Neil's direction and smiling a broad smile of recognition.

But even on close examination Neil did not, at first, seem to know her. For how could he recognise the young blind girl from Rona as this wee princess in the flowing gown, all scrubbed clean and shining like a new button, who was now moving towards him.

'Catriona – is it you?'

Fumbling for Neil's hand, she knelt down and kissed it as though he were a Prince.

'Catriona!'

He pulled her to her feet and knelt down himself. Brushing back the dark curls, he could see that little sightless creature again. Smiling through tears, he hugged her a long moment, repeating her name over and over.

She spoke to him in the Gaelic, an earnest look on her face, then smiling too.

Neil looked up at Coll for the English.

'She says that she iss overjoyed to meet with you again, and to know that you are safe. She wishes to thank you for saving her from the soldiers.'

But Neil did not understand, for he had feared the worst for the little Catriona.

'We went back to find her!' explained Coll. 'The soldiers had taken her to the mainland, unharmed. There she wass looked after by a family of MacLeods. But she did not like it much there, so we haf adopted her.' Coll paused, a great beaming smile breaking out upon his face. 'Or, more likely, I should say, it iss *she* who hass adopted *uss!*'

Catriona looked up at the big fellow, saying something to him in the Gaelic.

Coll pulled a stern face and bowed politely. 'She hass

reminded me that I haf a wee bit beesness to attend to,' he informed them, smiling. Then, taking the wee lass by the hand again, the gentle giant gave his guests a leaving wink and promptly left the encampment with his little princess in close attendance.

After a few moments silence, Ross got up and came over to where Neil was standing, still in a kind of shock.

'What was that you were saying about savages? Something about no loyalty! No compassion!' He shook his head disappointedly. 'Ah well, now isn't that the truth! . . . '

Loch Beoraid flashed sunlight like a heliograph as Ross MacLean, eyes half-closed against the glare, strived desperately to decipher the coded message that was coming to him from the surface of its undulating water.

The moor, which had lay sombre all week under a sullen sky, now in the bright afternoon sun came suddenly to life in the transfiguring light. All around him as he looked, purple bell-heather rang silent in the wind and the creeping carmine fingers of thyme flourished on the shore where peewits played 'Dead Wing' with their neighbours. And all the while, that urgent 'Peep! Peep!' of the oyster-catcher stabbing and stabbing in his brain.

The evening shadows found Neil Cameron wrapped in his warm tartan plaid. Lying cosseted by the glowing fire, he was blissfully asleep. But there would be little sleep for Ross MacLean tonight, for the afternoon signals from the loch had brought forth the memory of a promise yet unfulfilled; the little matter of a certain letter from an old friend which had been burning a hole in his pocket for five long months. And Mhairi lived but a short distance across the mountains . . .

At the edge of the pine wood a shaggy-haired Highland garron grazed unfettered. The MacLean's eye swept it keenly. There might never be a better opportunity . . .

Warming himself by the fire, unobserved, Coll MacDonald sat quietly watching his guest examining the sturdy little horse.

'You'll pe planning a wee fisit to your kin, I'm thinking!' guessed the big man intuitively.

Ross wheeled round, startled by the suddenness of the voice behind him. 'He's a fine beast!' he said admiringly.

Coll beamed one of his mischievous grins through his great ebony beard. 'Och, go on then, you can borrow it!' he said reading the other's mind. 'But it'll need to pe tomorrow' he added with a finger. 'For tonight, we haf a wee bit beesness!'

Coming over to warm his hands at the fire, Ross gazed up at the tree-tops, where he could see that the wind had dropped, the hills were clear of cloud, and the encroaching darkness showed a harvest moon, hanging like a lantern in the sky.

'Himself iss sleeping, then?' enquired Coll, nodding in the direction of their prostrate friend.

'Aye, like a bairn.'

'Aweel, he's needing it all, iss he no!' And lifting his black eyebrows. 'Will you partake of a wee sensation wi' me?' he asked, now showing his guest a bottle of fine malt whisky from his considerable cellar.

Ross nodded enthusiastically, and soon the two Jacobite warriors were touching glasses over the camp-fire and giving the world and all its problems the benefit of their Highland philosophy.

'Och, man, man, it's a sad day we left the croft bonnie lad!' complained the MacDonald with a regretful shake of his tousled black head. 'If yon foreign lairdie had bided where he pelongs, we'd all pe the petter of it!' he growled scathingly. 'Yon high-and-mighty blethering at Loch Shiel, and grown men ass should've known petter, standing agog in the pelieving of it!'

The two men exchanged guilty glances.

'And you're looking at one of them!' admitted Ross, sheepishly.

'Aye,' returned Coll. 'And you ken fine you're looking at another!'

And to this mutual condemnation, the two men looked into the fire and shook their heads all the more.

'I've neffer met the man yet ass could match hiss exploits to the boasting of hiss tongue!' declared the big fellow. 'We should haf called it a day at Edinburgh, split the Union once and for all, and our man would haf had hiss crown!'

Ross nodded thoughtfully.

'It was a kingdom too far, Coll. My father said it back then and he was right!'

'Aweel,' concluded the MacDonald. 'It's all bye the bye now. But we made a damn good fist of it for all that, did we no!'

And with not a little pride, Ross raised his glass in salute:

'Scotland has few peers when it comes to spectacular failure! I've heard more songs sung to defeat than ever to success!'

'Aye!' agreed Coll, clinking glasses. 'I'll drink to that!'

There fell a rather long and pensive silence before the big man moved again to speak, and when he did so, it was in an altogether more serious tone:

'There's a bee in my bonnet and it's peen stinging my conscience awhile concerning yon sickly lad,' said he, nodding in the direction of the sleeping Neil. 'It's a queer day, Ross lad, when the hawk flies wi' the dove! And yet, there's peen much talk of it.'

His guest showed him a furrowed brow.

'A Campbell and a MacDonald,' explained Coll, 'haf peen spying the coast and passing tales down the glen to Scott and yon spendthrift Earl Albemarle!'

Ross MacLean looked suddenly awe-struck.

'Aye!' confirmed the smuggler. 'I ken fine you canna pelieve it, but yon clique got our man arrestit and that's a fact – ass sure ass I'm here!'

Ross shook his head, unable to take in this impossible revelation:

'No, Coll, it can't be true! A Campbell running with a MacDonald? It's unnatural!'

'Och, man, man, dinna remind me!' growled the big man, clapping a hand over his eyes in despair. 'I canna weel sleep at night for the shame of it!'

On the turn of midnight, Coll and his men slipped out of camp on 'beesness.' Where they were headed and to what purpose, Ross never asked. Sitting quietly under a tree, warmed by the camp fire, he stared into the flames still disbelieving. A Campbell and a MacDonald – had things really come to this?

Throwing another log on the fire, he pulled his warm blanket plaid against the cold night air and pondered the day ahead. For tomorrow, he would deliver the letter . . .

The hardy little horse turned off the old drover's road into a glen, deep and dramatic, stretching into the savage solitude of the hills. Across the rabbit-nibbled turf, a thread of bridle-track conducted him through the chaos of fallen rocks and boulders to where a salmon river tumbled to the sea.

Guiding his horse's heavy feet into the roiling river, he forded the shallows at the narrowest crossing, each hoof kicking up a thin veil of brown water as he went. On the far bank opposite he picked up the trail again, following the route onward and upward, climbing ever higher. All around, peaks of red sandstone and grey granite towered against the deep azure sky. Ahead, the mountains loomed steep and magnificent.

High on a rocky knoll a red deer stag roared defiantly, his hot breath steaming like a dragon's in the crisp mountain air. Motionless, this sentinel of the herd stood ever-watchful, then turned his royal head disdainfully, the tremendous sweep of antlers catching the early morning sun as he lurched silently away.

As the little horse walked slowly on a loose rein in the hot stillness of the afternoon, the creak of saddle-leather and the clink of stones the only sounds, the Highlander was suddenly seized by an overpowering sense of watching eyes and, looking up, he saw a golden eagle swoop from its lofty perch to glide majestically; the wing-tips arched upwards as it circled overhead, shrieking an ominous warning to the bold intruders below.

He was into the mountains now, high in the haunts of the blue hare and ptarmigan, way above the treeline, where the frost-bite chill in the air carried the warning that the first snows of winter would not be long in coming.

By late afternoon the horse's broad head was dipping into a wide strath, green and pleasant, where a shady stream, born in the upper reaches of the glen, meandered lazily. And below, standing proud against the emerald of grass and the purple scattered fingers of heather, lay the object of his journey. The faint wisp of grey smoke from a peat fire curling upwards from a solitary croft, where goats grazed unfettered and unconcerned.

Pulling the rugged little horse to a standstill, Ross leaned forward in the saddle, gazing down at the familiar places of his childhood. And for a timeless moment, lost in the memories of the past, the Highlander could forget the troubles of the present and the future . . .

Then with a quick tap of the heels, he urged his horse forward.

Under the heather thatch, a young woman stood in the doorway with a hand cupped against the sun. Nervously, she observed him closely as he approached, an infant hiding behind her skirts. She uttered something in her native tongue then broke into a wide smile of recognition:

'Ross . . . Ross MacLean . . . iss it you?'

Dismounting, the traveller advanced towards her, smiling. 'Hello, Mhairi!' he said, pulling his bonnet from his head so that she might know him better.

Rushing forward, she embraced him warmly. 'For a moment my heart leapt in my breast,' she exclaimed, in her soft West Highland tongue. 'For I thocht it wass Calum come home!' Then she broke from the embrace, looking mournful. 'It hass been twelve long months since he and the others went down that road,' she said pointing. 'Not one hass returned. Efery day I look in hope but nobody comes . . . '

She touched him, affectionately, on the cheek and, feeling the warmth of his skin, she smiled, happy in the knowledge that he was indeed mortal and not some spirit visitation. 'But you haf come home Ross, and it lifts my heart to see you,' she murmured, taking her visitor by the arm and leading him indoors.

'And this must be wee Ewen I see!' grinned the visitor, catching up the child in his arms and holding him so that the light from the little window fell upon the young lad's face. 'Why, he's the image of his father, so he is!'

'Aye, and he hass hiss father's ways, the wee rasscal!' she laughed, tickling the boy and chasing him playfully from the room.

Exchanging brief smiles, Mhairi invited her guest to sit at the table.

'It iss like old times Ross!' she reminded him, sitting opposite. 'You haf been gone too long.'

'Aye,' he replied wistfully.

'And you are an Invernessian now!' she smiled. 'Hardly a trace of the West left on your tongue. They talk the proper English there, I haf heard!' she teased. 'Fancy you of all people, talking like an Englishman.'

'Och, Mhairi!' he scolded. 'I would cut off my tongue if I thought it were so!' Feeling suddenly awkward, he looked around for something to say:

'Are you managing the place on your own?'

'But of course!' she replied. 'I haf the goats for milk! And peat for the fire iss plentiful!'

She showed him the ingredients of the broth she was preparing. 'I grow my own fine vegetables, and fish from the burn are easily caught when I need them!' she declared proudly. 'I am fortunate to haf the help of good neighbours! Your cussin Tonald and hiss wife are a great comfort to me. Tonald mends the walls and cuts the peats whenefer I run low.'

'Aye,' agreed Ross. 'He's a good man, Donald! – And is he still making that explosive whisky of his?'

They both laughed.

'Are you here on a fisit to your cussin?' she inquired.

Ross did not at first answer. He had travelled a long way but would have wished, at that moment, to be anywhere other than here with the unpleasant news he was duty-bound to deliver:

'It was you I came to see, Mhairi,' he said. 'I promised Calum I would come.'

Mhairi felt a knife stab and twist in her heart. It was the moment she had come to dread, knowing instinctively that the words carried with them an inevitable truth – she would never see her husband again, she was sure of it.

Removing the distressed envelope from his coat pocket, Ross handed it across the table. Mhairi stared stone-faced at the stained and crumpled piece of paper. For an instant she wished it away. And she wished the messenger away. Then, closing her eyes in stoic resignation, she reached out and took possession of the letter.

The squiggled handwriting was unmistakably Calum's. She fingered the wording of her name, tenderly, as though sensing that some essence of the writer might somehow still remain.

'I am afraid it has lived rather badly with its keeper these past months,' Ross said, apologetically.

Opening the envelope carefully, Mhairi read the letter while Ross sat watching. He could only guess at the contents, yet the tears never came. She looked up when she had finished.

'I should like to read it to you,' she said proudly.

But Ross looked doubtful. 'It is personal,' he objected.

'No matter. I should like for you to hear it,' she insisted, then proceeded with an authority of voice her listener could only marvel at:

Mhairi, my love, if you come to read these words, then it will mean that my good friend in whose care I haf entrusted thiss last letter, will haf survived the ordeal that awaits uss across the moor, and I sadly haf not.

I know that I haf been a poor hussband and father. Our time together hass been too short; but pelieve me when I say that they haf peen the happiest years of my life.

When wee Ewen iss old enough to understand, tell him the truth about me; the reassons why I left home and the cause I felt important enough to give my life for. With the passage of time, he will pe petter placed to judge for himself whether or not my actions were justified.

Ass the years go by, Mhairi, you may find a place in your heart for another; do so with my blessing, for you should haf company ass you grow old and the boy a father to guide him.

Tell that man Ross MacLean to stop hiss restless wanderings. He should put down roots pefore it iss too late! Bully him Mhairi for he will listen to you!

All that remains iss for me to tell you that I love you dearly and it will always pe so. Please forgive me for I haf broken my promise to you . . .

Your loving hussband,

Calum . . .

Mhairi glanced up from the page. 'He promised me faithfully that he would return,' she explained, with the shadow of a smile. 'It iss dated the sixteenth of April,' she added.

Ross reached over and took hold of her hand, squeezing it gently and wishing with all his heart that he could remove some of the pain she was so bravely trying to conceal.

'I am sorry that I had to be the one to bring this unhappiness to you, Mhairi,' he sighed. 'I wished it could be otherwise . . . '

'I am glad that you came, Ross,' And screwing up her courage, she held the letter against her heart. 'I will tressure it always!' she said.

Though he tried many times to leave, she begged him stay longer than he would have wished. Yet such was the depth of her pain behind the warm smile she presented that he could scarce deny her. And so it was, after many hours had passed, his head filled with tales of the old days and no small measure of old Donald's whisky, that Ross, with a heavy heart, took his leave . . .

It was well into the night when he arrived back at the smuggler's lair. Coll MacDonald and his men had left for the coast on 'beesness,' but the embers of a camp fire still smouldered and a welcoming brew bubbled invitingly in an iron pot. Pouring a large measure of the aromatic infusion into a metal cup, the weary traveller drank deep of the herbal tea as he sat admiring Coll's *Cridhe* sword, stuck proud in the earth where he had left it the previous day.

Neil, listening anxiously for his companion's return, emerged from the pine wood and stormed over to where Ross was sitting. It was clear from the look on the young Cameron's face that he was in high dudgeon:

'Where in God's name have you been all day!?' he demanded.

Ross chose to ignore the question, and the high-handed tone of its delivery, and continued as before to enjoy his refreshment.

'I have asked you a question!' Neil reminded him. 'Kindly have the decency to grant me a reply!'

Ross glanced up at his interrogator. A Cameron by birth he might well be, but his haughty manner was altogether too condescending to be worthy of that name. Nor, it seemed, had he been blessed with his father's depth of understanding. Perhaps his association with the Big Wigs across the water had elevated him to a higher station.

'I was delivering a letter, if you must know!'

Neil stood speechless for several long seconds, seemingly unable to answer.

'Ten short miles from our destination – and you go off into the back of beyond to deliver a letter?' He fell silent again as though waiting for the full impact of his own words to sink in. Then:

'The life of our Prince in danger! Every second vital! And you go off delivering foolish letters!' And at the sight of his friend's apparent apathy, Neil's overstretched composure snapped completely:

'For pity's sake, Ross – Don't you care?' he implored despairingly. 'Have you no feelings at all?'

In the twinkling of an eye the MacLean's quiet manner and

inscrutable face changed completely, and in those intense blue eyes something almost malevolent stirred:

'No feelings?' he thundered, springing now suddenly to his feet and flinging his metal cup with such force that it bounced off a rock like a cannon-ball quite some distance away.

Neil reeled back with the shock as Ross snatched up Coll's *Cridhe* sword in a moment of blind rage and pointed it menacingly at his accuser's heart. For a terrifying instant Neil Cameron thought his life in mortal danger from the very man who had once come to save it.

'No feelings!' erupted the swordsman, and wielding the great weapon in the air overhead, he turned on his heel and launched himself at a nearby sapling, striking it first one way then the other, continuously, and with such force that in no time at all, huge chunks of it lay hacked and severed on the ground.

For a timeless moment he stood rooted to the spot, staring down at his handiwork in a haze of subsiding fury – then, coming slowly to his senses, he cast the offending sword aside as though it were infected. Somewhere in the swirling mists of confusion, the memory of his father, and of Calum, and of his dead comrades, came sharp to his mind. And most recent and poignant of all, Mhairi and wee Ewen too.

Turning once more to face the cause of his outrage, he gazed with blank eyes at the spot where Neil was standing, still in shock. A moment ago, he could so easily have run him through at the point of the sword for his callous remark. But now, seeing again his companion's broken fingers, and his gaunt, haunted expression, he remembered that this young man too, had suffered much for his Prince.

'No feelings, you say,' he mumbled, the fire of rage gone from his words. 'You can accuse me of many things, Neil Cameron,' he said, his eyes falling from the other's fearful gaze as his voice sank to a whisper. 'But don't ever accuse me of that . . . '

Not another word passed between them, and with the MacLean Highlander sitting once more by the fire with his head inclined downward, both men were soon overtaken by a profound silence.

18

Early the following morning, Coll and his gang of smugglers
returned from their nocturnal activities, heavily laden with
many creels of West Coast cuddies for the breakfast, and the
exciting news of two French ships in the neighbourhood!

Expertly prepared by Allan-nan-corc (Allan-of-the-knife),
the fresh catch of sea fish proved a delicious meal to start the
day, washed down with a generous swallow of hot *drammach*
and a rich *crannachan* to follow.

Despite this hearty breakfast, Neil amused them all by
complaining bitterly that he had not yet tasted a plate of
porridge in all the long months he had endured in his native
Highlands.

'Porritch!' spluttered Coll in amazement. 'If it iss *brochan*
that you want, then you had petter go eat with the poor folk,'
said he, pulling a freshly 'caught' bottle of the *uisge-beatha*
from a creel, to hoots of laughter. 'For thiss, laddie, iss where
the gentry dine!'

But not to be outdone, and seeing the big fellow in good
fettle from his recent enterprise, Neil insisted that he and
the others drink a toast in the Gaelic to the health of their
King across the water. And, although much of that rash
adventure still rankled with the giant Highlander, he could
scarcely deny his overseas guest this otherwise simple pleasure.

With all glasses duly raised in salute, Coll gave forth in his
native tongue a heartfelt toast to the King and to all the good
men and true who were out in the '45! And now, addressing the
bottle of *uisge-beatha*:

'*CHA MISHDE THU-SA E, AGUS'S FHÈIRRDE MISE E!*
YOU ARE NONE THE WORSE OF IT, WHILE I FEEL
ALL THE PETTER OF IT!' he gave in English, with a
provoking smile.

Receiving the gift of a knapsack, brim-full of newly baked

oatmeal bannocks, and a warm embrace from the fair Catriona, Neil and Ross were ready for the off.

Bidding Coll and his men a fond farewell and, taking their opinions on the safest route to the coast, they set out with all speed for Loch Nan Uamh.

Darkness pressed on all sides as they proceeded and the overcast sky threatened rain. And though it was no time of day to be out on the hill, it suited their purpose to be early afoot while others slept. Neil stopped frequently to check his father's watch, for time was growing short and news of the French ships – stormbound in coastal waters – would very soon reach enemy ears too.

During the night a gale had sprung up, and while it had subsided a little, now in the hours before dawn an incessant slanting rain was attacking them full in the face. All around them there appeared the dark outline of great hills and rocks, and the sound of rushing water. But without the kindness of sun or moon to guide them, nor any sign of path or track to follow, progress was slow and arduous and, above all, downright dangerous.

Coll had warned them to keep a sharp eye out for the many dawn patrols in this part of the glen, and all too soon the hot pace they had set themselves began to take its toll. But as it drew on to morning and the darkness began to lift, the fear of discovery gave renewed flight to their slowing feet.

Drenched by rain or burn, knee-deep in bog, or just plain broken with fatigue, Neil's thoughts would run back to Coll's log fire, a soft feather bed, or a sunny foreign shore some-where – anywhere that was as far removed from this God-forsaken place as it was possible to be!

All around them as they ran, the country was so bestrewn with bog, boulder, and burn that pretty soon Neil had their Gaelic words forever etched in his brain, for so often had he heard his fellow traveller pour out the vials of his wrath upon each and every one. Here to the right, a *creachann* (rock). There to the left, a *coille* (wood). And all the while, closing in about them, a dense *ceathach* (mist).

For all his fine tutoring in Europe's halls of learning, the young Cameron could seldom wish a more graphic illustration of this most descriptive of languages than when uttered from the lips of his frustrated companion during that headlong dash through the darkness.

In a fine wood of birches, growing on a wee bit grassy side of a fast flowing river, they at last stopped to take shelter from the rain, and a much needed rest. Here, they took some of Catriona's freshly baked bannocks and a spiritual uplift of brandy from a bottle Coll had tucked in their knapsack, unbeknown to them.

Neil had time to recover his breath, but little else, and would gladly have lingered awhile in the sanctuary of this leafy bower. But his taskmaster had other ideas and was all too quickly on his feet again with his determined face to the rain.

'Come on, Cameron! Move yourself! It'll be daylight soon!' His voice, swift and rough, left no room for argument and Neil, albeit reluctantly, found himself once more running off down the glen before he had thought to complain.

Sunrise found them on the leeward side of a hill with the boiling mists of morning rising out of a deep glen far below. And the Atlantic gales, which had battered the coast relentlessly throughout the long night, now suddenly dropped to an eerie silence.

At that first peep of dawn, the sun's rays, coming over the high peaks behind them, shot through the morning gloom and flooded the entire hillside with its blinding light. Neil caught his breath, in that instant, for up here in the high country where the cold biting winds put a rusty tint on September leaves, the scattered trees of birch and rowan came suddenly ablaze with colour!

'Over the hill and we should see the coast!' cried Ross and, dropping to the heather on all fours, they struck out for the summit.

Within an hour of this breathless climbing, they at last gained the top, more dead than alive, and had their view – a panorama of endless ocean stretched out before them as far as the human eye could see. Here and there, great lumps of islands reared out of the sea. And below, in the sound of Arisaig, two fine ships lying at anchor in the deep waters of the loch.

Neil Cameron was ecstatic:

'We've done it!' he proclaimed wildly. 'My God – we're here!' And falling back on his heels, 'Loch Nan Uamh!' he whispered reverently.

'Aye,' confirmed his companion with a little quiet satisfaction of his own. 'The loch of the cave, and not a moment too soon, by the looks of things!' Pulling the little brass telescope from his coat pocket, he proceeded to study the two French vessels through the glass.

But Neil could scarcely contain himself. The tang of the sea had come sharp to his senses as all along the coast great waves came rushing against the rocks, breaking and booming defiantly. And the morning, now so bright and clear after the storm, made it seem another world they gazed upon.

'Aye, they're Frenchmen all right!' confirmed Ross after some moments' close examination. 'And flying English colours at their mastheads!' he observed with a wry grin.

Neil was for going down immediately, but Ross counselled that they should linger awhile and think upon their situation. His observations through the telescope had revealed the few men of an anchor watch on board both vessels, indicating that the crews must be ashore. It was decided, therefore, to rest up and take what provision Coll and Catriona had provided for their journey.

Emptying the contents of their knapsack, both men stretched full-length in the heather for a well earned rest and a chance to dry off their clothes in the warm sunshine. Despite his excitement, Neil very soon fell asleep, as was his usual habit.

But Ross, though equally worn out, was still ever-mindful of the constant dangers that lay in store for the unwary traveller and, consequently remained watchfully half-asleep – with one eye closed and the other open, but with the incessant shrieking of sea birds overhead and the nearer annoyance of his companion's loud snores of contentment, his own broken slumbers proved worse than useless.

The place where they had concealed themselves was all heather, full of great stones and crevices in the face of a round-top hill, with some scattered trees interspersed. A fine herd of red deer had come on to the hill opposite to look at the strangers. But seemingly unimpressed by what they had seen they promptly trotted off again to view some more interesting spectacle.

After a time, a faint chatter of trickling water sounded close by and, crawling in the heather, Ross soon located the source of the fresh-water spring and began drinking generous handfuls of it to quench his thirst.

On the hill beyond, immediately below where the deer had stood only moments since, a brace of red grouse exploded from their cover. A flash of sunlight nearby caught the Highlander's keen eye and in an instant he was fumbling in his coat pocket for the telescope.

The lens picked out a small party of men descending the hill opposite, and at no great speed.

'Lochiel!' whispered Ross under his breath, for he was certain that he had recognised one of the party as the man himself! But whether or not the Prince was with them was difficult to tell. For at this most crucial moment of all times, the contrivance of the sun and the previous rain upon the glass caused the lens to come over all misty with condensation. Cursing his luck, Ross threw the little brass telescope down in the heather with a tirade in the Gaelic, all of which brought Neil out of his slumbers with a start.

'What – what's happening?' he spluttered, still half asleep.

'You've just missed your chance to see your clan chief!' muttered Ross, over his shoulder with a scowl. And then, gazing up at the position of the sun, he concluded that it was now time to leave.

Neil pulled out his pocket-watch to check the time more accurately but to his great consternation, discovered that in the heat of their headlong flight that morning he had forgotten to wind it! This caused his companion no end of amusement:

'Sometimes I find it hard to believe you are your father's son, Neil!' he said in a rare moment of laughter. And Neil, to his credit, and notwithstanding that the object of this laughter was his own good self, could only laugh also.

Their decision to descend was hastened all the more when a swarm of rapacious midges began to settle about their heads and devour, most savagely, every nook and cranny of human male flesh that it was possible to imagine! Deeming discretion the better part of valour, the two promptly retreated down the hill with Ross complaining that he would sooner face a Campbell charge with broadsword and dirk, any day, than a plague of Highland *malhoulakins*.

At the foot of the hill they came out upon the road to Arisaig that took a wide sweep round the headland. A few hundred yards, and they stopped where a dusty track turned off to the left. With a spring in their step now they headed towards the tang of the sea and the sound of the waves.

They arrived on the beach in the gold of evening, tired and hungry, but much relieved. Many gentlemen of the Rebellion were already present among the welcoming party; Lochiel, Cluny, Lochgarry, John Roy Stewart, and Doctor Archibald Cameron. And others, who had come out for the Prince, now came out again to avail themselves of the opportunity to escape. And still others, who had been skulking in the country of Morar, Moidart, and Arisaig, getting wind of the French ships, came along too.

But alas, no ship had yet been built that would carry them all!

Neil, in spite of himself, rushed off searching eagerly for the Prince. He very soon found him in deep conversation with the ship's captain and a certain Colonel Warren. Although they did not at first recognise each other – for so much had they both changed – their affection for each other, when they did, was plain to see.

Ross, who had remained apart from the others on a slight

219

eminence above the shore, watched, with a certain quiet smile of satisfaction, the Stuart Prince greet the young Cameron like a long-lost brother. And Lochiel, too, when introduced to his kinsman, seemed equally pleased to see him.

Presently, after much ardent exchange of words between the three, Ross could see his young charge pointing in his direction and, to his great consternation, the Prince himself approaching! Seized by a sudden panic, he agonised over what he might say to the man. So much had changed since that day on the moor. So much bitterness and recrimination. So much anger. He was no longer sure of his own feelings.

'Less said, sooner mended!' his mother had always advised. Better then, perhaps, to say nothing?

The Prince, when he stood before him, looked much changed within himself; unwashed and unshaved, weary and careworn. Hunger had reduced him considerably. Gone too was the suit of fancy clothes. In truth, the reality seemed at that moment a long way removed from the legend.

'I hope that isn't pity in your eyes, Captain?' he said intuitively, 'For . . . hardly a Prince you see before you. I fear that my fine clothes and courtly bearing have all but gone . . . '

The Highlander bowed politely in the royal presence. The man's shocking appearance and self-deprecating manner pricked his conscience more than a little.

'Our young friend has only just confirmed a most unbelievable tale! You have my deepest admiration, Captain.'

He turned from the Highlander then and looked out across the islands, watching the sun go down on the horizon; a shimmering orange ball half-buried in the sea and sinking. Rapt in silence, he stood for an age, it seemed, before the voice came again, his words heavy and beset with emotion:

'My ship leaves with the tide . . . Soon my days of living like a hunted deer will be over . . . ' He paused, looking around, taking in the rugged scenery. 'God, but I will miss this country! Its wildness . . . Its beauty . . . Its people . . . I fear, once I leave . . . I may never return! And yet, still my heart will always be here . . . ' He turned hesitantly, his eyes cast downward, as though searching the earth for something lost. And when he lifted his gaze once more to look, there was a gleam of moisture there:

'Can a man live without a heart, Captain?' he asked. Then, placing a hand rather affectionately on the Highlander's shoulder, he went quickly down the beach and into the waiting arms of his anxious companions.

All this time, Ross had stood lost in his own private silence. All the dark thoughts he had carried in his mind since that day on the moor, and all the harsh things he had thought to say in lesser moments he found now had seeped away in the listening and the seeing of that greatness humbled.

'Two fine ships!' exclaimed Neil, coming now towards his friend, excitedly. 'The *Prince de Conti* and *L'Heureux*. All of sixty-eight guns between them!'

But of this great stir Ross heard little, so deeply entrenched was he in his own pensive wanderings – until the young Cameron touched his arm and snatched him back from that distance:

'Why don't you go with us, Ross?' he begged.

'Go?' said the other, looking up dreamily. 'But where?'

'Why, to France of course! It will be safer for you there,' Neil reminded him.

'But you forget, Neil: I gave my promise to Alice, and I intend to keep it.'

'Indeed, but when news of the Prince's escape reaches London and the dust of rebellion settles . . . You can return! Please Ross, think of yourself for once! Come with us!'

But his friend did not answer, for already his eyes had switched their gaze beyond that argument, drawn now to those haunting hills, and glens, and islands, that it would break his heart to leave.

'I am a Highlander, Neil,' he answered softly, and with a glint of a wistful smile in his dark eyes. 'And here is where I belong.'

And though a greater pull prevailed upon him now, here,

standing on that leaving shore in the afterglow of sunset, Neil could feel that beauty too.

'Aye,' he sighed acquiescently. 'And more fool me to ask.' Hands deep in pockets now, the young Cameron turned back to face the MacLean Highlander, shrugging his shoulders a little, as though himself reluctant to leave.

'Go on now!' urged his friend. 'Before your fine ships leave without you . . . '

There fell a long silence, wherein all things that had passed between them came vividly to mind. They had travelled a long road of danger together since first they met that night on the scaffold. And yet not one word had been spoken about it. For such, it seemed, was the Highland way.

Then in a sudden surge of emotion, Neil caught up his companion in a long embrace:

'This is farewell then, my friend! Take good care of my sister!' And all at once he was gone: down the sand and into the little boat that would carry him to his ship.

About a hundred men in all went out in the boats, and for those that remained behind, the Prince left a pretty speech:

'My lads, be in good spirits. It shall not be long before I shall be with you, and shall endeavour to make up for the loss you have suffered. I have left money for your subsistence – you that are officers – and have also left money to provide meals for all the private men.'

There followed more heartfelt exchanges as the last of the little boats pulled clear of the shore.

Ross stood on the beach watching, with the others, the slow rise and fall of the oars as the rowing boats drew away. From the little boat where Neil Cameron was seated, there could be seen an arm raised in farewell; alas now . . . too dim and distant to distinguish.

Then all fell silent, and empty, and dark . . .

Early next morning as the dawn was breaking, the 'Prince de Conti' set sail for France. Behind her, in the deep waters of the loch, the heavily-gunned frigate 'L'Heureux' slipped anchor and gathered way as the wind of the morning filled her white canvas sails with the promise of fair weather.

As the hills of Moidart fell astern, Neil Cameron looked back for his last glimpse of Scotland, and wept. And there was a tear too for the MacLean Highlander he had left behind; standing now on the crest of a hill, looking out to sea with a kindred heart.

And there he stood, a long time watching, until the ship, now a mere speck on the horizon, vanished from sight . . .